MW01242471

Praise for Cold Crossover

"Cold Crossover is a riveting mystery based on the drama of small-town high school basketball, complete with the missed shot no local will ever forget. Along the way, Tom Kelly takes the reader from the Northwest's wild frontier days to its equally crazy present as a real-estate mecca. Kelly weaves the ferries, crabbers, and timber-men of his region into a timeless and page-turning tale."
—Jim Ragsdale, Minneapolis Star-Tribune
~

"A long-time coach goes on a search for the best player he ever had in a mystery that will keep you reading deep into the roots of its Pacific Northwest setting." **—Danny O'Neil, ESPN**
~

"Award-winning real estate writer Tom Kelly makes a terrific transition into fiction, offering a small-town hero as the center of a big-time story. Kelly clearly knows his territory, including the energy and emotions surrounding a state high-school basketball tournament. A successful merging of past and present, Cold Crossover catches some colorful characters along the way to its captivating climax."
—Alan J. Heavens, Philadelphia Inquirer

The Ernie Creekmore Series

The Ernie Creekmore Series features a longtime high school basketball coach who calls upon his years of experience, resources and small-town logic to help his fishing buddy and the county's chief criminal investigator solve murder mysteries. The books contain basketball and murder and much more. They are about boys and men, sons and parents, and the confusions of love when we are no longer young.

In the first book, COLD CROSSOVER, initially published in 2012 and rewritten in 2020, Linnbert "Cheese" Oliver, a hard-luck hero in the Northwest town of North Fork, is reported missing from a late-night ferry. And for Ernie, his father figure, friend and former coach, the news hits hard. Ernie's suffered too much loss and pain in his life—his wife, a state basketball championship, a serious medical malady—and he just can't accept the idea that Cheese might have taken his own life. "The Cheese" was the best basketball player Ernie Creekmore coached in his nineteen years at Washington High School and the best shooter Ernie had ever seen. The unassuming great-grandson of the town's founder, Linn Oliver could do no wrong. He was the talk of the town—until he missed the final shot in the 2000 state championship game. Working with the county's Harvey Johnston, Ernie uses his new contacts in real estate and old hoops resources to trace Cheese's movements. Meanwhile, hints at possible foul play turn up in pieces of North Fork's rough-and-tumble history in fishing, logging and railroading and the past and present violently collide in a series of heart-stopping moments that peel back layers of secrets, gold and twisted family ties that refuse to stay buried.

The second book, COLD BROKER, rewritten in 2020 and initially published as Hovering Above a Homicide in 2014, finds Ernie trying to solve the murder of a "helicopter" parent whose body is discovered in a vacant home for sale.

The third book, COLD WONDERLAND, Ernie, from rainy North Fork, Washington is offered a golden opportunity in the Golden

State to get back into his beloved game, guiding a team of elite young athletes to the prestigious Pacific Waves basketball tournament. But the beach trip quickly tips off into trouble. Some of the kids can't handle the dark temptations of this sun-kissed paradise. Ernie can't seem to handle his own love life. And soon he's got his hands full trying to handle unfinished business from its past as it blasts back into his present.

Purchase the other books in the series:
Cold Wonderland- Now Available at Amazon.

Cold Broker - Pre-Order Now on Amazon.
Releasing January 26, 2021.

Cold

Crossover

Cold
Crossover

AN ERNIE CREEKMORE MYSTERY
BOOK 1

T.R. KELLY

Crabman Publishing ● Rolling Bay, WA

Published by Crabman Publishing Rolling Bay, WA

Copyright © 2020 by Tom Kelly
Book design by Alicia Dean and Kathy L Wheeler. Cover design by Victoria Cooper. Cataloging-in-publication data is available from the Library of Congress. 978-1-7361611-1-1 Printed and bound in the United States of America

Cold Crossover, An Ernie Creekmore Mystery

COPYRIGHT © 2020 by Crabman Publishing

Dedication

For Dickie – "Dickels"
Ukuku!

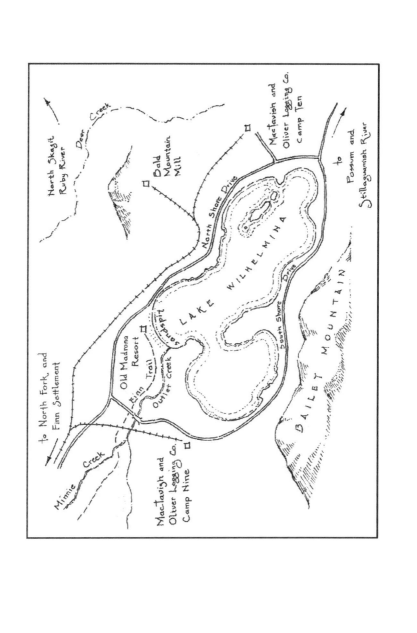

ONE

IF THERE WERE AN ALL-STAR TEAM FOR rotund rear ends, the guy with the Harley Davidson jacket hunched over the center of the bar would've been the captain. He was taking full advantage of the time of day when opinionated working men drink faster and talk louder before realizing that they should have been home sooner.

"I'm tellin' ya," Harley said to a pair of work-booted buddies. "The frickin' guy was the best high school basketball player I ever saw. And Lord knows I've seen a lot of 'em." He offered a palms-up proposal to his partners. "Of course, if you can suggest somebody better, I'm all ears."

I dropped my fork and peeked around the partitions that divided the dining room from the bar at Tony's Place. All I could see were the backs of heads, all with hair spilling out from under greasy hats atop bulky bodies in overalls. The man on Harley's right nodded. "I saw that kid in a regional playoff. Good player, but not great. Had trouble on defense. Seemed to get lost trying to find his man. But, yeah, he could shoot it."

Harley scoffed and stirred his drink with a crooked index finger.

"Heard you guys talking," another man said, planting a cowboy boot on the brass rail beneath the bar. I leaned around two room dividers but saw only *Fighting Crabs* stitched across the back of his red windbreaker. "I know you aren't from around here, but we had a player at the high school a few years back that every college in the country was after. He could score from the parking lot."

"Lot of kids got range," Harley replied. "Most float around at the top of the key and just call for the ball."

The man in the windbreaker pointed the neck of his brown bottle at the bartender: *Give me another.* When he did, I recognized the two sagging chins. "This kid could do it all," Mitchell Moore said. He stared high into a far corner. "Score, pass, defend, help ... Got free for his shots with this wicked crossover dribble. First time anybody'd seen a young white player with that kind of a move."

Labeled "Wide Load" for his ample middle and for the bright yellow sign that hung from his backhoe trailer, Moore was the bombastic treasurer of the Washington High School Fighting Crabs Booster Club and its vainest contributor. He spent many of his days in direct reflection of how the Crabs performed the previous evening and the cash he had won or lost wagering on games. For more than a decade, he found subtle ways of letting all of the school's head coaches know about it. While he owned a ton of heavy equipment, including a cement mixer and a septic pump rig with the banner THIS TRUCK SUCKS and a vanity license plate, SHTOGO, his most prized possession was an old league-championship wrestling trophy anchored on the mantel above the fireplace in his dumpy log home.

The third man in Harley's posse tossed back the remainder of his gin-and-tonic and nodded at the bartender for a refill. He rose to his feet, stretched his arms toward the ceiling, and gripped the side of the bar with both hands.

"I know who you mean," he said. "I heard a lot of people talk about him. Cheese somebody. Great kid who'd run through a wall for a win. Played for the Huskies for a couple of years, but his knee was gone by then ... Wasn't he the kid who missed the final shot in the state tournament? Could have won it all. Heard the coach didn't help him much, either."

I was no longer hungry. Outside, on Division Street, sidewalks were speckled with the glow of early streetlamps and windblown value coupons from the *Skagit Valley World*.

"Best player ever to come out of this county," Moore said. "Some people say the entire doggone state. His great-grandpa was one of the first pillars of this community. Kid got hurt and was never the same after that. Cost me a ton a dough, too. Bet the farm on the state title game, and he choked. Hell, bookies took me for a buttload of cash. Dumbshit coach also made him do too much."

I knew it all too well. Linnbert "Cheese" Oliver was the best athlete I ever coached in my nineteen years at Washington High in North Fork, Washington, home of The Fighting Crabs. Patient, easygoing, and humble to a fault, he did things on the basketball floor nobody else could do. He was the best shooter I ever saw. For years, I'd feared that the only thing he couldn't do was to accept his limitations after a logging injury before his senior season. And the bar talk had merit. I could have called a timeout late in that title game and set up a better play. I felt the decision in the bottom of my gut every day since, five years later.

The conversation reminded me that I hadn't seen him in several weeks. I missed his energy and insight. After taking in a prep holiday tournament early in January, we hadn't sat together in the stands and critiqued teams or shooters as we usually did.

"Coach? Coach?" The waitress had been hovering close to my table. Curiously, my feet now felt buried in sand, and the tips of my fingers tingled. Maybe the bar talk aggravated my multiple-sclerosis symptoms. "When's the last time you didn't finish? Aren't you even gonna look at the dessert menu? Skagit pear pie on there tonight ..."

"Not tonight, Polly," I said, embarrassed by my zone-out. "Got to get on down the road. I'm headed up to the lake tonight and don't want to feel too heavy on the way." I glanced at the food. "Mind putting this in a doggie bag? I know I'm going to want it sooner than I think."

Moments later, a voice, sounding barely old enough to be served alcohol, emanated from the far end of the bar. "I went to Washington High." A young man with patchy facial hair pushed up the brim of his Mariners' baseball cap.

Several heads turned his way. "So what?" Harley winced, appearing upset that his closed circle had been breached. "Who are you? Beaver Cleaver?"

"Played a little football till I broke my leg sophomore year," the kid said.

"And?" Harley said incredulously.

"And I was two years behind Cheese Oliver in school."

I began to rise but sat back down and slid the doggie bag on to the chair next to me while I squinted to try to identify the speaker.

Harley swayed on his stool. "Congratulations. I'm sure a bunch of kids were." His gaze returned to his buddies.

"Got a cousin in the Washington State Patrol," the kid said. "I talked to him about thirty minutes ago."

Harley grinned and checked his audience. "Well, I know they weren't lookin' for me. I served my time. Believe me. Paid my debt to society and walked out free as a bird seven years ago."

After a few snickers from the bar gang, the kid said, "No, it was about last night."

Harley wiped his mouth on his sleeve, smacked his drink down, and swiveled his stool toward the youngster. "OK. What about last night?"

"My cousin said the WSP had to tow Cheese Oliver's rig off the Bremerton ferry. All of them in the office were saying he jumped off that boat in the middle of Puget Sound."

TWO

THE UNFATHOMABLE POSSIBILITY THAT Linn Oliver would leap off a ferry tore at my gut and elevated my guilt for not reaching out to him for several weeks. I left Tony's Place and drove my sputtering truck—an ancient International Travelall my dad left me when he found a newer model to work our Yakima orchard—past the Shell station where Linn worked part-time. Finding it closed, I headed east past Skagit Valley College, then south toward Lake Wilhelmina where some dock work, a favor for an aging booster, awaited me in the morning at the Gustaffson place. It sat across the lake from the Dolan cabin I had listed for sale—and rented out in the meantime to Linn Oliver. Dolan's had no phone. The entire lake valley relied on the payphone at the Mountain Market. As I drove I became more restless, stunned that any rumor about Linn, especially one of this magnitude, would reach a kid in a bar before me.

Rambling past winterized, deserted cabins—Hogerty's Hideout, Saul's Never Done Inn, Me and Mrs. Jones, Stan's Hog Heaven—I flip-flopped between radio stations wondering if the news of the star-crossed player had become public. Finally, I stopped at Mountain Market, and after a few calls from the payphone, I got the gist of it.

One of my former players, now with the WSP at its Seattle headquarters, informed me that Linn's car had been abandoned late last night aboard a Seattle-to-Bremerton ferry. The trooper said that the yellow Subaru was locked up tight, with a bloody towel on the shotgun seat. But Linn had not been located.

I figured that Linn either forgot that he drove on the boat and then walked off with the rest of the crowd—commuters do it all the time—or he let a buddy borrow the car. The blood didn't bother me. Knowing him as well today as I did when he was in high school, I guessed that it came from a wild elbow to the cheek during a rec-league game or a random cut suffered while working on a vehicle at his service station. Linn certainly caught his share of nicks and stitches over the years. I figured he'd turn up, embarrassed and apologetic over causing a fuss. That is, if he were even behind the wheel in the first place.

I could see how people would look at the circumstantial evidence and conclude the worst, but that was crazy. People didn't know Linn Oliver the way I did. Coaches often understand and influence kids on a different level. But with this young man, a part of me operated on an even higher plane. More like a father knows his son.

It was dark and damp by the time I rolled down the driveway to Jim Dolan's waterfront home on Sandspit Road at the far end of the lake. I'd known the property and the Dolans for decades. Last year after Labor Day, I listed the place for sale. The decision saddened the lake community. The family had owned the property for more than sixty years, and it had been headquarters for major summer shenanigans. Sadly, one of the parents had recently died in a tragic accident, and two of their four kids needed the money from the sale. When the house didn't sell by the end of September, I suggested to the Dolans that Linn move in and watch after it in exchange for a bargain rent. Linn needed a place to live after his family's home in North Fork sold shortly before, and his parents retired to Arizona.

I had always known I would go to the mat for Linn. He was the type of kid a coach gets once in a career. Maybe once, period, if they were lucky. Polite and easygoing off the floor, he'd cut your balls off for a victory on it. On anything. Buckets, ping pong, girls. Didn't matter. It pissed some people off because they didn't expect that level of intensity from someone so nice. We often butted heads when my game plan didn't solve the opponent's strategy. Somehow, he knew what was coming better than I did, the ultimate court visionary and opportunist. He ran the floor like a four-star general in the Situation Room and locked down the opposition's best player with DEFCON 1 efficiency. Score? From the parking lot. Each shot had impeccable form—eyes, shoulders, feet, and extended right arm always aimed at the basket. He mastered an imposing dribble-drive that forced his opponent to the baseline before quickly rising and squaring up to the basket. Defenders floated by.

College scouts from every region in the country descended upon North Fork early in his sophomore season. My phone at school and home rang off the hook. Recruiters said no schoolboy—even in Indiana and Kentucky—drew more attention. I heard longtime fans and scouts compare him to Jerry West and Rick Mount.

Even before I saw Linn on a basketball floor, I found him to be an attentive, interested listener, the likely result of his place as the last of four kids. His elementary school teachers considered him an old soul at a young age. He hated to waste time on information that appeared logical or already known and always seemed to be two pages ahead of everybody else. His intuition and instincts were uncanny and primary contributors to his athletic prowess, allowing him to excel at every sport he attempted. Basketball, though, held a special place in his world.

He was the talk of the town, the unassuming great-grandson of the town's founder. Linn Oliver could do no wrong. Then he missed the final shot in the state championship game.

THREE

THE DOLANS' FRONT PORCH LIGHT was out. I smirked and shook my head. That was part of my rental agreement with Linn Oliver; he was to keep at least one exterior light glowing when he was away, to provide a sense that somebody was looking after the place.

I grabbed a flashlight for a closer look. The ground near the two-story wood-clapboard home had been busy with boots and vehicles. Cars carved deep ruts into the muddy parking area, including one distinctive pair of tracks left by a larger vehicle, perhaps a fire truck or emergency-aid car. Several different sets of footprints remained on the wet lakeside lawn leading to the dock. A green spike near the beach still held my Big River Realty sign, alerting late-season boaters that the place was for sale.

I discovered that the porch light fixture with its half-moon frosted glass had no bulb. Kids often didn't notice such things, and I had to tell myself that Linn Oliver was still a kid. The lockbox allowing real estate agents to show the home was still strapped to a front-porch post. I shooed away a lake otter that had gotten comfortable in a stinky nest of sticks and leaves, punched in my combination, and removed the house key.

I figured the police had poked around and probably cleared their entry with Dolan. But I also knew Harvey Johnston. The county sheriff's top detective did things by the book and would not conduct a thorough investigation until someone had gone missing for a full twenty-four hours. Even a local celebrity. The way I figured it, Harvey's official clock still stood short, so any cops who entered would have only tiptoed around.

They also hadn't coached this kid or knew what made him tick.

My usually nimble hands fumbled then dropped the key to Dolan's front door lock. I fanned out the fingers of my right hand, hoping to relieve the cramps. Instead, I discovered a peculiar painless shaking, not unlike what I experienced at Tony's. The key tip dinged several spots around the lock before I successfully guided it into the deadbolt. Knowing this would not be a regular Realtor walk-through, I pulled a pair of painter's gloves from my hip pocket.

I flailed my arm in tiny arcs on the knotty-pine wall before I found and turned on the kitchen lights. A jumbo jug of Heinz 57 anchored most of the week's issues of the *Skagit Valley World* on a round oak table. A fry pan floated in an inch of water in the sink, topped by a plastic plate with solidified drips of grease and mustard.

The downstairs bedroom carried the familiar smell of a young athlete on the move—a combination of gum wrappers, unwashed gym clothes, and Axe body spray. Draped over the closet door rested Shell station work garments, while jeans and t-shirts covered the chair and ottoman. A golf shirt rested on the arm of the reading light. A green, unzipped sleeping bag lay atop the tartan bedspread. Loose change, crumpled fast-food receipts, and a couple of pens took up most of the bedside table.

Behind the chair, a mound of purple practice jerseys and shorts rested against a wall. Dirty socks and jocks lined a section of the closet floor while several pairs of partially laced Adidas high-tops took up the remainder. I lifted one of the newer shoes, recognizing it as the same model he'd worn in the state final and heard the "ching" of loose change in the heel. Beneath a few dimes and nickels lay scrap of paper, a return slip from J.C. Penney in North Fork. Scribbled on the back was *Holly, 9, Bremerton.* Dusty cordovan oxfords were the only street shoes. Various jackets and windbreakers hung between two wool Pendleton shirts and three pairs of jeans. Typical young-man threads—and still on hangers. So, Linn had changed on the fly for days, maybe weeks, in a row. What kid didn't?

The green top to the Gillette Foamy rested underneath the bathroom sink, and the cap to the Crest toothpaste was missing. What a surprise. No curious prescriptions or questionable over-the-counter drugs. If Harvey Johnston and his guys were here with their A-game, this stuff would've been bagged and tagged.

The three upstairs bedrooms were spotless and likely untouched since Labor Day weekend. Same with the bathrooms. As I grabbed the stair railing, I heard a creaking sound like a linebacker leaning back in a rickety wooden chair. I applied more pressure to the bannister but could not duplicate the noise.

When I re-entered the kitchen, a cold breeze knifed in from the back porch. The mud-room door, closed when I entered the home, now swung slightly back and forth. As I approached the door, I noticed the floor was slightly bowed, the plywood and linoleum curved from seasons of freezing temperatures and little crawl-space insulation. My steps brought the same creaking sound I heard a moment before.

A powerful car engine rumbled to a start as I darted out the back door.

"Hey!" I yelled, sprinting toward the road. "Get your butt back here!"

The car peeled rubber and whipped around a bend lined with tall firs three driveways down before I could even guess at a make or model. Its red taillights glowed high on the limbs of the evergreen canyon fashioned by North Shore Drive. Attempting pursuit in my ancient truck seemed ludicrous. The car would be halfway to North Fork by the time I got the big rig rolling.

Careful to sidestep the random ruts in the sloping driveway, I went back inside and took one last look around. No telltale mud from other boots or shoes; no pried locks, or jimmied windows. It also appeared that Linn had restricted his living to the kitchen, the downstairs bedroom, and bath. I turned out the lights, locked the door, and removed a glove to return the key to the lockbox. As I did so, I thought of the number of times I had forgotten to repeat the routine at other properties, leaving fellow agents stranded with customers in tow.

A light rain had begun to fall, chilly enough to bring a few snowflakes to the top of Bailey Mountain. With the flashlight beaming the way, I briefly flashed the home's siding and roof before moving to the wooden shed on the road side of the lot. The structure, more of a fall-down than a tear-down, was too small to shelter an automobile. A small rusty spike in the circular latch held the two barn-like doors closed. I pulled the spike. The place smelled like the half-dozen musty canvas lifejackets hanging from the rafters. Fresh footprints led to four large cartons on top of the workbench I'd never seen. On the shelves above, glass jars in a variety of sizes held nuts, bolts, screws, corks, and fuses. Wrinkled clothes filled three boxes. The fourth proved the biggest and heaviest. A gold-plated figurine shooting a basketball protruded through the flaps. I unraveled the four overlapping sections and immediately recognized the trophy mounted on a nicely finished wooden base.

Linnbert "Cheese" Oliver

1977 Washington State

3A Player of the Year

Smaller plaques, plates, medals, ribbons, and framed pictures surrounded the trophy. A leather binder with plastic-coated newspaper clippings, photos, and programs, starting with Linn's third-fourth grade team at St. Brendan Elementary School in North Fork, sat deeper in the box.

One picture showed him among the skinny arms and legs of his teammates at the annual Husky Hoop Camp on Whidbey Island, the same week he received his peculiar nickname. I was a camp counselor assigned to coach one of the eight-man teams of elementary school kids and handle all transportation for the campers. The camp's supervisor nearly fell over in laughter when he read the youngster's name at the meet-and-greet lunch that kicked off the first day of the session.

"Linnbert Oliver? What kind of name is that? You gotta a brudda named Chedda? What was yo momma thinkin' . . ? OK, here's the deal. I've heard your buddies call you Linn or Linnie. From now on, you are just 'Cheese.' Got that? Cheese Oliver."

Linn's elementary and middle-school basketball games were legendary. I attended as many as I could. He innately found a way to score nearly at will and provide backdoor passes to teammates while handling the ball at the foul line. Unlike most other kids, he dribbled confidently with either hand and consistently surprised opponents by favoring his left side. A gifted leaper, his incomparable skill clearly lay in how quickly he could rise from the floor and release another machine-like shot. He took his camp coach's advice and made it a central part of his game:

"It's not how high you jump, son. It's how fast you can get off the floor."

I rolled up my sleeves and ran a gloved hand down the side of the box to the bottom. I gripped the last set of publications, pulled them through the other memorabilia, and set them on the bench. My legs wobbled slightly. I reached out to the bench and steadied myself. I clutched my chin, momentarily forgetting how different the glove's surface would feel against my face. The brittle, blond rubber band that bound a dozen copies snapped when I removed the top one.

Washington State Interscholastic Activities Association
1977 State Basketball Tournament
University of Puget Sound Fieldhouse
Tacoma, Washington

I took a deep breath, but the hurt returned anyway. The best kid I ever had got us to the ultimate game, and I blew it. Too stubborn to change defenses. Too reliant on a star with a sore knee. Why didn't I call time-out in the final seconds? It wasn't Linn's fault his final shot didn't fall. I should have adjusted sooner and never have put him in that position.

For years, I secretly harbored the concern he'd never put that moment behind him. And now, after the bar talk and the tournament memorabilia Linn chose to drag with him all these years, I wondered how tightly he'd turned that screw.

I put everything back and replaced the spike in the door.

A police car coming the other way blew past me as I drove to Gustaffson's to bunk down before tomorrow's dock repair.

I rocked all night in what usually had been a comfortable bed.

Who in the hell is Holly?

FOUR

THE TRUCK'S RADIO RECEPTION as I drove back down to the Mountain Market was remarkably clear, but there was no mention of a missing basketball player on any of the morning news broadcasts. I parked and headed for the payphone, eager to get Harvey Johnston's opinion. But I had to settle for his dispatch center.

Returning to the cabin, I geared up for the original reason for the trip and spent the next few hours sinking a new pair of two-inch steel pilings to support the original fir posts at the end of the Gustaffson dock. I also spent time admiring the scenery while concocting a few more positive possibilities about Linn Oliver's disappearing act.

A beaver's wake was the only disruption on the glass-top lake, and I followed the gentle wave until the last of the V dissipated near the middle of the emerald bay. I was the morning's only interloper and felt like apologizing to the deer, chipmunks, eagles, and fish each time the sound of my sledgehammer reverberated through the valley. By the time I trudged back to the cabin to clean up, my thermal underwear was soaked with sweat beneath my chest waders.

I glanced at my watch. Of course I was behind schedule. A quick stop at home to change before the office meeting was out of the question. The clothes I had with me at the lake would have to do. I knew I'd get hammered by my no-nonsense boss for holding up the show and picked apart by our two elderly agents for my choice of clothing combinations, which usually included crumbs and stains from a recent meal. Today, a blotted, greasy lasagna spot. Even if I appeared in a new Nordstrom pinstripe suit, either Edith or Martina "wouldn't care" for the color.

On more than one occasion, they'd looked me square in the eye and said, "Coach, you could use a wife." *What does that mean?* I had one, a good one, and when she passed away, I knew I'd never find anyone like her. What I wouldn't mind was a little feminine company at dinner, followed by a two-way intellectual critique of a new film. Who knows what could happen after that? Most of the time, I shielded myself by being clueless about dating. Did mature adults actually date anymore? It seems they simply converged on bars and restaurants in packs, like college kids.

I pulled into the paved lot off Main Street and jogged to the back door at Tony's Place in work boots, an unbuttoned, untucked plaid shirt flying behind me and a manila folder under my arm.

The downtown eatery and watering hole dominated the corner site of a century-old block once occupied by the MacTavish & Oliver Mercantile, the first retail outlet built on the banks of the Skagit River in 1877. It was the only North Fork riverfront restaurant and bar that did not rely solely on the transient business from the Greyhound station two blocks away. Tourists and other wayward customers gravitated toward the national chains on the edge of town. Summer boaters and fishermen tied up to a floating dock, schlepped their empty five-gallon gas cans up the gangplank to the Shell station for refilling, and then strolled to Tony's outside window for a Bud, a burger, and the always tantalizing but later troublesome garlic fries.

I operated under the impression that the only person who believes a regularly scheduled meeting will begin on time is the one who schedules it. Come to think of it, the only detail that I truly had cared about most of my life since Cathy passed away was whether the lights in our steamy gym, Washington's High's legendary Crab Pot, beamed brightly enough above the baskets. Since I retired, I rarely made a decision that couldn't easily be put off until sometime next month.

"Ladies and gentlemen, if the world were to end tomorrow, Ernie Creekmore would have another week," said Elinor "Cookie" Cutter, the broker at Big River Realty. "I give you our guest speaker for this month, the tall, angular— and tardy—Coach Creekmore."

The eleven full-time agents—plus a few office staffers, local builders, property managers, and drainfield designers— reluctantly wrapped up their conversations at the silver coffee dispenser, snared one last sugar cookie, and moseyed to their seats.

I tried to tuck in the tails of my blue-black check shirt as I ambled toward the front of the room. Martina caught my eye, slowly shook her head, and glared down at her nun-like shoes. Cookie, Napoleonic at five-foot-two, stopped me near the back row and grabbed my arm. I was fourteen inches taller and who knows how many pounds heavier but somehow I never felt I was looking down at this miniature dynamo.

"This better be good," she whispered as heads turned our way. "Or I'll fry your fanny for lunch." She smiled for all to see.

"Thanks for the resounding support."

I tossed my presentation and handouts on the speaker's table and began erasing the blackboard in the room that felt like the den of a second home. The restaurant's proprietor, George Berrettoni, also owned Big River Realty and once taught math at Washington High. As I began to speak, George removed his white apron and slid into a chair in the back of the room. He mouthed: *Where's Linn?*

I shook my head, offered a palms-up, no-idea gesture, and plowed into my presentation.

"There is so much waterfront here that our local buyers have become spoiled," I said. "They have been around water all their lives and take it for granted. Friends from out of town often remind the locals how special our waterfront property really is."

Many of my associates, especially the younger ones, looked as if they had dates elsewhere. Or wished they did. They picked at their clothing and glanced at their watches.

"Think about it." I pointed to a colorful map of the lower forty-eight states that Cookie had brought. "Where else in the country can you find affordable salt waterfront and fresh waterfront, mountains, streams, in a decent climate? New England? Too cold and expensive. Miami? Often muggy, no fresh water. San Diego? Crowded and expensive. San Francisco? Cost-prohibitive ..."

Cookie chimed in, confirming that Puget Sound residents who were seeking a residence on the water or second home already had waited too long. "Coach's right," Cookie said. Two agents looked at her as if she just dropped in from another planet. "The Good Lord will not be making any more waterfront. With the number of new people discovering the area, only people with real means will soon be able to afford these lakefront homes."

I mentioned that many of my customers had not come close to entering the "rich," "wealthy," "well-heeled," or "doing extremely well" bracket often associated with waterfront buyers. The landscape had changed. If I did happen to land a big-bucks, out-of-state, high-maintenance buyer, it would be the lucky result of a cold call I took—not dialed—while working a shift as the floor agent in the office.

"Keep it moving, Coach," Cookie mumbled, whipping a finger like an egg beater. I sensed she wanted some motivational material straight from the old locker room. "Perhaps you could spend some time talking about networking or people skills."

"Sure," I said. "Well, I'm a word-of-mouth guy. Customers need to believe that your handshake is genuine and that you will battle for their interests. I also feel it's a two-way street. While I'm always mindful of my sales commissions, I refuse to accept a property listing if the seller is asking far more than a realistic price for the parcel. I once told a pompous seller who wanted to list his property for three times its appraised value to get another agent to bear the burden of his greed."

"OOOkaay," Cookie said. "Maybe that's enough for today. Any questions for Coach before we adjourn to go out to list and sell tons of real estate?"

The newest member of the staff, a retired Army officer named Ted, held up a reluctant hand close to his shoulder. He had to be six-six, maybe a tad taller. We hadn't formally met, but I heard he'd played two years of college buckets at Butler before zeroing in on ROTC.

"Forgive me, Coach," Ted said. "This is a bit off topic, but I've heard so much about some of your old teams. I was wondering what you've heard about Linn Oliver? Have you spoken with anyone who's seen him lately?"

I swallowed hard. "I've got a feeling there's a simple answer to this ferry thing you probably heard about from Cookie. Or the newspaper. Or George." George stood, incredulous. He winced and shook his head, big hands waving a not-me signal. I sighed and continued. "It's some sort of mistake. He's probably off playing hoops someplace. But I should know more soon."

"Well, I'm glad to hear he's still playing," Ted said. "Heard a bum knee might have done him in. I'd like to meet him someday. A friend of mine said he's the best shooter he'd ever seen."

FIVE

A BALDING REP FROM THE county's building department wrapped up the Big River Realty sales meeting with a synopsis on the state's "exciting" new law. The excitement? Requiring that all private septic tanks be pumped upon the sale of residential property in order to obtain an approved onsite sewer treatment certificate. Martina led a threesome of white-haired agents to an early exit, snipping to Cookie on her way, "We'll just skip the latest on potties, thank you."

I motioned to Cookie to meet me in the bar. I knew if I didn't bring her up to speed on Linn Oliver and she heard another story from someone else, there would be more than hell to pay. As I made my way out of the private dining room toward the bar, Mitchell Moore bounced out of the men's room, still struggling with the button-up fly on his Levi's.

"Holdin' it together, Mitch?" I said.

While I appreciated his tireless fundraising efforts for the high school, he was a power broker who could turn on a coach if you didn't see things his way or if you lost two games in a row. But all was well when the Fighting Crabs were winning and topping the prep headlines on local websites and in Saturday morning papers.

"Coach! Hey, glad I caught you." Mitch looked down, realized that the middle brass button on his fly had missed its slot, but simply let it be. He raised a hand as a cautionary signal, then let go a sneeze so ferocious that it sent his head rocketing to his knees. Unfortunately, a blue paisley handkerchief arrived too late from his hip pocket. He swabbed his drippy nose and mouth. "Say, want to join our poker group down at spring training?" Mitch surveyed the hanky. "That new Mariner complex near Phoenix. Should be a gas. Sun, baseball, who knows? We might even find a beer. Those young M's should have a decent team this year and ..." He stepped away, arched his back, and blasted another big-league gesundheit into his hands. The tattoos on his stout forearms displayed his passions; a gold Navy anchor rested on his right, and a snarling Dungeness crab stared up from his left. The sneeze sparked a trickle of blood from the gaping twin cones leading from his nose. I sunk back on my heels, repulsed and amazed at the same time. I rushed to the restroom and grabbed a handful of paper towels.

"Thanks, Coach," he muttered through the soggy cloth. "Can use these as backup."

"No worries," I said. "I heard you guys might be heading down to the desert. But that's the state tournament week. Can't miss it."

Like a school kid yearning for June, I couldn't wait for the depths of winter. Basketball is a winter game. High school buckets are all about jam-packed gymnasiums like Washington High's legendary Crab Pot and shivering lines of parents, kids, boosters, and community leaders desperately waiting to leave the biting cold and enter a familiar, raucous sauna-like gym. While I'd been approached about job openings in Las Vegas and Tucson, I'd always thought coaching hoops in the Southwest was backward; it's unnatural for people to escape the heat outside in order to attend a basketball game played between two rivals in a chilly, air-conditioned building.

"Tell you what," Mitch said, holding his head back long enough to get the words out. "The boosters will even pick up your airfare." He dabbed his nose. "That's the least we can do for all of your years of service."

His offer—and explanation—came as a complete surprise. The boosters had showered me with gifts and freebies at my retirement dinner. And, just about everyone in the county knew I hadn't missed the state tourney in thirty years. Even so, it had been awhile since I felt flattered.

"Very tempting, but I'm afraid I'm going to have to pass," I said. "A lot of the old boys would wonder what happened to me if I didn't show up at state. You guys have a terrific time. And get some sun for me."

Moore shifted his weight and poked me in the chest. "Ah, c'mon Ernie. What's it going to take to get you down there? You know they'll be some great after-dinner hoop talk. Bring back old times. I'll even pick up your hotel, and we'll have plenty of cars to get everybody around. Whole time won't cost you a cent."

"Like I say, it's not the cost but the time. If the dates were different I might."

"Just forget it," Moore growled, waving a hand. "You're one stubborn sonofabitch. Always have been." He leaned in closer. "Wouldn't even change defense when everybody in the building knew better. You go fuck yourself on your own time 'cause we'll be having a big time without you."

I stood open-mouthed, unsure if I could even muster a reply. Head cocked back, he waddled toward the parking lot, passing Cookie coming from the other direction. She cringed, backed against the wall, and lifted both hands as if being frisked, allowing Moore as much room as possible to pass.

"Don't need those cooties. Eww!" Cookie took a moment to rebound then angled her head toward the dining room. "Let's you and me go find a table." She took a step, then turned and faced me. "Talking about tables, Peggy in our office said Mitch made a killing the other night at the casino. Sucker couldn't lose." She pulled a yellow notepad from a white patent leather purse that could have held my entire wardrobe. "How long do you think this is gonna take?" she said over her shoulder. "I've got a customer who's been circling on a home at Big Lake for weeks and who might be ready to make an offer, with a little coaxing."

I stopped in my tracks.

"You know, Cookie," I began, as she eyeballed the dining room for a spot with a clean tablecloth, "why do I feel like you're doing me a favor lately every time I ask to see you?"

She snickered. "When did you become so touchy?"

"Am I not hitting the numbers you expect, or is it you feel I have little to say?" She curled her lip and hurriedly primped her silver-streaked hair before taking her seat—a dark, high-back chair that I was late tugging back from the table.

"A gentlemanly thought," she smiled. "But slow." After a moment, she said, "Regarding work? We can all do better."

I snorted at her familiar line, and then I gave her a blow-by-blow of the previous day. Cookie tapped her ballpoint on the tablet. "Has any competitor called, saying they were headed out to show your Dolan property?"

"I usually hear about it when an agent takes somebody up there," I said. "The house simply hasn't gotten that many showings since the first of the year. You know how it goes up there in the winter. Most of the people who do look are neighbors driving by. Too cold and nasty for the big-city people."

She dug back into her bag. "Tell me something. Have you heard of any break-ins at the lake? Stuff gone missing?" She unfolded a cocktail napkin with scribbled notes. "A broker said one of her owners thought some heirloom place settings were missing. Old Maryland, engraved. Expensive, I guess. Custom water skis gone from another home. Yamaha outboard from a shed." She took out a pencil and checked the list. "Here's a Mastercraft ski boat reported stolen on the north shore. These ring any bells?"

"No, but it sounds like kids. Happens sometimes. I don't see them hocking silver, though. Anyway, what's good flatware doing at a lake house in the first place?"

"Retired couple. Sold their Seattle mansion and moved up there pretty much full time. Oh, well." She shook her head, dumped the paper in the purse, then pulled out a small gold compact with the same motion. "All right, let's try this. Get Dolan on the phone. The cops might've told him something was up. Let's reassure him that the house looks fine and that things will work out with Linn. And be low-key. That poor Dolan family has had enough drama."

"I'll say. It's been two years since the accident in Mexico."

She popped the compact's top and rotated her face in front of the tiny mirror and made sure I was looking her way. "Level with me here, Ernie. What's your gut tell you on this? Could Linn have been running with the wrong crowd?"

I looked around the dining room. A young waitress folded napkins on a far table preparing for the early dinner crowd. "He's smart enough to stay clear of the riff-raff. Sure, there were a few keggers and joints along the way, but I'm fairly certain you would see that just about anywhere. The youngsters he hung around with were all pretty good kids. He really got hammered over in Stanwood one night, though. It was not long after his surgery because he was still in a cast. His girlfriend called me at home, saying Linn didn't want to give up his keys at a beach party. I drove the bus down there and took a bunch of them home."

"Did Dr. Oliver find out?"

"Never did. Barbara called there first, but he was at the hospital, and Linn's mom was out of town. But I honestly haven't seen him in several weeks and can't really say how he was doing."

"Well, I heard through the grapevine that the young man was very despondent," Cookie said. "From what I understand, he no longer can make a lot of baskets. Something about him not being able to properly shoot the ball or run as fast. I don't know. I just hope he wasn't so discouraged that he ..."

I didn't want her to finish the line. "I think every good player goes through a tough time accepting a decline in skills," I said. "I know he's tried several anti-inflammatories and some have worked well from time to time. He's biding time at the Shell station now, but he loves those big trees. Even after he got hurt that one summer. Probably end up in the family timber business, eventually."

"Wait a minute," Cookie said. "The UW said he was completely healed. I understood the university conducted a thorough examination before awarding him that scholarship. Besides, he had that very impressive senior year."

"Yeah, everybody thought he'd be fine. Make a full recovery. But the truth is he was never the same player after he tore up his right knee when that choker cable slipped in the forest. Frankly, I think it started to show in the state final. When he got to Washington, he could no longer play hard on it every day. Took a while for him and his coaches to figure it out."

"Well, even so. After all this time, you would think his own uncle would at least give him an office job," Cookie said. "I just hope he lands on his feet—and soon."

I leaned in closer. "When he lost his scholarship, he left the UW and never did get a degree. He told me he was really just drifting for more than a year. Couldn't get motivated to graduate. He didn't think it was right to drop out then be accepted into the family timber business just because his name was Oliver."

"Interesting, especially since his dad had no involvement in the company. I'm still not clear on how all that happened."

"That's a long story, but Dr. Oliver started in the logging camps with the rest of the family."

Cookie peered at her Mickey Mouse watch, centered on a beaded bracelet, and bounced out of her chair. "You can fill me in some day, but not now," she said. "I gotta go."

"OK. I'll find out from Harvey Johnston if he knows who was up there last night and check with my ferry guys and the state patrol," I said. "I promise to keep you posted."

She dug into the purse for a silver canister of lipstick and slapped on some deep red. "By all means. I'm going to go grind on that lakefront buyer to make a move."

"On you, or on that house?"

"Drop dead. Better yet, go and sell a piece of real estate for me before you do."

ON THE DIVISION STREET BRIDGE above the mighty Skagit, I watched the river run fast and high, the result of melting snow on the eastern slopes. Random branches and logs created floating snarls. The drive to the office took fewer than five minutes. I slipped silently through the back door. Off-the-cuff clothing critiques would just have to wait. I didn't have the energy for creative comebacks; couldn't rally the resources to be scintillating. Ted the Army Man's last statement hit too close to home.

I heard the kid could really shoot it.

Edith was the agent on the floor. Her drawn-on eyebrows arched up as I sneaked into the office meeting room.

"Oh, Ernie," Edith said in her not-so-endearing singsong manner. "I seeee youuuu. Now, let me tell you something for your own good." Curtness cut into her voice. She pulled a pencil from the white hair above her ear. A heavy gabardine skirt started too high above her hips and extended to her mid-calf. It looked like a drape yanked from a medieval manor.

"Not now, Edith. I'm preparing for a client call. Please ask the others not to disturb me." I nearly lunged at the doorknob.

"You really should stay away from large checked patterns. Especially blue and black above your waist. They do nothing for you. You need to get your colors done. Women prefer ..."

"It's plaid, and there's some red in there too," I said.

"If you weren't so snippy, I would have told you earlier that there's a nice gentleman asking for you or Cookie in the lobby," Edith said. "She's not back yet, but you might pay attention to how he chooses to dress. Unlike yourself, his shoes are actually shined."

Mark Rice was one of the good guys who always finished first—except in the eyes of the two women he left at the altar. A tireless worker and former all-state shortstop, "Pee Wee" became the top producing agent in a huge Redmond-based multi-office brokerage by spending more time in his cavernous Cadillac than he did in any building. When a customer wasn't opposite him in the comfy shotgun seat, he'd often yank the cigarette lighter and use it as a microphone as he mimicked Jim Morrison down I-5. Slick yet authentic, he reserved his library of ridiculous pickup lines for female strangers while remaining earnest and honest in his business dealings. I'd never been paid faster, or better, for a referral.

After the usual intro pleasantries, I said, "What can I do for you? Do you happen to have another Bellevue attorney who needs a mansion with a private dock to accommodate his yacht?"

"Actually, I did have another person who's looking for a second home to send your way, but she wanted me to conduct the tour," Rice said. "Can you imagine? I hope to hear from her tomorrow and then cover a lot of ground up here in the next couple of days."

"Does not surprise me at all," I said. "I'm betting you'll cover more than ground."

Rice grinned and rotated one of his gold cufflinks. "Don't think she's going to be the future Mrs. Rice, but you never know. She's an intelligent person and fanatic about the Mariners. You have to admit, brains and baseball can be a decent foundation for a long-term relationship and, hey, spring training's just around the corner. Throw in a bubbling personality and looks that could ..."

"Listen to you." I laughed. "I thought you were done with long-term relationships after that second time you couldn't find your way to the church."

"New confidence, Ernie. You're lookin' at the brand-new me. Got a handle on the nerves. No more problems down the road. Or down the aisle, for that matter."

I smiled and looked at my watch and then to my second-string Nikes. They were no match for his spiffy Italian imports. "Good to hear, Pee Wee. Really, it is. Now, can I get you printouts of some properties?"

He raised his chin slightly. "Coupla of things. I was going to show this woman your Dolan listing at Wilhelmina. Does the place still look OK? I haven't been there since October."

I stared off over his shoulder, wondering when the cops might take another look.

"I was up there recently, and the home looked fine," I told him. "It came through the hard part of winter in great shape. If you can, give me a holler before you make the decision to go up there."

He nodded. "Say, talking about decisions, when are you going to make the move back into coaching? I know I'm probably not the only one asking."

"I like the scouting work I'm doing now," I said. "Although there are plenty of real estate agents here that wish I was back in a gym instead of taking up space here. Maybe I'll get involved with a select team. You never know. We'll see."

I wished Rice the best and sent him on his way. The farewell felt awkward yet cordial; all threshold conversations that included coaching seemed to be that way. Perhaps I underestimated my need to be back on the bench, diagramming plays on a whiteboard, and encouraging exhausted young men to somehow find the will to continue.

The conference room remained vacant, and I was eager to secure its privacy and telephone. I dug the Dolan folder out of my file cabinet, hustled down the hall, and closed the conference room door behind me.

Jim Junior's Bellevue telephone number was listed below his signature on the last page. He was the oldest of the four Dolan children and held power-of-attorney for all matters regarding their Lake Wilhelmina cabin. I recalled the reason for the action. Jim Dolan, Sr., and his wife, Martha, two of the more popular characters at the lake, accepted an invitation for an extended vacation in Mexico with two other couples. Martha never returned.

According to police reports, she died in a scuba diving accident. Jim Dolan, Sr., ridden with guilt for partying in a sea of gin and tonics at the time of the incident, never fully recovered. Senior told me he couldn't bear the thought of being at the lake for more than an afternoon visit without Martha, so he deeded the cabin to his four children.

The Dolans had rented their place out a few weekends in the past, mostly to other lake families and their friends for special occasions. There was an unwritten "trade it forward" environment on the lake, allowing longtime residents to take a summer week or a long weekend free of charge in return for the reciprocal use of their cabin for a special occasion at a future date. The only time real cash actually changed hands occurred when out-of-towners insisted on fair compensation for wonderful accommodations they couldn't have secured without the help of a lake neighbor.

Since Martha's death, the Dolans were always giving and never using. The kids reluctantly decided to sell. They replaced some of the rounded cedar decking on the lake side of the property and had Mitch Moore bring in his backhoe to extend the drain field. Last September, they called me, and I listed it for sale. Linn Oliver moved in later that month to watch over the place.

I reached Jim Junior at home, explained that I had been unable to contact Linn, and had stopped by the cabin last night.

"No problem, Ernie," Dolan said. "I heard from Harvey Johnston yesterday. One of his guys came down here around noon for a key. I never expected Linn to be there all the time anyway. I mean, what is he, anyway? Twenty-two or twenty-three?"

"He's twenty-three."

"Well, what kid didn't disappear for a few days at that age? Good-looking young man like Linn probably has a ton of girls. Probably whisked one of them away for a romantic interlude."

"I hope you're right," I said.

"That sounds right to me. Is he still going with Barbara what's-her-name? That cute brunette?"

"Sylanski. Barbara Sylanski. They've been on-and-off since they were kids. Mostly on." But I recalled, again, that I hadn't seen either in several weeks.

"Well, there you go. That's probably where I would focus my attention. Perhaps he had a hoop game in Seattle. I know he's played a lot at the Montlake Gym in Seattle and probably just slept over instead of driving that nasty lake road."

"I hope that's the case," I said.

"Maybe he joined a traveling team to Portland or Spokane," Dolan said. "Players pick up and go in a heartbeat. I'm sure guys like him get last-minute calls all the time."

"I've making a list of some of his basketball buddies," I said. "Just haven't gotten around to calling them."

"If I were a betting man, Ernie, I'd say Barbara whisked him off to a hot time between the sheets, and Linn let somebody use his car while he was gone. Kids lend out their cars these days like women lend out scarves. Some clown probably had too much to drink and left that little wagon on the boat."

"We'll see," I said. "Pretty early in the evening for a kid to be hammered."

"C'mon!" Dolan laughed. "You ever see how fast they drink after work?"

We turned at the rustling in the hallway outside the conference room. I could make out at least one man who was wearing a brown suit and gold necktie. Several people were talking at the same time, like students outside their next classroom waiting for a long-winded professor to finish. A woman said, "Didn't you reserve it?" The door opened slightly and then closed.

"Say, did I ever give you any extra key to the place?" Dolan said. "I gave the one on my key ring to Harvey Johnston's guy."

"Nope, took the one from the lockbox and put it back," I said. "Used it last night."

"OK, I'm glad that one's still there," Dolan said. "I've been trying to reach my dad to see if he has any extras, but he must have gone fishing. The place looked pretty good, right?"

"Looked great, Jim," I said. "Linn really only uses the downstairs bedroom, the bath, and kitchen. The rest of the rooms all show well."

An office associate opened the door wide enough to mouth *We have reserved the room*. I held up the black receiver and pointed to it, indicating I was on a call.

"Well, I can't ask for much more than that," Dolan continued. "I'm happy to help the kid in any way I can. His family, especially his great-granddad, did a lot for families in this area. The guy was the Father of North Fork, for chrissake."

SIX

"SKAGIT GOLD GROUP FORMING. Inquire at the front desk."

Henry Oliver tucked the note in his shirt pocket and headed for the wooden staircase that overlooked the lobby and saloon of Murphy's Hotel in Calaveras County. The short, squatty proprietor had taken a liking to Oliver since the young man prepaid four nights' lodging upon his arrival from San Francisco. Henry, though born in Maine and raised in Wisconsin, was interested in understanding the components of mining and panning, plus the other materials that hardworking men needed in their gamble to find and process gold on the West Coast.

Henry found the proprietor in a tiny office behind the front counter, nose-deep in the hotel ledger. He closed the large cloth-bound register and removed his delicate wire-rimmed spectacles as Henry approached.

"One of my employees accompanied a party led by a man named McBee to an area north of Skagit a few years ago," the proprietor said. "I'm told McBee is considering another journey. You mentioned visiting the gold country north of Seattle."

Henry was more than intrigued. Such a trip would place him in the middle of the latest gold territory and allow him to estimate the number of gold seekers and the need for future supplies. Henry realized that if the throng was significant in size, his personal strike would come from selling the gear and services those people needed. His mind raced with possibilities, boom or bust.

"Last time, they all returned with gold," the proprietor said. "But my man said McBee turned selfish and reclusive. He will not work for him again."

Henry nodded. After arriving in San Francisco by steamship, he'd explored the California gold country for two months, astonished by the numbers of mesmerized prospectors, and the scope, placement, and variety of their bizarre claims. He understood how greed could cloud judgment and damage partnerships. "Do you know when this group is scheduled to depart?" he said.

"Fairly soon, I would assume. The rivers have begun to slow from the winter rains. I'll send word of your interest to my employee."

That evening, Henry Oliver met with Ernest Twombley, the hotel cook who joined Angus McBee's first of two trips to the Skagit gold country. The men talked long into the night about Twombley's experiences during the rainy summer of 1872. The transporting of gear was far more arduous than he had ever imagined. McBee hired native guides to paddle the party and supplies up the Skagit River to a wide clearing known as Goodman's Trading Post. The most difficult portion of the trip was the twenty-mile trek along the river's rocky cliffs from Goodman's that led to prime gold-panning river sites. Twombley said that the backbreaking work, pitiful return, and constant bickering among team members had turned McBee into a drunken conniver.

Twombley told of one particular afternoon when Angus, six-five and two hundred and forty-five pounds, got in the middle of a fight between two miners over borrowed goods. Clubs and fists landed on faces, legs, and shoulders. A wayward fist crushed McBee's nose. He gashed his hand falling on the jagged shale. When the fracas finally ended and the fighters had moved on, Twombley sewed up the hand with fishing line.

"Angus was covered in blood," Twombley said. "Spewed from his huge nostrils, and his hand. It took a long time to close that wound. I watched as he washed his bloody face and hands in a spring near the riverbank. At first, it appeared blood from his hand had dried on a rock, giving it a deep-red tone. After rinsing, the color remained. He slipped the stone into his pocket. I didn't think anything about it until we returned home. The rock he discovered that day was a precious, fiery ruby worth more than his home and farm combined."

Twombley revealed to Henry that McBee planned to parlay his ruby with other discoveries and buy hundreds of acres along the Skagit River where he could prospect and farm for the rest of his life. Twombley said McBee returned to the same location on the river three years later, this time in secret without partners.

"The man wanted to keep everything to himself," Twombley said. "He'd dig a hole and hide it before he would split any gold with anybody. Selfish bastard. Only reason he needed anybody was to carry his load."

McBee reportedly named the creek meandering from the spring "Ruby River," and focused his digging and exploring in the area near his original find. Twombley said McBee collected a significant amount of gold by panning smaller tributaries above the confluence of the Skagit and Ruby rivers.

"If you go, know that the river changes Angus. It makes him a different man."

In 1877, Henry, age twenty, signed on as McBee's professional assistant. McBee was adamant that he keep confidential their business—and ultimate destination. When the pair arrived at Goodman's Trading Post in mid-June, the river bank was already brimming with nearly forty newly built canoes, along with calloused miners, surveyors, panners, guides, and a variety of restless chickens, horses and goats.

"We're headin' up river tomorrow," McBee told Henry. "No use lookin' for any nuggets in this sorry crowd. Now, don't go tellin' anybody because we don't want to be followed."

For two days, they coaxed stubborn pack mules through rocky crevices above the river. Exhausted by the journey, McBee and Henry finally approached the natural spring where Angus had discovered the most valuable asset he'd ever possessed. Instead of tranquility and seclusion, they encountered three men from Colorado camping on the site.

"You boys best move along," McBee said, sizing up the trio. "I staked this claim years ago, and anything taken from around here is mine. I understand if you didn't know, but ..."

"Name's Tyler," said a wiry man, who Henry took to be the oldest. Henry also heard that three brothers named Tyler had instigated a fight at the trading post for refusing to pay "injuns" for hauling their gear upriver. "I've got all the proper papers," the man continued. "Show 'em to ya if you like."

As Tyler retreated to his tent, McBee pulled a gun from his satchel and fired wildly into the night. The bullet whizzed past Henry's ear as he raised his hands to cover his head. Tyler raced back from the tent, leaped upon McBee's back, and drove a rusty oyster knife under the big man's ribcage. McBee shrieked, turned, and before he could raise his weapon toward his attacker, Tyler jammed the blade into McBee's ample midsection. McBee collapsed backward like a falling hemlock, his panicked face highlighted by the glowing fire. The three men quickly rifled through McBee's pockets and tossed his worn leather shoulder bags into their tent.

"Get out of here, kid," Tyler told Henry, the oyster knife dripping with McBee's blood. "If you ever say anything about this, I'll cut you right down the middle."

SEVEN

I NEEDED TO KNOW WHICH COPS had cased the Dolan place, what they found, and how long they were there. After I hung up with Jim Junior, I cruised back across the river to the cop shop in the dreary county administration building. Like many small-town municipal complexes that designers deemed modern and impressive at one time, the sprawling campus of shaded windows and skinny Roman bricks is what you'd now expect to find inside a barbed-wire fence. Interiors bathed in brown and off-yellow cried out for light; the hallways were as stale as an old man's closet.

I found Harvey Johnston behind his desk, scratching his balding head and dragging an eraser over his three-day whiskers. The pencil tip at the other end was dull and needed sharpening. From his tone and demeanor, so did his day.

"Ernie, when's the last time we caught a fish?" the county's chief criminal investigator said, arms crossed over his chest. "I take that back. When's the last time we even got a line wet?"

I hadn't expected the first question of the meeting to be about fishing. Nonetheless, the topic deserved careful attention. And immediate planning. "Well, let's see." I said.

"We didn't get out on any river in January; rivers were too high to fish. So it must have been late last year. Maybe that week before Thanksgiving?"

"That's poor," Harvey said. "Piss-poor. For years it was every other weekend."

The question was merely small talk, probably to avoid aggravating bigger talk. Harvey had built his reputation on thorough research, a network of resources, unfailing logic, and a memory like Dick Clark recalling oldies rock and roll. Harvey instantly remembered evidence from cases he studied, observed, or read about more than twenty years ago, including every run-in with the law involving one of my players. He always provided an early heads-up and even let me help him investigate some of those cases in which I had access to a tribal community, like troubled kids, that were sometimes out of his questioning reach. We became friends and fishing partners along the way. Harvey had risen through the ranks, cracked a handful of high-profile state cases, and become so revered nationally that he could telephone law-enforcement officials, physicians, and academics throughout the country at any hour. They all took his calls, then asked why he hadn't accepted a big-city job. "No steelhead streams in that city" was his stock reply. He fiddled with his pencil and thumbed the top page of his notepad over, exposing a fresh one.

"When I heard you were coming in, I figured it wasn't about fishing or basketball," Harvey said. "I did go by the Dolan place at Lake Wilhelmina late yesterday, but I wasn't happy about going up there."

I rose out of my chair and circled behind it. Confused by his apparent lack of interest, I gripped the brown fabric on the top of the chair with both hands. "Harvey, this is a great kid that everybody knows."

"Look, as much as I know your concern for Linn, he hasn't been missing long enough for this office to get hot and bothered about it. I mean, we usually don't even pay attention until a person's been gone for twenty-four hours."

That wasn't good enough. Not for this kid. "Harvey, we're coming up on forty-eight."

"I understand that. And that was yesterday and today is today."

I bit my lip and pushed the chair until it bumped against the front of Harvey's desk. "I don't get it," I said. "If Linn's disappearance failed to meet your minimum time requirements, why did you bother to drive that awful road and come home after dark?"

Harvey rolled his eyes. It didn't happen often. "The state patrol made the mistake of broadcasting the result of the license-plate inquiry. It went out on the cop CB early yesterday. One of our guys heard it, drove up there, and patrolled the lake all day asking about Linn. Word got around. I got some calls. I went up there to calm people down."

I figured as much but didn't want to say so. "Tell me something," I said. "Were there other county vehicles with you last night at Dolan's? Maybe a truck from the lake's fire department?"

Harvey pushed his hands together like an altar boy, then lifted his fingers to his lips. "I got there first," he said. "And Deputy Dawson met me there a few minutes later in his patrol car. There were no larger vehicles when we were at the site, but I did see some fatter tracks."

"Dawson . . ? The man's a meathead. A real walking weasel."

"Whoa, Coach. Take it easy on the guy."

"Harvey, Arnold Dawson probably already bragged the news about Linn to some teenagers, trying to impress them. Did he show you the box of Snickers under the front seat that he saved for young girls?"

Harvey coughed at the thought and shook his head. "You've never thought very highly of him, have you? And, I grant you, he did make a mistake here letting the word slip. Did you have a few run-ins with him at the high school, or is it something else?"

"He flirted with the girls and bullied the guys," I said. "Really upset them, but they felt they could do nothing about it. My players said he tailed them home from games—especially if they had a date. Stopped them for no reason but to check out the tops on the females."

Harvey appeared surprised, but I knew he really wasn't. Besides, a supervisor wanted only so much criticism about one of his own. Even from a friend.

"I looked around a little bit inside Dolan's place," Harvey said. "I didn't bring out the magnifying glass, just putzed around. Dawson stayed outside."

"Great decision. Keeps him from stealing televisions. I hope you had him counting raccoons."

"Help me think this through a second, Ernie. Linn either works or plays basketball. That's it. I wonder what Barbara thinks about that and him living up there?"

"When I rented him the place, they thought it would work," I said. "But he moved in September, and that's a heck of a lot different than the cold of February. I'll make a point to see her and ask about the past few weeks."

"Maybe he took her skiing in Whistler. They've opened a bunch of new chair lifts up there. Who knows? Possibly he drove to a hoop tournament in Missoula."

"You been talking with Jim Junior? That's about what he said."

"Yeah, I spoke to him," Harvey said. "Had to get the OK to go in to his lake house. But you know, he's probably right about Linn's whereabouts."

"Then how do you account for his abandoned wagon on the ferry? It feels like people are trying to explain that away before there's anything to support their explanations." I knew I sounded like Sherlock.

"That's one of the things I like about you. Always looking at the possibilities. It's your coaching background, dissecting routines and tendencies. You see stuff others don't."

"You should tell that to the old biddies at the office," I said. "They think I'm blind to colors, stains, and anything on a calendar."

"They could be correct."

"Well, this might surprise you," I said. "But I did see something you might have missed last night at the Dolan place."

Harvey spun the pencil on the yellow notepad in front of him, leaned back in his chair, and maxed-out its spring. His head rested on the office wall behind his desk. His collar was frayed; battered by years of stubby growth.

"Wait a minute," he growled. "You were in there *after* I left?''

"Hey, I'm a licensed Realtor, a dues-paying member of the MLS who simply entered a house for sale. You never know when I might have a potential--"

"Dammit, Ernie! I hope you didn't touch anything."

"Why? I didn't hear anybody say it was a crime scene. Besides, I had gloves."

"Right. You just happen to wear latex gloves when you're out on tour?"

"Wasn't on tour. I was up doing some dock work for a friend. And they were painter's gloves."

"Well, at least you were covered. Look, I don't mind you asking your former players, coaching buddies about Linn, but leave the heavy lifting to us. Particularly if this becomes an official investigation and we start gathering evidence. I don't want to be lifting your fingerprints from every place I go."

I smirked and bent over to tie one of my desert boots.

"Are we clear on that?" Harvey said.

While still hunched over, I laughed. "Crystal."

"I'm serious. I love your intuition, but I can't have you walking into buildings looking for clues and interrogating people. That would be extremely confusing and a huge mistake."

"A clue is simply a mistake by another name."

"Arthur Conan Doyle, The Hound of the Baskervilles?"

"No. Ernie Creekmore. Real estate agent. North Fork, Washington. Let me tell you what I yanked out of one of Linn's sneakers at Dolan's."

"Now, that's exactly what I'm talking about! What the hell did you take?"

"Didn't take anything!" I said. "I was looking over one of his high-tops in the closet. Same shoe he wore as a Crab. Found some loose change and a note with *Holly, 9, Bremerton* written on it.

"Well, there you go, amigo. Just as I thought. Our boy's got a new flame, and she's a babe from Bremerton. Probably zipped sleeping bags together last night and fell asleep at her daddy's fishing cabin out on the Hood Canal."

"Yeah, right," I scoffed. "Then why didn't Linn drive off the ferry?"

"Maybe he was so hot to see her, he forgot all about the station wagon and walked off into her arms," Harvey said. "Linn's car could have broken down or been borrowed or stolen. I've asked the state patrol to run the license plate again and have a local mechanic look at the car."

"What about the blood on the gym towel?" I said.

"Slow down, Mr. Sleuth," Harvey said. "Could have been anybody's. Maybe he sopped up a teammate's gash. If the car was jacked, maybe the guy was bleeding and desperate. We just don't know. A couple of my cops just got back from lunch at Tony's, and neither of the Berrettonis has heard a thing about anybody borrowing cars or blasting out of town. And those guys know everything."

"I was down there today, too. Thought it was too early to be asking around about Linn, especially to that crowd. Didn't want to start a ruckus. But I'll try and get a hold of Barbara today just to help ease my mind."

Harvey sat up and held up a finger, signaling an idea. "Her mother asked me to make a crime-scene presentation to her elementary school class, so maybe I'll stop by the house when school gets out. Anyway, I've got a four-thirty up in Burlington and I'll hit the Sylanski place on the way. I'll tell Barbara you're looking for her, if I see her."

I'd also planned to reach out to my contacts at Washington State Ferries, state patrol, and the newspapers. You get to know some people after coaching kids for nineteen years. Turns out some of today's important guys in the area once played for me; others were the kind you simply couldn't find when you needed to. Like Linn Oliver.

"And, Ernie," Harvey said. "The next time we talk, have your calendar ready. The kids gave me a new carbon rod for Christmas, and it's been sitting in the closet. Thing was made for the Skagit and the North Fork of the Stilly."

EIGHT

THE BLISTERS ON HENRY OLIVER'S heels bled through his heavy wool socks. At daybreak, when he waded into the chilly Skagit River, the torn skin waved in the current like circular white caps covering bright red jam. His broad shoulders burned from the sweat-soaked strap of the dusty bag that held all his possessions.

Henry had run as fast and far as he could from the ugly scene at Ruby River, but the unbalanced load soon ruined his rhythm, drained his energy, and kept him from covering more ground on the flat plateau. When he reached the steep cliff trail, the loose gravel beneath his oversized boots slid on every step, taxing his ankles. He sunk to his knees often, feeling with his hands in the dark for the path's next switchback. The gruesome night was finally behind him.

"Pretty early to be goin' for a swim, ain't it, son?"

The rangy rider stood atop an outcropping above the bank. His white hair fell to his shoulders. All else was black and proper—hat, shirt, vested suit with string necktie, shiny boots. His snorting black horse bobbed and glistened in the sun. He dismounted and held its reins as he walked it to a nearby pool. "Looks like you're about done, and the sun's just said hello."

Henry turned and began tiptoeing out of the water, his arms stretched bird-like as he balanced his cautious steps over the slippery stones.

"Came down out of that canyon last night, sir," Henry said, unrolling his damp pantlegs. "Planned to have something to eat and make my way down to the trading post. Then, don't know. Maybe Seattle."

The stranger bent down and scooped his hand into the water, lifted it to his lips, then shook away the remaining drops. "Looks like you're travelin' light. Did you already make your fortune and just leavin' the rest for others?

"Job didn't work out, sir," Henry said. He eased his bottom on to a large boulder, drew his left foot into his hands, and cringed at the open sores. "Looks like I came a long way for nothing." He reached into his pack for salve, dipped a slippery glob on his index finger and wiped the wounds. The harsh-smelling liniment quickly brought water to his eyes.

The man placed a boot in a stirrup and hoisted himself into the saddle. "Tell you what. If you're not set on pannin' or diggin', there's a mill that's hirin' a ways downriver from Goodman's. The boat captain'll know the place. Ask for MacTavish. Wallace MacTavish. Call him 'sir.' He'll like that. Man's got big plans."

Henry stood, relieved and surprised. He rolled up a sleeve and rubbed the remaining ointment on his forearm, keeping his eyes a safe distance away. The possibility of more suitable employment quickened his movement. "I will do that, sir. Thank you. I know a bit more about cutting trees than I do looking for gold. Speaking of gold, I see you're not packing a shovel or pickaxe. They seem to be the only thing people do up here."

The rider moved up the hill and now spoke over his shoulder. "Not in my blood, son. Just don't see spendin' a lot of time on a gamble. No, I just come around now and then, makin' sure a guy's diggin' on land that's his. Some claims in these hills were staked years ago and some folks don't care about who owns what. Take whatever they want to take."

The man in black was nearly out of earshot. "Sir!" Henry shouted. "Who should I say sent me to the mill? To Mr. MacTavish . .?"

"Sylvester. Just tell him Sylvester O'Leary."

HENRY TRUDGED ALONG the river to Goodman's Trading Post and gave most of his remaining money to the steamboat captain for passage to the sawmill, where he caught on as an office assistant. He worked long hours, offered creative suggestions, and displayed a personality that impressed his superiors. Especially its owner, Wallace MacTavish.

The Scottish entrepreneur had formed his own company to operate another mill and mercantile on a bustling waterfront near the mouth of the Skagit. After two months, MacTavish recognized that Henry clearly understood the needs, habits, and language of the miners and panners, and hired Henry to help manage the retail outlet. The store could not stock enough shovels, axes, manila rope, gunpowder, salt, flour, dried pork, smoked salmon, and lard for the increasing prospector population—let alone the needs of the fishermen who worked the rivers and salt waters of Puget Sound. An increasing number of hunters and trappers began to traipse the Cascade foothills east of North Fork for deer, black bear, and beaver.

The following summer, MacTavish rewarded Henry's energy and contributions by making him a partner in the growing operation. Henry grew the business and became popular with customers for establishing short-term credit accounts. Only one account, "Tyler," continued an outstanding balance.

NINE

3 P.M., THURSDAY, FEBRUARY 3, 1982

HARVEY EXCUSED HIMSELF FOR an impromptu conference with the district attorney, so I waited in his outer office. While thumbing through an old edition of *Field & Stream*, I found a map of western Washington rivers highlighted by an inset of the Stillaguamish. Plopping the magazine in my lap, I recalled some of the exceptional people and extraordinary fish that flowed through different phases of my life. I had worked nearly every pool of the Stilly with my father and planned to do so with my own son. That wasn't to be.

I was fortunate, however, to try a few spots with Linn Oliver.

One memorable day he selected a copper-hued nymph fly and started down through the brush to the river, circling the east end of a wide pool. I recalled the first time I slogged away in heavy waders from my father, choosing for myself the place to firmly plant my feet in the hypnotizing current.

Linn turned suddenly and called out, his right hand on his hip, his left pointing the rod toward two o'clock. "You know what I loved, Coach? I loved sophomore year. That was somethin' else. Nobody expected us to do much, and we just rolled into districts. All the laughin' in the locker room after winning the league title. That's what I remember most."

"Special days," I yelled. "With special players."

Head down, he returned to his tromping, pushing aside replanted seedlings above a tiny peninsula where swift swirling water rested into a quiet pool. I gazed at the pool with a mix of excitement and gratitude, knowing Linn was alone in the sun, standing in a spot that held the best opportunity for a steelhead in the entire river. I stayed above the pond and worked a tiny rapid, partially guarded from Linn's view by a peeling birch.

The fiberglass pole looked comfortable and light in his hand. Linn watched his line as the current drew it in and deftly angled the fly toward the active water. He repeated his casting routine. When the line hit the water, he allowed the current to carry it until the fly slid toward the lower end of the silent pond. The screaming of Linn's reel began losing yards of line until magically pausing when a fish soared three feet out of the water, trying to shake the hook from its angry mouth. I caught a breath in deep pleasure.

Could it be that big? That colorful?

I stepped downriver to a cleared rocky section of bank. When the gorgeous creature splashed back into the river, the reel continued squealing, relinquishing foot after foot of line as the fish headed to the safety of a small rapid. The top half of Linn's rod was a throbbing crescent, pointed downstream at a moving target that seemed to spend as much time out of the water as in it. While Linn reached for the reel's tiny pearl handle, the fish suddenly leaped. Beneath the evergreens, the wet silver flash made a complete tailspin, throwing crystal drops in a wide arch.

Linn raised the tip of his rod, enticing the fish toward him before it broke the surface again, diving toward the end of the pool. The black-speckled torpedo shot away again, the line carving a small semicircle on the surface of the glassy water. This time, the fish slowed. Linn lifted the rod high over his head. The steelhead moved on its side toward Linn's boots in the ankle-deep water. He crossed the rod from his right hand to his left, then slid two fingers of his free hand into its pink gills and carried it up the bank. I couldn't remember a time on the river when I was more delighted.

"Now, that's how you do it!" I roared. "What a fish!"

I sloshed down the shallows in my waders. Linn's smile said it all. The fish was a grand specimen, about twelve pounds, and fresh from the sea. A trace of crimson blood trickled from the hooked corner of its jaw. Its small head and wide, square tail were separated by a massive yet supple spine mixed with black, violet, and silver. Linn set a small piece of driftwood under its white-silver belly, raising its middle slightly higher than its head and tail, accentuating its girth. Thousands of black diamond dots appeared over its shiny body as if dusted by some heavenly ash.

After removing the hook, he rearranged his backpack and cinched up his hip boots. Rod in one hand and prized catch hanging from the other, Linn began his triumphant march along the riverbank toward the Socrates Pool, where we would share a sandwich and discuss the details that led to his catch. I followed, shaking my head in amazement and gratitude.

Along the shady path, I became aware that he'd experienced no such days with his father, the ever-scheduled physician ostensibly on call every weekend. I'd been his basketball coach but also his teacher of river etiquette. I'd taught him principles usually reserved for a father or grandfather, such as to never fiddle with his gear while another fisherman was upstream moving in his direction. I stressed that the first fisherman to the water had first shot at a specific pool, yet one pool did not stretch the entire length of the river. I reminded him to always maintain a reasonable distance between himself and the next fisherman downstream, and to never overstay his time. Work the bank in slow, steady strides. Just like basketball, he picked up suggestions instantly.

A rowdy argument was developing on the far side of the river. Bart Knight, looking rough around the edges in torn bib overalls and no shirt, was in another man's face about trespassing on his fishing territory.

"Don't you be fishing down through my water, fella," roared Knight. "It ain't your pool!"

"You're dead wrong, Bart. I was here first, upstream of you, and did not take five steps before ..."

Knight looked up and locked a glare on Linn. Suddenly, any breach of protocol did not seem so important. The other fisherman simply shook his head, reeled in his line, and began making his way up river.

"Is that Linn Oliver over there, taking a beautiful fish out of my river?" Knight said. "You gotta be shittin' me. I wouldn't think you could catch a cold."

"I can fish some." Linn smiled and looked down at his catch. "It's just been a while."

My mind raced back again, to the years when everyone in town cared what Linn did and where he was. On or off the court, he was front-page news. Boosters jockeyed to buy his lunch. People he didn't know slipped him money in a sweaty handshake, hoping he would remember a particular college when it came time to choose his next stop.

"Yeah, well, I heard it's been a while since you've done anything right," said Knight, leaning against a riverfront alder. "Washed out in college, don't wanna work the forests. So, you thought you might just come out here and take your dinner from my river."

"Well, if you think people are trespassing around here," said Linn, "then spend some money and put up a few signs."

"What?" Knight said. "A wise guy to boot? You bet your sweet ass you're on my property! And your family sure as hell tried to ruin it."

I took a deep breath and tried to relax the tension in my shoulders. I hadn't realized how tightly I was gripping my pole. Bart Knight's presence had a similar effect on me just about everywhere I went. When he attended basketball games, it was simply to yell at coaches and referees. He once built an ugly metal workshop just to block the mountain view of one of my customers. The woman, a retired second-grade teacher, enjoyed bird-watching, but Knight contended that she had been spying on him and examining his property with powerful binoculars.

"Slow down, Bart," I said, taking three steps closer to Linn. "He's got as much right to fish this river as anybody."

"Well, now," Knight said. "What do we have here? From Coach to Mister Real Estate Rip-Off. Once a loser, always a loser."

"Look, Knight," I said. "I've fished this river for years, and you know it." I set my gear on the bank and folded my arms, knowing if Linn hadn't been there, my fists would have been slamming both sides of Knight's face. "This is not private property, so just leave us be."

"Kiss my ass, Coach. Actually, I don't even have to call you Coach anymore, do I? Thank gawd you're no longer on that bench. Cost us a frickin' state championship."

Knight locked his right hand on his hip and aimed his bloodshot eyes at Linn. "No wonder you had nothin' left in that title game, kid. Coach stunk the place up." Knight bent over and spit brown tobacco juice between his hip boots. "Know what? I think I can smell you both from here."

Linn dropped his fish, clenched his fists, and took two quick steps up the bank, searching for the quickest route across the river. I grabbed him by the back of the shirt. Linn's muscles stood out through the sweat of the blue cotton.

"Oh, so you want some, do ya, kid?" Knight said. "Well, bring it on, son." He signaled the young man to come closer. "You punk, I'll kick your ass from here to Arlington."

I blocked Linn's charge and pushed him away, pointing him downriver. Linn quickly pivoted and returned. I tried to restrain him with both arms, but he forearmed me aside, his entire weight behind the drive. He jogged through the shallow water and launched a huge right fist to Knight's left cheek, propelling him backward to one knee. Water rushed in and over his pant leg.

"You sonofabitch!" Knight barked. 'Pullin' some kind of sucker punch like that. You're screwin' with the wrong hillbilly!"

"Just get back up, old man," Linn sneered. "I got a lot more left for you right here, right now."

I dashed across the river as Knight wiped blood from his nose on an open hand. His uneven teeth were stained a light brown, and he reeked of alcohol. I tugged at Linn's arm, twisting him away.

"Let it go, Linn," I yelled. "Now!"

He turned and glared at Knight, still recovering from the power of the blow and the speed with which it was delivered.

"You're better than this," I said. "It's just talk. Some people like him never change."

We spun around, crossed the river, and headed up the bank.

"You better watch your back, kid," Knight called out. "My people ain't good at forgettin' shit like this."

As I swung the truck through the Stillaguamish Valley road, I welcomed the warmth of the afternoon sun on my face. Linn's eyes were closed, opening only when his chin bobbed abruptly toward his chest. He held his breath and stretched long and hard, all limbs extended; his right arm fully outside the shotgun window, the left behind my headrest.

"Talk about outfishin' a guy in his own backyard," I said. "That is some fish to be taking home. You have to be pleased."

"Thanks, Coach," Linn said. "Truly enjoyed it, except for what Knight said about my family. I know the old loggers left a lot of stuff behind in the camps, but I never heard that they damaged any property."

"Gotta take everything with a grain of salt," I said. "Especially when you're talking about a guy like Bart Knight."

TEN

WHEN HARVEY HADN'T RETURNED after a half-hour with the DA, I left. I figured I'd tour two new listings on the Sauk River submitted over the weekend by a Darrington agency. A couple of old flycaster friends of my dad would probably make offers if the roofs didn't leak and the septic systems passed county inspection.

I ducked into Tony's and jumped on the pay phone. The dark cubby between the bar and the restaurant was like a second office. I'd often reported box scores and offered game quotes to newspapers on Friday nights while a cold mug of beer sat precariously perched above the coin slot. I made appointments to preview new listings and held heated discussions over counteroffers with fellow agents. Then there were the late nights I dialed home just to listen to Cathy's rendition of a Hank Williams tune she'd left as a message while visiting her folks. *"Hey, good lookin', what's you got cookin'?"* I hadn't thought of a good reason to erase it.

I dialed information and got the number for the Montlake Gym. The way I figured it, his teammates were the last ones to see Linn Oliver before he headed to the ferry.

"Cheese Oliver?" said the gym manager, above the din of players demanding equipment. "The guy can still shoot it. You should have seen him last week. Man *could not miss.* He probably--"

"I'm sorry," I interrupted. "I'm on a pay phone. Can you tell me the name of his team?"

"Let's see," the speaker said. I could hear shuffling papers and then a muffled "shit!" when an object apparently crashed to the floor. "Yeah, he's with Fool's Gold. That league runs Tuesday and Thursday nights. Elite Division."

"Thanks," I said. "What time are those games?"

"Got one at seven and another after that, usually around eight-thirty. Schedule says Fool's Gold goes at seven tonight."

"Great," I said. "Is there a team contact person?"

"Lemme look. Says here, captain's Garcia. Ronnie Garcia."

"Really?" I mumbled. "Gotta number for him?"

A moment later I dialed but hung up after a dozen rings.

ELEVEN

5 p.m., Thursday, February 3, 1982

BARBARA SYLANSKI SLOUCHED INTO their corner booth at Tony's, watching shivering boaters glide under the Division Street Bridge. The "their" had suddenly become frighteningly singular now that Linn Oliver was missing. Her once-perpetual smile made fewer appearances. Her gentle face attempted to hide a profound sadness and invited sympathy. She'd grown tall and athletic, and now had to downplay a figure that never had an extra inch anywhere. The ends of a classic bob cut curled above a charcoal cable sweater.

"Thanks for taking the time to see me," I said. "I've been worried about you."

A smile played at the corners of her mouth. The gray eyes lacked their usual sparkle. It became clear there had been no romantic getaways to Canadian ski slopes or elegant downtown hotels.

"It's been so hard, Coach. It really has ... just not knowing. I mean, I've looked everywhere the past two days. And his Subaru on the ferry? I woke up last night just screaming. I get these images of Linn's body washing up on some isolated beach." She removed an embroidered beige handkerchief from her sleeve and interrupted a falling tear. "I can't remember ever being lonelier or more scared."

The rumors of Linn's disappearance, now confirmed in the news and by local law enforcement, stunned the entire town. For his long-time girl, inquisitive eyes locked on her everywhere she went. People stared and whispered.

Barbara stirred a diet soda with a pink swizzle stick and waited for her Crab Louie, the restaurant's blue-plate lunch special for February. She'd spent countless hours in the popular gathering place over the years; dinner with Linn after Fighting Crabs games, the occasional brunch following Mass at St. Brendan's. The early dinner buffet tables overflowed with several varieties of pizza, steaming stainless steel trays jammed with fresh vegetables, Italian sausage, pasta primavera, eggplant parmesan, and wicker baskets lined with white linen and loaded with sourdough rolls. Barbara chose to order off the menu.

George Berrettoni balanced a salad on a brown oval tray and strutted through his bar and into the restaurant. His father, Romeo, still frisky at seventy-seven, shuffled a few steps behind, his white smock tied around his ample middle. Two waitresses in white hats remained near the tent-like oven hood, pairing huge squares of Romeo's homemade lasagna with dripping slabs of hot garlic bread for an off-site catered banquet.

"Our best salad for our prettiest girl," George said. He swirled the chilled dish in front of her. "May I sit and finish my lemonade with you?"

"Of course, George," Barbara said. "And, I am so honored to be served by the proprietor. Will Mister Berrettoni consider spending a few minutes, too?"

Romeo beamed at Barbara, twirled his thick mustache, and slid in next to his son. A freckled-face waitress with a tight-curled perm instantly appeared with Romeo's iced tea. George waved off an offer for a lemonade.

The two Berrettonis had always considered the Sylanski women as family, particularly since the loss of Barbara's father. Ross Sylanski was a gregarious, third-generation crab fisherman who worked the Alaska king season from October through January out of Dutch Harbor. He came home just in time for the prep basketball playoff tournaments in February, then fished for Dungeness in Puget Sound during the summer months. A small-time car nut and mechanic, he cherished the navy blue '57 Chevy Bel Air two-door hardtop that took up half the space in his spotless garage. Ross swapped George Berrettoni fresh crab for pizza and salad at Tony's and usually delivered the crab in the Chevy so George could again remind him how badly he wanted the car. This continuing arrangement allowed Barbara, her sister, and mother to dine for no charge in the restaurant at any time. The meals came in handy, especially when Ross was at sea.

In the winter of 1980, Ross Sylanski did not come home from the Alaska King Crab season. His 86-foot boat *Shamrock* began listing in twenty-two-foot swells in the Bering Sea after he radioed a mayday message to the Coast Guard station at Cold Bay. The bodies of the five crew members were never found. His death hit me like an uppercut. Ross taught me the tricks of the crab trade—how to work the afternoon flood tide, where to snag free salmon heads for bait, the proper way to position the pot on a sandy, grassy bottom. To countless crabbers who tried to guard their favorite locations like fishermen who protect their favorite stream, Ross Sylanski always offered a rhyme that locals recalled every time they cracked a fresh Dungeness:

"A secret crab hole keeps for only a day;
Because your buoys always give it away."

"How's your lovely mother?" Romeo said. "She hasn't been in for more than two weeks. Please tell her that I miss seeing her here."

"I will do that, sir," Barbara said. "And thank you. You are one of my mother's favorite people. She's taking some time away to visit my aunt down in Oregon. She's been in Bend and loving the sun."

We quickly covered the obvious topics. George groused over the week's weather. Romeo bemoaned the high school's dwindling basketball playoff chances. Both recalled Barbara's athletic passion had been cross country, and she still ran long distances on weekends. She picked at a chunk of crab. She dropped the folk and lifted her napkin, then shyly looked away and dabbed the corners of her mouth. Clutching the linen in her hand, she spoke softly. "Mr. Johnston came to my home today," said Barbara, holding back tears. "He said he simply doesn't know much about Tuesday night. Nor has anyone turned up to say that Linn lent him his car and that they just walked off the ferry and forgot about it. There's been no sign of Linn's clothing, gym bag, wallet, turning up anywhere." She took a deep breath and interlaced her fingers on the table like a schoolgirl instructed to sit up straight and tall. "I went to the Montlake Gym Tuesday night."

I could feel my mouth open. What *else* didn't I know?

"Mr. Johnston was quite interested to hear that, but I'm certainly not trying to hide anything. The truth is, it was the first anybody asked me about it."

Romeo's charcoal eyebrows arched skyward, like two small Cs capitalizing.

"Sweet one, what did you talk about?" Romeo asked. "Did Linn seem out of sorts in any way?"

"That's just it," Barbara said. "I never got to see him. One of his teammates told me Linn had another game he wanted to play. He left the Montlake game early and took off." She dipped her shoulders and glanced briefly out the window to the river. Her deep sigh seemed rooted in frustration and confusion. I wondered why the couple hadn't coordinated. Barbara seemed to know what I was thinking. "Earlier Tuesday, we had an awkward conversation. He'd called me from the pay phone at Mountain Market, and it turned into more of an argument. I decided later to go to the gym to see if we could get things sorted out."

"You guys seemed to be good about hammering stuff out," George said. "A lot of times, right here in this booth."

"This was different," Barbara said. "I had seen Ronnie Garcia a few times. Linn evidently had gotten his nose out of joint about it."

Where was this going? Barbara and Ronnie? Linn and ... *Holly?* I could not remember seeing Barbara with a steady guy other than Linn Oliver. They went through stages when they were "just friends," but most of the time they were so close that their classmates referred to them as "Cheese 'n' Cracker." They giggled; big eyes, and bigger smiles, eating Romeo's pepperoni pizza after games until the cook shooed them out at midnight. Linn talked of Huskies, Cornhuskers, and Blue Demons; Barbara passed along her dreams of exotic places. Her real dream was to own a used bookstore in a nearby storefront.

A moment later, she lifted a reddish-brown notebook above the lip of the table and lightly brushed the magazine-size cover with the front of her hand. The back cover, with one corner missing, appeared stiff and discolored as if left out in the weather. As she carefully opened the book, I noticed that some of the pages were stuck together. The ones that remained separate and independent pages were brittle and faded and crinkled when she delicately turned them.

"Linn and I found this diary under the trestle at the bottom of Brookens Gorge the night after we graduated from high school," Barbara began. "It was the Senior Lockout, the last time a lot of us were together. The party was supposed to be on the lake, with pontoon and ski boats, but we got in a hassle at the boat launch before we could get started. We ended up lugging all the beer and food down into the gorge from the North Fork road and camping out. When Linn and some of the guys were digging a fire pit, setting up beach chairs, he hit this with a shovel."

She ran her fingers of her left hand over a slight indentation on the front cover while holding a place in the middle of the book with her right. "It belonged to a single mother in one of the logging camps," Barbara continued. "She includes details about her daily chores, some of the possessions workers left behind at different sites, a hospital stay at the old clinic. Seems some pages are missing, from what I remember. Anyway, Linn and I promised ourselves we'd try to locate the old sites, but the years went by, and we never did. I put the book in Mom's garage and forgot about it."

George shimmied closer to the table. "I know this is a personal matter and not really any of my business," he said. "But how high on the jealousy scale was Linn regarding your involvement with Ronnie Garcia? I mean, you might want to think about how you present that to the cops. Envy always has a way of tweaking their interest."

Barbara tugged on her thin silver bracelet then spun it slowly. "Bart Knight and some of his bad-news friends have been harassing the Latinos. Knight's guys had even been cruising the parking lots at Skagit Valley College, looking to pick fights when kids get out of class."

"So, what does all this have to do with the young mister Garcia?" Romeo asked. Both Berrettonis were good at interrogating. It must run in the family. I wondered if they were ever cops.

"Ronnie wanted to organize a group to arm themselves and fight back," Barbara said. "I told him it wasn't a good idea. The last thing he'd want was to be known as a gang leader. Maybe Linn thought there was more to it than that. I just don't know. If so, I hope he didn't think it would push our relationship apart."

News of the taunts and fisticuffs did not seem surprising to the Berrettonis. "Brown-faced kids have always gotten the short end of the stick around here," Romeo said. "Even some of the Italians kids have been called wetbacks, or worse. This guy Knight has always had a temper. Likes his Beefeaters, too. We've had to ask him to leave the bar more than once."

Barbara said tensions were escalating between Knight's cronies and the Hispanics. "One of those jerks pulled a knife on a kid and sliced his baggy pants as he walked to his car. The boy wasn't hurt, but he was afraid to tell the police, fearing more would be done the next time." Barbara began folding the ends of her napkin on the table. She ironed the white triangle with her palm and spent an extra moment looking around the restaurant. "Mr. Johnston also asked some specific medical questions about Linn. I really didn't know what to tell him. Linn simply wanted to play without pain. I think he'd accepted that his days as a star were over. He seemed desperate for an alternative to a second surgery— he wasn't sure how much the first one actually helped."

The Berrettonis squirmed at "desperate."

"This is difficult, sweetheart, I know it is," George said. "Tell me only if you feel like it ... But do you think Linn was to a point where he could have possibly taken his own life?"

Barbara eyed me warily and said she'd lost sleep mulling the same question. "When I spoke to him on the phone, his knee had been bothering him," Barbara said. "He was down about that. He twisted it again moving some old material on the Dolan property." She swayed and frowned. "But his outlook on life was consistently positive after he returned from Mexico. The trip changed him. I think the heart-to-heart meeting in Scottsdale with his father after the stroke also had a big influence."

Robert Oliver once mentioned the same thing to me about the Mexican trip on the phone, but I had yet to hear details.

"Doctor Oliver tried to make Linn's games," Romeo said. "But I don't think he had lot of time for anything else but work."

Barbara nodded slowly. "Much was said at his parents' home in Arizona that never had been said before. It was the last quality time I know that they had together. Something clicked. He telephoned me saying he wanted to return home, get a job, and make plans to get married. He also asked me if I remembered the old diary we found. You should read it. There are some great images and names from the logging days." She stopped sadly and looked down. "The only wild card for me was if one of those Seattle doctors he was seeing prescribed a different drug. Something that would affect his mood, personality."

I felt uneasy and considered the possibility of a new mix of drugs jostling around in Linn's body—and mind.

"Linn just seemed to be exhausted all the time," Barbara said. "Working too much at the service station, playing in I don't know how many rec leagues, making that drive to the lake in all sorts of weather. I've never seen Linn really out of sorts, yet I do know that some drug combinations can make some people crazy. They do things they normally would never do."

TWELVE

MIKKO KURRI CRADLED THE DELICATE porcelain teapot like a newborn child. A similar glazed piece highlighted his grandmother's mantel in his homeland, thousands of miles and now two years away. The young Finn grew restless stocking the counters and towering shelves that lined the MacTavish & Oliver Mercantile. He preferred the heavy lifting in the company's barn, where the fifty-pound sacks of feed, flour, and salt brought needed exercise for his imposing frame. Still, he was grateful to have a job. Like many newly arrived Scandinavians promised employment at the shipyard adjacent to the sawmill on Bainbridge Island, he'd become frustrated and gone broke waiting for the heavy European machinery the yard needed to open.

"I never expected so many trained shipwrights to become farmers and fishermen," Kurri said. "It could be another year—maybe more—before that yard opens. It's time we put our efforts in the land."

"We will make a list of the provisions you will need," Henry Oliver said. "You can repay the store when you are able. I've seen what you can do, and I'll take your word for your food and supplies."

At Oliver's suggestion, Kurri obtained a homestead for a hundred-acre parcel a few miles northeast of the tiny outpost of McMurray, one of the new clusters of activity springing up south of North Fork that was soon served by railroad.

Kurri cleared a portion in the southwest corner and built a cabin from local cedar and fir with the help of his cousin Anders Gustaffson, who continued as a deliveryman at MacTavish & Oliver Mercantile. Soon after the home was completed, they set out to find the source of the steady creek that had been providing them with water, fish, and soothing comfort for tired limbs after long days of building and farming. Directed by Wilhelmina, their neighbor and daughter of a German pioneer woman and a native Sauk chief, Anders and Mikko followed the creek bed for three hours and discovered a gleaming lake several times the size of their homestead and rimmed to the south by a steep ridge covered with fir.

To the east rose several Cascade peaks. The northern wind, coupled with the natural movement of the lake toward its only outlet, had created a sweeping crescent sandspit on the northwest shore. The outlet converged with several creeks and streams from nearby hills and tumbled west through valleys meadows, and fields, including the Kurri homestead. The idyllic lake and sandspit beach were ideal for camping, swimming, and fishing, and were only a few hours' trek from their home. The Finns named the enchanting place Lake Wilhelmina in honor of their Indian friend—her name was also a German word for "protection"—and the stream that ran through their homestead was named Minnie Creek.

"Few of my people have ever seen the hidden lake and its outlet," Wilhelmina said. "The creek provided the fondest memories of my youth."

Mikko's relationship with Wilhelmina deepened and flourished. Two years later, the two were married near a community retreat they built on the sandspit. The Finns and Wilhelmina hand-peeled and milled every log, forming sturdy pole trusses. They bound the poles with resilient reeds gathered from the lake shore and caulked the gaps between the logs that made up the walls with gray mud scooped from the lake's outlet.

The men cleared a level area on the beach and cut cedar shakes for the community cabin. A few of the larger bolts, tossed into random piles on the sand, rolled into the lake water and floated toward the outlet, eventually finding their way into the main section of Minnie Creek. Mikko later discovered them floating in his farm's diversion pond several miles below the lake. Not only did the woods adjacent to the lake have an ample supply of cedar, but the creek also served as a transportation system that carried the valuable wood to the homestead. Mikko, Anders and two other families soon established a milling area near Mikko's farm, complete with a makeshift drying shack and a small loading dock. The shipwrights-turned-farmers were suddenly and unexpectedly in the cedar-shake business and were now deluged with requests from friends, neighbors, and the merchants in North Fork, particularly MacTavish & Oliver Mercantile. The Finns also anticipated the increasing demand for roof shakes in towns along the planned railroad that would head southwest from Sedro Woolley and skirt Mikko's original homestead.

"We need more of your cedar in our store," Oliver said. "I will pay you to widen and improve the trail to the lake in exchange for exclusive sales rights to your shakes and bolts. The trail would enable a steady flow of material without having to rely on the creek."

"I recognize your proposal will also increase my business," Kurri said. "It is I who should be grateful to you."

"A wider trail also will bring more visitors to the lake," Oliver said. "If you wish, our company will enhance the community grounds and assist with other buildings you deem necessary."

By 1889, the commercial cedar-shake undertaking had moved a few miles north to the Bald Mountain Valley, where Gustaffson was the manager for their expanding processing business with financial partner Henry Oliver. Wilhelmina and Mikko Kurri became hosts at the lake retreat they named Madrona in honor of the two swirling, sturdy, peeling-red madrona trees stationed at each end of the curving sandspit that defined the boundaries of the community.

The couple soon added their own little cottage down the sandy beach from the larger resort. Wilhelmina's flower and vegetable garden stretched from the cottage to the base of the northern madrona, where Mikko's wicker swing hung from a knotted branch. Wilhelmina's extended family, expert fishing and hunting guides in the region, regularly arrived with supplies and surprise gifts. The visits and exchanges became so frequent that Kurri petitioned the county representatives for a United States Postal Service station at the lake. The request was approved, largely because one of the voting commissioners in Seattle was an associate of Wallace MacTavish and had spent more than a few nights at the resort.

"Madrona, Wash." was proudly embossed on postal stamps and became a much-desired Cascade oasis; invoking warm, vivid experiences for those hardworking people desiring a respite from their routine lives.

THIRTEEN

THE PROSPECT OF RONNIE GARCIA on the same Seattle basketball team as Linn Oliver weighed heavily as I darted out my back door after a quick dash home.

A tough but marginal high school player, Ronnie was two years ahead of Linn in school. A couple of gym rats, they were friendly competitors for years and part of a core group that showed up for full-court buckets on Wednesday nights and Saturday mornings. Things began to change during Ronnie's senior season, when he took to calling Linn "Headlines" for the amount of media attention Linn received. I heard rumors the two had drifted further apart after Linn suffered his knee injury in the woods. Everybody knew that Ronnie and Linn were choker partners that summer; one stretched the main winch line to the farthest point on the setting while the other wrapped individual choker cables around each log and secured them to the winch line. Since the day the winch line snapped, whipped across Linn's knee, and sent him to the hospital, I never saw them together again.

I left the truck in the garage and swung my 1972 Volkswagen bus south toward Interstate 5. The bus was a gutless but comfortable old friend. I never needed to go fast or corner on a dime. It carted dozens of amped-up players, hosted mobile chalk talks, transported boxes of jerseys and balls, and served as a portable hotel room for out-of-town coaching clinics. The players razzed me about my ancient tapes but most young passengers couldn't wait to rummage through the cluttered glove box to find a favorite.

Well, I don't care if it rains or freezes
'long as I got my plastic Jesus
riding on the dashboard of my car ...

The Montlake Gym near the University of Washington campus is the cornerstone of Montlake Playfield, a gem of an urban park, complete with a football field and outdoor tennis courts that once boasted the smoothest surface in the city. The familiar brick structure sits tucked away on the shore of Portage Bay and across the Highway 520 concrete causeway from the luxury yachts belonging to members of the exclusive Seattle Yacht Club.

The gym sits a few a few blocks from Hec Edmundson Pavilion, home to the Huskies and the drama that is Division One college basketball. Montlake's modest basketball court attracts a radically different type of player from the collegiate crowd across the bay. I played in a few Over 30s leagues there years ago, back when my knees had discernible cartilage. Pickup games typically include no-name gym rats, former high-school showstoppers, and aging Huskies looking to break a weeknight sweat. Teams of knee-braced warriors appear nightly, resplendent in tattered tank tops and scuffed-up sneakers. It's a stark contrast to the button-down shirts and high heels found in the boardrooms at the nearby yacht club or the silky, shiny warmups covering spotless uniforms donned in big-time college arenas.

At Montlake, there are no realistic hopes of making headlines; no frantic reporters racing from a jammed-packed house to beat deadlines with an exclusive story about the next can't-miss superstar. Linn Oliver was a celebrated former blue-chip prospect, one of a very few white kids from the Northwest invited to prestigious national basketball camps during his high school years. Every player in the recreational park leagues like Montlake secretly wanted to discover what Linn Oliver had that he did not. Opponents cranked up their intensity level when they played against him. I've seen this peculiar athletic stage render an intriguing combination of pent-up curiosity and runaway testosterone.

Since his forgettable last days on campus at the University of Washington, the Montlake Gym was one of the few places Linn Oliver was still consistently referred to as "The Cheese." He told me he wished the nickname would go away, along with the chronic pain in his right kneecap. Still, he wanted to play, and there was always a game at Montlake.

I aimed the bus into the parking lot, under one of the light standards that needed new bulbs. Inside, Fool's Gold walked through the motions of a lazy layup drill at the far basket, its team members far too cool to actually break a sweat before a rec game. Ronnie Garcia was not on the floor.

A familiar kid with a smooth shot nailed three shots in a row from the left corner. Austin Ragsdale was a decent player and a likeable logger from Aberdeen I'd seen in a state tournament. He was a close friend of Linn's; the two had roomed together one year at the UW. Linn brought "Rags" to a couple of our practices at Washington High during winter break. As I approached, I said, "Guardin' Austin is just exhaustin.'"

He stopped his next shot in mid-motion, held the ball at his waist, and squinted in my direction. "Coach Creekmore. I'll be darned. Been a while since I heard that kinda talk." He tugged up his droopy brown sweat pants and extended his right hand.

"Good to see you, Austin. Wasn't sure if you would remember ..."

"You've got to be kidding, Ernie Creekmore, coach of Washington High Fighting Crabs? I'm sure a lot of the guys in here'll spot you."

I hesitated and looked away. "Because I lost a state title game with Linn Oliver? And, that's *former* coach."

"Not what I was gonna say. Linn said you did things the right way. 'Sides, I bet you're back into coaching soon."

I faked a snort, but I knew I wanted back in to the game I loved. The smell of the gym, players preparing to run the floor, refs asking for the game ball. I loved it all. I refocused on Austin as the game's referees strutted to midcourt and summoned the captains from both teams. "Say, you heard from Linn?"

"Nah but heard another guy on our team was trying to track him down. He'll probably blow in the door sometime in the first quarter. Like Tuesday night. He changed in the bathroom, pulled on his jersey at our bench and was on the floor for the opening tip."

"Anything different about him that night? How'd he play?"

The officials waved players to midcourt, impatient to start the game. One shouted again for a Fool's Gold captain. The other practiced his two-handed toss in preparation for the jump ball.

"Where's Garcia?" one of Austin's teammates asked. "It's time to rock 'n' roll."

The stocky player, nicknamed Sweater for his body hair, looked around the gym. "I guess I'm your captain again tonight." He reluctantly jogged to center court as the designated leader. The two captains slapped hands.

I stared at Austin. "Ronnie didn't make it Tuesday night?"

"Nope, didn't show at all. Anyway, you asked about something different. When I saw how tired Linn was, I told him to take the night off. The team we were playing was easier than a third-grade crossword puzzle. But Linn wouldn't hear of an early exit. Said he wanted to loosen up for a game later in Bremerton. Christ, get on a boat to Bremerton?"

"You thought he was serious about going all that way to play in another game?"

"Said some team at Silverdale Community College needed bodies." He stopped stretching, and yanked his sweatpants, one leg at a time, over his bulky high-tops. "Can you believe that?"

I walked with Austin to the sideline where he fired his warm-ups under a metal folding chair. "Did Linn say anything about how he was feeling?"

"He said he got a new drug for the knee. Made him crazy sometimes, but it helped him sleep better." Members from both teams shot us hurry-up looks, eager for play to begin. The official scorer made a whirling motion with his finger.

"But how'd he look?" I asked.

"He always seems whipped, Coach. Like nothing's in the tank. He's working all day at the Shell station, then driving to hoop games at night. I just hope he doesn't screw up somebody's car at work."

"C'mon, Rags," Sweater yelled. "Ref's gonna give us a T if we wait any longer."

As Austin jogged away, I said, "Did you ever hear Linn talk about a girl named Holly?"

"Nah, doesn't ring a bell. Barbara, but no Holly."

"Do you think he left in time to catch the ferry?" I asked.

"Should have," Austin said over his shoulder. "He knocked down three long-range bombs and was out the door before halftime. But, hey, stick around. He should be here. You can ask him yourself."

I hung around until midway through the third quarter, but Linn did not show.

The hour-plus ride home did me in, thanks to the perpetual roadwork in south Everett. I pulled into the driveway and noticed a package under the light on the front porch. I took the box inside. It was a small white carton from an auto parts store. Ripping off the tape, I found it was filled with crushed Dungeness crab shells and a yellow piece of binder paper with a barely legible message blotched in black ink:

It's been five years, but it seems like yesterday. Thanks for the memories, asshole.

I slumped into the couch, clutching the paper in my hand. As I eased my head back on the cushion, I noticed a set of car lights moving slowly up the street, stopping in front the house. I stood and squinted through the window, trying to make out the model, but the car pulled quickly away.

FOURTEEN

THREE DAYS AND STILL NO WORD. Dr. Robert Oliver left a message on my home phone saying he was catching the next flight from Phoenix. It was time for me to dig out my ferry contacts and learn more about Linn Oliver's evening boat ride across Puget Sound.

Willie Colegrove was the type of player a coach tried to keep on a team. Wild Willie couldn't shoot a lick and was too slow to guard an old nun in full habit, but he could fire up a locker room like nobody else. He'd show up ready and on time, had a non-stop motor, and was more than willing to tell Larry Bird he had no game. *Nothin', man. You got nothin!* Like many other alumni, he returned to witness our 1977 state championship game.

Willie became one of four family members to land a job with Washington State Ferries. His dad worked the San Juan Island run out of Anacortes when the kids were in school, and the family still lived in North Fork. When the children left the family home, the folks moved to nearby Guemes Island, where the dad skippered a nine-car county ferry, and the mom operated the community store and boat lift. I dialed her there.

"Coach Creekmore, you just made my day! Tell me you're comin' to Guemes." I immediately pictured the squatty woman with the raspy delivery, the product of years of Winstons and Wild Turkey.

"No, ma'am, I'm not, but I sure would like to. Some fine fishin' spots on the west side of your island."

"You got that right, Coach. Couple from Victoria rented a kicker boat this morning and hooked a twelve-pounder 'round noon. Real shiny blackmouth. Say, are you coachin' anywheres?"

I took in a lot of air and let it out audibly. "I gave up coaching at the school a few years ago. Didn't see any more Colegroves coming through the ranks. Mostly scouting now. There's talk about helping with a county all-star team, but that'll be down the road."

"You were always good to them, Ernie. I will always be grateful for that. A little sassy to the parents, though."

It was time to curb the cordials. "Mrs. Colegrove, I was wondering if you might know Willie's work schedule? I heard he recently moved to one of the Seattle runs."

"That's right. WSF moved him from Mukilteo last month. He's working swing shift on the *Storm*. Call the main number in Seattle to get the boat rotation. You don't want to get on the wrong ferry."

"Thanks. Say, is the *Storm* running to Bainbridge Island or Bremerton?"

"I'm sorry, Coach. I could've at least told you that. Willie's on the Bremerton run."

A COLD WIND WHIPPED through the canyon of Seattle buildings, clearing the sky of winter rain clouds. The majestic Olympic Mountains dominated the horizon, seemingly rising from the saltwater west of the Kitsap Peninsula. A few private boats bobbed in a light chop among huge international freighters and container ships in Elliott Bay. I paid my car-driver fare at the curb and took my place in the Bremerton line at the south end of the parking lot on the pier. Vehicles loaded several minutes late for the 4:20 p.m. sailing, but the views of the Seattle skyline and Puget Sound eased driver anxiety. A deckhand directed the bus up the ramp on the starboard side, where I jerked the hand brake and climbed the stairs to the galley.

"Willie Colegrove?" I said to the cashier over the heads of two twin boys in matching soccer sweats who couldn't wait to purchase a greasy bag of popcorn and two small sodas. The kids dropped handfuls of sweaty coins on the counter.

The cashier frowned. "Second mate's office. Port side."

Roger that.

Willie huddled over a green picnic-style table surrounded by light brown wall lockers piled high with gym bags, heavy coats, and boots. He glared down at a piece of binder paper and held a black CB-like microphone in his right hand. When he spoke, his voice streamed from the speakers throughout the vessel.

"Will the owner of the black BMW with the California license plates parked in the center section near the stern please return to your vehicle and secure your alarm. Folks from California—no one is stealing your designer sunglasses. The motion of the ferry activates your alarm."

"That's our Willie," I said. His pudgy cheeks accentuated a wily smile. He stared, trying to recognize me in an out-of-place setting.

"Coach! How ya' doin?" He landed a roundhouse handshake then slapped me on the shoulder. "Whadda doin' on this dump?"

We grabbed an empty booth near a window in the passenger cabin and reminisced about old times and former players. Willie graduated from high school before Linn

Oliver enrolled. Like other hoop fans, Willie followed Linn's career and was interested in his whereabouts. He knew nothing of Linn's disappearance—until I told him. Linn's car had been towed off the boat and sat in the Bremerton parking lot for a few hours before the state patrol ran the plate. By that time, the *Storm* had begun its return trip to Seattle.

"You gotta be kiddin' me, Coach," Willie said. "I can't even believe this. I remember the night and the car, but I never saw Cheese. It was a cold, nasty crossing. One of the worst I can remember."

"Bad enough that waves came over the bow?" I asked.

"You bet. Badass wind blowing like crazy. Boat was really rockin.' Lotta people losing their lunch. A seagull nearly shattered a window on the starboard side. Thing scared the snot out of a family from Poulsbo coming home from Seattle Center."

"So, anybody near the bow or stern could have been surprised by a swell?"

"Easy. Felt like a roller-coaster ride. First couple of rows of cars were sprayed with saltwater. Captain made two announcements for passengers to stay away from all railings."

"Was Linn's car found in the middle section or on one of the side lanes?"

"On the rail," Willie said. "Starboard side. I remember 'cuz the tow truck had little room to work. Took forever to maneuver the rig into place."

Willie talked of vehicles with all sorts of problems— dead batteries, flat tires, lost keys, empty fuel tanks, slumbering drivers, and goofy kids seeking revenge by locking out their parents.

"How often does a driver leave a car on a boat?" I said. "I mean, it must be a fairly rare occurrence."

"Happens all the time on these commuter runs. Most of the time, these people walk on, then walk off." He pointed to dozens of passengers in our vicinity. "Then one day they drive to work—or drink too much and simply forget they drove on the boat. They leave the car and walk off. When they get to the parking lot, it hits them."

Willie explained that a stalled or deserted motor vehicle on a ferry boat ranks somewhere between inconvenience and annoyance in the job description of veteran ferry workers. When a boat is in port and otherwise off-loaded, an abandoned car simply steals precious time the deckhands earmarked for a break before the loading routine begins again.

"That yellow Subaru station wagon was dusty and dirty," Willie said. "Interior like a dorm room—soda cans, pizza box on the floor; clothes all over the seats; gym towels and running shoes in the flat back. Had to be a guy's car. No chick would drive that nightmare. Wouldn't make that kinda mess."

"When do the fine folks at the state patrol get involved?" I said.

A wayward, curly-haired toddler laughed down the aisle, thinking she had ditched her mom. Mom hustled a few steps behind, diaper bag in hand. Too late, by my nose. Willie held his. "If we have to tow a vehicle off the ferry, the guys in the parking lot give the owner about two hours to show up. Some have sobered up by then. If they don't show, we call the state patrol. After that, it could get expensive."

"Just how expensive?"

"Well," Willie said, resting his boots on my bench seat, "depends how things unfold. State patrol researches the plate through the computer system and then tries to contact the owner or a family member. Obviously, we're talking about a well-known family name here."

"Say they couldn't find Linn, and his parents don't answer the phone in Arizona?"

"Then, maybe they try his uncle," Willie said. "The guy who runs the timber company south of North Fork. Somebody like that often knows where a kid might be."

"I guess when the state patrol calls a couple of people, word has a tendency to travel pretty fast."

"Got that right. You know, I'm kinda surprised you weren't at the top of the list."

I looked down at the graffiti-like specs in the worn linoleum. They looked like the tiny circles and squares my niece stuffed in my last birthday card, only faded by the sun. I dragged a tired hand over my forehead and felt as if my receding hairline had lost another inch in the past three days. "As you said, lot of Olivers in the area. Big family, certainly bigger around here before most of Linn's siblings moved away. Anyway, the state patrol had plenty of people to try before getting to me."

Willie pushed his hands into his WSF jacket pockets and tipped his head back against the top bench cushion.

"Well, if push comes to shove and nobody's got a clue where Linn might be, the Coast Guard gets involved with search boats," Willie said. "Maybe helicopters. If the feds put a bird in the air, we could be talkin' jail time or a big, fat fine. At least twenty-five large. Bad news for a drunk who forgot his car and left town."

"Ouch, that's quite a bite," I said. Harvey Johnston revealed that the license-plate search helped spread the word that Linn was missing. Nothing had been mentioned about the Coast Guard. "Do you know if they sent out boats that night?"

"It's SOP if nobody answers the call for the car," he said. "Again, if there's the slightest reason not to, they wouldn't. Costs too much."

"Should be easy enough to find out," I said. "I'll follow up with the Coast Guard when I get back."

"Mighty big chop on the water that night, Coach. And so friggin' cold. Anybody in that water would have been screwed. Some guy without a lifejacket ... matter of minutes." He lifted his legs from the bench, placed his boots firmly on the floor, and leaned toward me, elbows on knees. "Good Lord, Coach. Do you have any reason to think Linn leaped off this boat?"

"I don't. I'm also trying to figure out if somebody else might have been using his car."

"Entirely possible. Coach, I leech rigs all the time."

I glanced up at the clock on the back wall of the galley. Soon the skipper would ease back on the engines and slowly float into the dock. "If Linn was on the boat that night, is there anyone you can think of who might want to help him overboard?"

Willie stood up and tucked in his uniform shirt. "Hell no, Coach. No friggin' way. But I'll tell you what. The Sound was so rough that night, if he were walkin' around on deck, he wouldn't have needed any help."

FIFTEEN

WALLACE MACTAVISH GLARED AT HENRY Oliver across the polished mahogany table of his spacious upstairs office. "Are you more interested in the man as an investor or do you simply have an eye for his daughter?" MacTavish said as he clicked open his gold pocket watch, checked the hour, then slid the round piece into his vest pocket.

"Probably both," Henry said. He stood, walked across the room and peered out at the Skagit River and to customers coming and going to their North Fork mercantile below. "Do you think Fredrick has an idea that I am smitten with his Elizabeth?"

"Think! Good Lord, Henry." MacTavish removed his wire-rim spectacles, gently massaged his temples, and placed the glasses on the table. "Everyone in town has been talking about your involvement with this woman. I need not remind you that she is young enough to be your daughter."

Fredrick C. Linnbert left the outskirts of London to fund a coal mining operation in the hills of the upper Skagit Valley. Coal was in heavy demand in the 1870s, especially in the cities of Portland and San Francisco and to fire steamships and locomotives around the world. Anyone who could supply and deliver coal stood to make a tidy profit.

"Fools and dreamers seek their fortunes of gold," Linnbert said. "Wiser men choose the reliable rewards of coal. Coal heats homes."

After years of coaxing, Henry persuaded Linnbert, the patriarch of a prominent Seattle family and a pillar in the city's Capitol Hill neighborhood, to fund a series of railroad tracks into the Skagit forests. Through experience, Linnbert discovered coal required too much money and manpower to extract from the hillsides above the river.

Henry held an underlying and guarded excitement that every tree that was felled, every log that was milled, and every board foot of lumber that was produced could find its way to any country in the world.

"Northwest men prefer working in a forest rather than in the depths of a dark mine," Henry had told Linnbert in the large meeting room above the store. "Enormous trees are everywhere just waiting to be cut. When the region had massive quantities of both resources, why choose the more difficult one to harvest and ship?"

Linnbert's decision paid off, despite the difficult economic times of the late 1880s and early 1890s. Railroading was proving to be an efficient, cost-effective way to move people and product. North American investors began to flock to this mode of long-distance transportation when the first Canadian Pacific Railroad rolled into Vancouver from Montreal on May 23, 1887. Two years later, the Fairhaven and Southern Railway completed a leg south of Bellingham to two remote towns near Goodman's Trading Post. Another railroad was busy laying track south of North Fork to Seattle, picking up the growing waterfront town of Everett along the way. Everett was fast becoming a timber center and port, with the Snohomish River delivering logs from cutters in the hills to its front door.

Elizabeth Linnbert, the youngest daughter and the pride of Fredrick C. and Henrietta Linnbert, had failed miserably in two attempts at an East Coast finishing school. She preferred the backwoods, canvas trousers, and brushed-cotton shirts to polished storefronts, wire-rimmed dresses, and parasols.

"She might be a handful, Henry," her father said. "But like you, she's logical and loves this land."

The same year that Henry Oliver asked Fredrick C. Linnbert for Elizabeth's hand in marriage, the MacTavish & Oliver Logging Company became an official subsidiary of the Linnbert Railroad Company. Wallace MacTavish & Oliver were given substantial equity shares in the new corporation. MacTavish was still comfortable in his cozy office in the North Fork mercantile site and assumed an even greater primary role in the store's retail operation. Linnbert remained in Seattle to pursue other business opportunities, allowing Henry and his bride to remain free to monitor the logging camps, share meals with employees, negotiate land contracts, and fish the rivers and lakes.

SIXTEEN

4 P.M., FRIDAY, FEBRUARY 4, 1982

I DROVE NORTH ON THE SEATTLE waterfront from the ferry en route to the *Seattle Tribune* and was promptly blocked by a southbound freight opposite Pier 70. A smooth old number softened the setback. It was Old Blue Eyes' turn on the AM dial. Cathy loved this one.

"Yes, you're lovely, with your smile so warm, and your cheeks so soft, just the way you look to-night ..."

Good thing Greg Smithson's work schedule was flexible. Sportswriters worked nights and weekends. Rarely were any games played during the nine-to-five business day, and they usually had some downtime before the reams of game results came pouring in about nine. Smithson had more contacts in the high school sports world than any other journalist in the state. If anyone knew whether Linn Oliver was involved in any goofy extracurricular activities, Smithson was a great place to start.

And, not all of his sources made their living with a clipboard and a whistle. It's surprising how many successful business people, elected officials, restaurant owners, factory workers, firemen, accountants, dentists, doctors, mortgage brokers, bartenders, and cops felt the need to remain entangled in the web of high-school athletics. I got a taste of that when I was coaching—some people need to be close to those making the decisions. Others loved to read about themselves. I wasn't one of them. And that's probably why Smithson agreed to see me on short notice.

Cruising past the Space Needle, I turned right on Boren and found a parking spot on the street outside the 13 Coins restaurant, then jogged across the street to the newspaper. An elf-like rent-a-cop stopped me in the bright entryway. He sat at a long gray metal desk surrounded by black-and-white murals of old presses and Pulitzer winners and eyed me as if I'd just told him he had to work on Christmas Day. He scoffed and dialed up the newsroom.

I sat on a stiff bench and contemplated how much background I was willing to reveal to Smithson—and when. If I spoke off the record, I was confident that material would not show up in the newspaper until we agreed.

Smithson was *the* conduit to all things prep, and his followers were not shy about leaving him tips, confirming rumors on phone messages, or sending confidential letters about an underrated kid from a tiny school who "did not have the size to play Division One but was extremely coachable and would bite your leg off." His network included the old Husky underground, plus countless stringers, coaches, statkeepers, and diehard fans from his thirty-five years at the paper. Many of his unsolicited informants were former players who lived to be mentioned in his weekly column. Parents enjoyed his insights and positive suggestions, and old-timers appreciated his trivia and monthly trips down memory lane in his popular *Where Are They Now?* feature.

Smithson blasted through the double doors at the end of the hall. "Coach Creekmore!" Smithson shouted. "Sorry to keep you waiting." We smiled and shook hands. "Let's head to the cafeteria. Find a place to talk."

He hadn't changed since the last time I saw him: the ever-present *Seattle Tribune* cap atop his thinning hair; corduroy trousers, plaid shirt, and blue cotton pullover covering his familiar six-two, two-hundred-and-twenty-pound frame. He held a stack of *While You Were Out* phone messages in one hand.

We skipped down two flights of stairs to NewsBreak, *The Trib's* spartan basement eatery that also could be accessed by the public via a sidewalk entrance. Passersby glanced down into various groups of salespeople, reporters, and delivery drivers. Five grubby pressmen sat closest to the below-street door, commenting on the length of a young woman's miniskirt as she shimmied to the Metro bus stop.

We grabbed snacks, coffee, and a seat in the corner.

We hit several topics, including a few outstanding players and teams I'd scouted since the first of the year. Smithson whipped a reporter's notebook from his hip pocket and took some notes. The coaching fraternity appreciated his candor, respected his opinions, and—like his readers—considered him the answer man. A skilled evaluator of talent, he usually could tell immediately if a player was of Pac-10 caliber despite the insistence of a too-proud parent. The man wasn't easily swayed. He first saw Linn Oliver as a tenth-grader and joked to me that I should invest in an additional phone line dedicated to college recruiters. I twitched when I saw WSP scribbled in his notes.

"Did your guy give you any indication how much time the WSP spent trying to locate Linn before they called you?" I said.

Smithson rested a fist on his chin and squinted slightly, perhaps surprised I got down to business. "The state patrol said they only tried the numbers they had on record. I got the impression it was a short list."

"I'm sure they were out of date," I said. "The Oliver family sold the family home in North Fork last year, and I assume Linn's car was registered at that address. Other than a dorm phone at the UW, I don't know what other phone numbers the state could possibly have."

He sipped his coffee. "What about where he is living now?"

I told him about the Dolan place. Smithson sat up in his seat and nodded. "I tried to locate him about this time last year. We were doing a series on Skagit County's all-time great players. We never connected."

I pondered the timeframe. "Linn went to Mexico about then to see an old friend from UW. He stayed longer than expected. In fact, his dad was so worried about him that I even thought about making a trip south of the border. He finally surfaced. Just wanted some time to think about things."

Smithson took another swig and then lowered the mug with both hands. "Maybe we are looking at a repeat performance."

I shrugged and shook my head.

"Ernie, the last few times I actually spoke with Linn— more than a casual hello—he's been down in the dumps. After all these years, the first thing out of his mouth is still that he let his team down by missing that shot in the state final. Still frustrated and embarrassed for washing out with the Huskies. Especially after being cleared by the UW docs on at least two different occasions. Tell you the truth, I've been wondering how he's handled those setbacks for a long time."

I glanced away. "Don't think it's as bad as you think. I've seen him quite a bit the past several months. Three weeks ago we were at a game--"

"Coach, ten days ago I got a call from a UW sports medicine intern. Linn asked her about getting him a drug she'd never even heard of. The next day, a high-school coach who stopped in for gas at his station asked me if I thought Linn was suicidal."

Linn Oliver, suicidal? Obscure drugs? The recent lack of communication was starting to make sense.

"Given his background, you'd think he'd be the type of kid who could turn it around by now," Smithson said. "Lots of local support. Pressure, too, I guess. But I'll tell you what. That state tournament week was something else. In fact, I can't remember a community being more fired up.

SEVENTEEN

7 P.M., FRIDAY, FEBRUARY 4, 1982

IN MY HEAD, I REPLAYED THE state title game, especially the last minute, nearly every day. But Smithson's remark brought back for the first time in several years the surrounding festivities leading up to the main event. I thought about those days as I sat in the bus adjacent to *The Trib's* employee square, the park-like setting highlighted by weedless landscaping and a towering fountain that local kids regarded as a wishing well. Other than Cathy, the final moments in that game were the only things I truly wished I could have back.

Nothing beats watching local youngsters represent a one-high-school community in a prep championship tournament. Anybody in North Fork who had been involved with a youth league, or held a remote interest in supporting quality hoops or quality kids, got behind the Fighting Crabs that year before Thanksgiving and stayed with them through February. "Claw 'em, Crabs!" was the cry that rang from cars, pickups, and eighteen-wheelers early and often that season, the school's first state championship game—in any sport—in sixty-seven years.

Coaching in a state tournament is an absolute privilege. The energy in the crammed gym is genuine; the passion irrepressible. It is a tangible, primal attachment that a kid even at the end of the bench can take with him for the rest of his life. More importantly, the state tourney comes without the threatening cloud brought by big-time endorsements or long-term television contracts. It is four days of too-salty popcorn, off-key bands in ancient uniforms, broken hearts, cold hot dogs, impossible deadlines, buzzer-beating shots, unsung heroes, loyal parents, legendary old-timers, proud administrators, and sugar-crazed students who could not believe they were *actually excused from school* to attend this annual rite of passage. The week is the highlight of my year. How could I possibly be anywhere else?

The entire week before "state," newspaper reporters, radio and television stations descended upon the tournament-bound towns, providing daily features on players, coaches, and fans to their hometown readers, listeners and viewers. It seemed I was constantly posing for pictures and being hounded for interviews. Then, it was on to the tournament site, where coverage was magnified.

The teams in the 3A title game were dramatically different in how they carried themselves on and off the court. My underdog Washington squad was a mix of unassuming athletes with one extraordinary player. Flintridge High, led by Elliott, Justin, and Teddy Beach ("The Beach Boys") strutted undefeated into state tournament week. The Jackrabbits had no intention of losing to a bunch of kids from the west side of the state. It was an east-west thing. People east of the mountains view westsiders as soft, big-city suburbanites who spend their Saturdays sipping Chardonnay in Lacoste polos, trying to determine the proper way to slice brie. West of the Cascades, eastsiders are seen as booted, bumbling hayseeds who swap their straw farmers' hats for felt about the time they switch from beer to booze.

Elliott was the coach and father of Justin and Teddy. Justin was a tough, squatty, boisterous senior guard who was out to intimidate with his ever-present black whiskers; Teddy was a quiet sophomore swingman with long "surfer" hair always magically in place on the court. Coach Elliott—a sly, erstwhile hippie—attempted to bring some slickness to the rural region east of the Cascade Mountains. He once said he "missed most of the sixties" and refused to ride the team bus to and from games. Rumors were rampant that "Ol' El" was expected at a local watering hole long before the bus arrived back at school and that he fired up something stronger than Lucky Strikes in his Ford van on the way home. He predicted a state-title victory—even confided to coaches in his league that he anticipated a "cakewalk"—and suggested in the newspaper that the proprietor of Flintridge's Fine Cuisine put the champagne on ice.

"This game has got the community of Flintridge bouncing," Elliott proclaimed. "Can you think of another event when you would get out the champagne? This team has worked hard. This is our time. Flintridge time."

It was no cakewalk, but I'm told the drinks were on the house at Flintridge's Fine Cuisine after the game. The Jackrabbit players devoured huge steaks, compliments of the boosters. The cheerleaders and school band paraded around them and high-kicked to their fight song. I saw one of the starters about five years later, and he told me no team member has paid for a meal in the restaurant since that night.

For better or worse, state tournaments often define lives, especially in a small town, and always produce memories that outlast playing days. Each of my Washington players in that painful title game can recall exactly where he was on the floor when Linn Oliver's last-second jumper failed to go through the net. Parents, boosters, and alumni can tell you exactly where they sat and who was in the row.

LIKE ALL COACHES, I dissected all the "what-ifs" after losing a big game. A state title loss came in a completely different package of hurt and disappointment. I drew mild criticism for not abandoning my man-to-man defense after Teddy Beach penetrated the middle of the Washington defense for three easy baskets late in the third quarter. To hell with a zone defense; Flintridge might've picked it apart. I played the percentages, did what I felt was right defensively, and put our club in a position to win the game in the final seconds. I gave the best player in the state the final attempt. Who could argue with that?

"Washington inbounded the ball, and Linn Oliver came off a hard screen at the top of the key," Greg Smithson wrote in his Seattle Tribune column, detailing the last seconds of the game. "It is stunning that he was so open because everyone in the building knew he would be taking the last shot. It appeared he got a great look at the basket, but he didn't seem to get both legs under him when he let it go. The Washington star underwent knee surgery last summer but refused to offer any excuses after the game."

"The team ran the play just the way Coach drew it up," Linn Oliver told Smithson in the Washington locker room that the reporter described as "soundless." "That last shot was mine to make, and I just didn't make it. It didn't fall. That's it, pure and simple."

I cut out Smithson's piece and stuck it into a large wicker basket in the living room containing my semi-valuables, then flung the remainder of the next-day newspapers into the dusty clawfoot tub where they joined old issues of *Sports Illustrated,* in easy reaching distance of the toilet. After Cathy passed away, I only used the shower. I simply couldn't soak in there without her. Tiny bottles of her rosewood bath oils still rested on the ledge above the faucets.

For me, memories of that state tournament lingered far too long. I'm sure it was hell for Linnbert Oliver. I probably faked it better because I was old and calloused. His eyes gave him away. Delight had departed; the glimmer was gone. The weight of that night never truly lifted. I tried to carry that load for him in public, but I only coached the game. I didn't play in it. The consequences differed for me because I wasn't on the floor. I didn't take *the* shot.

I never saw Linn in his letterman's jacket again. It seemed that the bright red "W" became his own scarlet letter. While most of his future acquaintances and classmates at the University of Washington had never heard of his school or anything about his hometown, I knew he'd never escape the label of the star player who missed the final shot in the state championship game.

EIGHTEEN

WILHELMINA CRINGED AS ONLY part of the dark brown tobacco juice hit its target—a gold-plated spittoon in the corner of her Madrona Resort, packed with shivering vacationers who had scurried inside to dodge early summer hailstones on the north shore of the lake later named in her honor. Bunks along the walls and upstairs overflowed with mud-caked gear, damp blankets, and weeping children.

The spitter, a lean man in a full-length leather slicker, brushed raindrops from his shoulders with his Stetson. "I'll give a gold nugget for three beds," said the gangly, unshaven man, who arrived in the middle of the unexpected cold front with his two brothers. "First to speak up can take our place outside under that tree."

The announcement stunned the Madrona camp and sparked an unruly disturbance among parties who believed they were first to accept the offer. A finely dressed, middle-aged man rose from a wooden bench and ambled toward the speaker. An elderly woman gasped and leaped to follow him but was yanked back by her husband.

"You've got plenty of money, Luke," her husband said, as he pulled his wife close to his side. "Let one of the rest of us who don't have a big cattle spread have a little piece of gold!"

"You people can all go to hell," another yelled, strutting to the base of the stairs that led to the second floor. "I was the first to raise my hand and y'all know it. Right? Mister?"

"Tyler, Vance Tyler," said the cagey, mid-fifties man offering the nugget. "That there is Cody and Alexander. You know, I can't really say for certain who was first. Maybe you folks ought to settle it yourselves."

Four men argued in front of the fireplace, determined to say and do what they could to gain the gold nugget. A towheaded Norwegian fisherman not given a chance to state his case threw a punch at a railroad lineman from Vancouver. Kurri intervened and separated them, grabbing fistfuls of their shirts while straining to keep the combatants at arm's length. The fisherman froze, shoved Kurri's hand from his chest, and left the cabin without a word. A young couple, heads down, immediately followed.

During the commotion, Wilhelmina watched as a young girl broke from her father's side. She climbed the stairs and calmly removed bedrolls and clothing from three bunks at the far end of the room. The girl piled the gear at the top of the stairs, then marched down and rejoined the anxiety below. The youngster gathered her silky hair behind her head with both hands, zigzagged through the adults, and stared up at a startled Vance Tyler.

"OK, mister," the little girl shouted. "I've cleared you your three beds. Now you give that gold nugget to my daddy!" The room turned quiet. Kurri took a step toward Tyler, but Wilhelmina gently raised her hand, signaling him to wait.

The eldest Tyler formed a fresh tobacco plug deep in his string pouch, lifted it gingerly without dropping a strand, and fingered the wad into the side of his cheek. "Well, now, little lady," Tyler grumbled. "Looks like you got more brains—

and guts—than any man in here." He reached inside his slicker and plucked a small gold chunk from the side pocket of a battered vest, his filthy yellow-brown fingers pushing the nugget into her pale right palm. Eyes glowing, she cupped it tenderly like a tiny golden egg and edged slowly toward her parents, never looking away from her treasure. "It's yours now," Tyler said. "You do with it like you damn well please."

Wilhelmina observed how the five members of the little girl's family nuzzled together, trying to balance the delight and worry brought by their newfound prize. The mother snipped a square from the corner of her blanket and stitched it inside the forearm sleeve of her husband's extra shirt. When her daughter nestled the nugget into the protective pocket, her mother immediately sewed the flap closed as her two tiny sons questioned aloud the need for the unusual procedure.

"I'd make my man wear that shirt day and night," said an older woman, prone on an upper bunk. "Gold does strange things to people. Even in a friendly place."

The nugget-winning couple tucked their children into bed. The father then slipped to his knees, huddled close to the floor, and pulled his shirt over his head. His wife handed him the altered garment. As he buttoned the shirt over his bare chest, Wilhelmina spotted the small hump on the right sleeve. The man gently brushed the area with his left palm like a wary winner attempting to determine all the possibilities of his new prize, then lay back in his bed and stared at the ceiling. When Wilhelmina returned at first light, it appeared he had not moved nor closed his eyes. The family soon departed with most of the other guests, much to the chagrin of Wilhelmina, who had planned an afternoon of games and crafts for the children.

After two more consecutive days of hard rain and no fishing, Wilhelmina watched the Tylers become more and more restless. She overheard Vance and Cody say they planned to move on, setting out to break ground on a new mining site east of Birdsview and a mile from the Skagit River. They told the youngest brother, Alexander, to stay behind for a meeting with a Seattle banker scheduled to arrive in North Fork aboard a commuter steamer.

"You are the only one of us who can understand what that banker will have to say," Vance told Alexander. "Find out what the gold and the other bags are worth in Seattle and Vancouver. Me and Cody need to go stake this new claim. Now."

Dubious about its safekeeping at the resort, Alexander buried a large burlap sack containing several smaller packets of gold nuggets and gold dust at the base of a madrona tree at the west end of the sandspit. He hid a leather satchel deep in an old beaver hole at the base of a stump near the outlet creek.

Eager to explore the lake area after the rain clouds moved east, Alexander packed his climbing gear and headed southeast for Mount Higgins, a sheer rock face that towered above the magnificent valley named for the local Stillaguamish Tribe. His body, nearly picked clean by cougars and black bears, was discovered by deer hunters a week later on a shelf near the base of the mountain and brought to the Madrona Resort.

When word of his death reached his brothers up on the north Skagit, they hurried back to the lodge at the lake and nearly dismantled the building, seeking the precious possessions they had left behind with their younger brother. The Tylers interrogated Kurri and Wilhelmina, incensed that there were no specific instructions about their missing belongings. Bitterly disappointed, the two Tyler brothers eventually set out for Seattle to search for a particular banker.

NINETEEN

8 P.M., FRIDAY, FEBRUARY 4, 1982

SOME OF THE REFEREES AND COACHES I planned to call next about Linn were actively involved in the night's prep games. Most of them gathered at a popular tavern afterward, so I had some time to kill. I decided to catch the second half of the O'Dea-Roosevelt showdown in O'Dea's stifling bandbox of a gym.

I stood under the entry doors waiting for a stoppage of play to take a seat. Maroon and gold banners declaring *Metro Champions* in every conceivable sport wrapped the walls. Several boasting *State Champions* were mounted strategically above the baskets. I spotted one of the few remaining seats in the top row of the bleachers above the Roosevelt bench, and worked my way up during a timeout, trying not to step on jackets, shoes, and small children. I checked the ancient scoreboard as the seconds ticked down to the third-quarter horn. Two of the tiny red lights were out in the visitors' side "8" so that I had to look twice to make sure it wasn't a "3."

I smiled at the defect, knowing it was part of an imperfect package that made a cramped high-school gym so enticing. Since I left the classroom and full-time coaching, this was the type of place I chose to be on Tuesday and Friday nights. Witnessing how different coaches handled particular strategic situations became an intriguing chess match. How did the style of play in Seattle's Metro League compare with the hard-nosed rebounders in the Seamount League? Did the refs on the west side let the kids play, or were they control freaks? Did coaches respect their players, fans, and peers?

Gus Gables, the crotchety O'Dea coach, loved the old-school, tenacious man-to-man defense almost as much as me. Play rock-solid defense, block out under the boards, get the ball to the open man, take good shots, then get your ass back on defense and blanket your guy.

A whistle blew and so did Gus. "Baseline, Rocky! Do NOT give up the baseline!" On one knee, the coach turned to his players on the bench; a teaching moment. "The baseline is your FRIEND. It's like another defender. Take advantage of it and never give it up!"

I smiled in agreement and then was nearly knocked over by a man who tried to wedge his way into the seat next to me. "The program lists that Taylor kid at six-six but he is only about six-four." The comment tweaked a tender nerve, and I had a feeling the speaker knew it. I'd been known to list my players taller than they actually were in the state tournament program. He sat and shoved my shoulder.

"Doug Willis, the pride of Puyallup. I should have known." I stretched for a quick handshake.

"If it ain't Old School Ernie," Doug said. "How goes it?"

Most of Doug's hair had been gone for years. The few thin strands remaining composed one of the more talked-about comb-overs in coaching. His black leather bomber jacket was brand-new and carried a few raindrops.

"We've been lucky, Ernie," he said. "Won a couple of games we had no business winning, but made some free throws down the stretch. For some reason, the schedulers gave us a bye tonight. This might be one of my last real chances this year do a little scouting."

I'd been in Willis' position countless times—a night off in the middle of the season and a chance to check out an upcoming opponent. Generally, I tried to hit a contest that matched two teams I would meet in the near future so that I could return home with scouting reports on both clubs. I knew his school, South Hill, faced challenging road games at O'Dea and Roosevelt the last week of the league season, so Willis was killing two birds with one stone.

We watched and talked about the game for a while. Then Doug asked, "Do you have a few minutes to come down to the tavern after the game? Got a couple a things I'd like to talk with you about."

My day felt longer and harder than a triple-overtime loss. The hot gym drained what was left of my energy, and I was thinking about bagging the bar idea. But the potential for additional information about Linn coupled with my growling stomach sealed the deal.

"Sure, I'll come down," I said. "Save me a seat. I missed dinner and might get your take on something that's come up."

THE VENERABLE M&J Tavern on Fairview Avenue near Mercer Street was headquarters for high school coaches and visiting college assistants seeking to stay close to them. "The tav" was a stronghold for referees, sportswriters from *The Seattle Tribune* and *Seattle Post-Intelligencer,* high-school hoop junkies, plus blue-collar printers sweating through the swing shift at a book bindery across the street. A major draw was its location near the Seattle Center with easy access to both the northbound and southbound lanes of Interstate 5.

The cozy spot featured ice-cold Rainier beer on tap, well-placed televisions, pool tables with "shorty" sticks for shots close to the wall, lottery tickets, pickled pigs' feet, peanut shells on the floor, and the legendary Hazel's Special—a hot corned-beef sandwich on fresh rye bread.

But there was a different kind of emptiness in my gut. The longer I heard nothing to the contrary, the more I wondered, *Did Linn Oliver drive his car on—then jump off—that ferry?*

For all my fact-gathering, I felt I was no closer to an answer.

The immediate area surrounding the M&J smelled like the intersection of Deep-Fried Fish and Chips and Flame-Broiled Hamburgers. The particular combination conjures up a saltwater boardwalk with bikini clad-women or a minor-league ballpark on a hot summer day. The M&J is the only place able to pull it off in winter with ugly men wearing heavy clothing. This scent drifted from the kitchen and pulled me down the dark hallway leading from the spring-loaded back door that slammed and announced every new arrival.

When I reached the L-shaped main room, I felt like Johnny Carson walking onto the *Tonight Show* stage. Old friends greeted me with cheers and whistles; some stood to shake hands or slap me on the back. I raised a casual index finger to the bartender, and a frosty schooner of beer appeared seconds later. Frankie Laine belted out "Rawhide" from the jukebox near the antique pool table in the far corner.

"I'll get that, Ernie," said Doug Willis, billiards stick in hand. He ushered me down the length of the bar as I tried to put names to old faces now weathered by years, losses, and alcohol. "Keep your money in your pocket. I'm the one who asked you to come down, remember?"

Doug briefly leaned his cue against the table's middle pocket as he reanalyzed the scrambled mix of stripes and one solid. Black cigarette burns rested like dried caterpillars on the pool table's top rail, spoiling the glossy varnish. He frowned, used the cue as a pointer, and waved it toward the far corner. "Eight ball. Up there."

Hazel Sittner, still slinging sandwiches and pulling Rainier taps in her sixties, barged through three patrons, her brown tray stacked high with dirty plates and beer glasses.

"Welcome back, Ernie," Hazel said, setting the tray on the bar. "'Bout time Doug dragged some class in here. Do you miss being in the middle of the action, 'specially on Friday nights?"

"Thanks, Hazel. Yes, and no. I miss being around the kids, but I don't need those helicopter parents always hovering over the program. Also I don't miss the college assistants who refuse to leave players alone. Call all hours of the day and night."

Hazel smirked and pulled an order pad and pencil from an apron pocket. "Well, I hope you get back into it at some point. We need guys like you not just as coaches, but as mentors. We've got too many young guys now who think coaching is all about screaming. Gonna eat?"

"Yeah, soon as this pool hustler here finishes his work."

"Perfect," Hazel said as the cook appeared and restacked her tray with more food. "Just holler. Say, there was a guy lookin' for you earlier tonight. Don't know his name, but I've seen him before. Not a regular, though."

"OK. I'll ask around. Gotta be one of these coaches."

Hazel checked her order and lifted the tray now jammed with four platters, anchored by mammoth hamburgers and one fried-egg sandwich. A few french fries slipped off a plate on to the floor. She turned into the crowd and hoisted the tray even higher over her red curls.

Doug dropped his forehead to the green felt after missing his game-winning shot. I offered a polite, bad-luck cringe, sipped my Rainier, and pointed to a corner table. "Let's sit," I said. "You can drown your sorrows."

He nodded and returned his pool cue to the chalk-dusted wall rack. As we ducked between patrons, he said, "I've always wanted to ask you. How in the hell did you get to Eastern Michigan University from Yakima, Washington?"

I laughed and faced him. "Only school to offer me a scholarship, Back then, if you didn't make the state tournament, no coaches knew about you. The assistants didn't scout like they do now. I wasn't even on the Huskies' radar."

"But Eastern Michigan ... I mean, that's not just around the corner."

I half-gagged a mouthful of beer. "Crazy story. I'd just graduated from Yakima High, working in the apricot fields for my dad. A buddy drafted me to play in a summer-league tourney over here at Bellevue Community College. The Eastern Michigan frosh coach just happens to be in the area for a family reunion."

"So the coach ends up at the BCC games?"

"Right. Our team played three games in one day—you know those goofy schedules—and I got a bunch of rebounds. Couldn't shoot a lick, even back then. Next thing I know, this guy is asking me if I wouldn't mind playing college ball in Ypsilanti, Michigan."

"The coach signed you that night?"

"Yeah, right there in the locker room. I was still wringing wet from the final game. Called my folks from the gym and told them I had a free ride to play college basketball. They couldn't believe it. Neither could I."

Doug shook his head. "Unbelievable."

As we sat, a cluster of guys at the adjacent table bemoaned the cuts in school district resources that meant fewer paid teacher-monitors at games.

"Hey, I'd do it again," I said. "Community was great to me. Met my wife there, got a degree, played with some good guys. Brutal winters, but no complaints."

"Are you still playin' at all?"

"Yeah, we've got the same group still showing up on Saturday mornings at the high school. Mostly older local guys who know how to play, get up and down the floor. A lot of them can still really go. Some of their kids even show up now when they're in town."

"Well, keep it going for as long as you can. Our weekly game went downhill in a hurry. We had some younger guys show up that didn't work out. Grab shirts. Never give up the ball. Lots of elbows and assholes. The veterans didn't need that and finally just stopped coming back."

Doug cupped his beer glass with both hands and laid his forearms on the table. "Look, I know you are close to Linn Oliver. I saw him the other day. Dark circles under his eyes, lethargic. I'd never seen him like that. I was concerned about him and wanted you to know. Then, I heard about this situation on the ferry."

I lunged forward. "You saw him? When?"

"God, I don't know. Early last week. Maybe Monday or Tuesday."

I winced and gazed out the window. "I was going to ask you if you knew of a tourney out of town. Maybe something one of your former players headed to? Fact is, I've seen very little of him in the past three weeks."

"Not off the top," he said. "Tell you what, though. I was really surprised by his appearance. Maybe he's trying to do too much at night after working all day. I know it can be difficult playing less than second fiddle when you've always been the go-to guy."

Two men nearby hollered as one of the teams in a televised pro game completed a stunning comeback with a Tom Chambers dunk. Doug broke the conversation, glanced up at the screen, then continued. "Anyway, I've got some elementary-school clinics coming up, including one at spring break. I'd like to offer Linn a paid position to help run them.

He would be a terrific teacher, and he would certainly bring in more kids. In fact, having Cheese on the staff would be the best advertisement we could possibly have."

"Sounds like a winner. He'll probably welcome the deal."

"But more importantly, I wanted a chance to talk with Linn about my experience. I went through the whole injury thing, then dealing with the prospect of never playing again. I was hoping my story might help him in some way."

I slid my glass toward the middle of the table, leaned back in my chair, and wondered just how far hurt might have pushed Linn Oliver.

Doug waited until my eyes returned to his. "Candidly? I can't hire Linn with him looking like he does now. It wouldn't shed a positive light on our clinics, and it wouldn't be fair to the campers."

He was right. You can't trot out a down-and-out legend in front of a bunch of impressionable little dribblers. I'd seen it before, and it ruined the camp's future and a coach's income. What families would be willing to plunk down their hard-earned cash to have their kids learn the game's fundamentals from a player who had lost his way? What was worse was that I couldn't believe Linn would ever fit into that category.

"I'll see what I can find out," I said. "I assume you have Linn's phone number at the service station in North Fork, but I will tell him to get a hold of you if I see him first. Those hoops clinics could be a real help to a lot of people, including Linn."

"That's one of my problems." He leaned closer, then checked over his shoulder to see if someone else could hear. "He won't return my calls. His boss at the gas station said he is tired of making excuses for him. Is it just me, or does the kid really need help?"

Doug raised his glass and signaled Hazel, who made her way to our table and took our orders.

"By the way," Hazel said. "The guy I said was lookin' for you? Well, he's now over talkin' on the phone."

I started to rise and was immediately eased back down by the handshake of a coach-turned-motivational-speaker I hadn't seen in years. In his life, everything was "super." We shared updates about a retired principal while I tried to be as subtle as possible in glancing toward the green wood-box phone booth pushed against the wall near the men's restroom. Two rangy loggers wearing plaid Pendletons blocked my line of sight. I managed to see that the collapsible window door of the booth was closed, and the light was on. I casually swayed, shifting my weight, trying to peer into the booth.

"What's up for the rest of the weekend, Ernie?" the pro mouthpiece shouted over the music, television, and elevated conversations. "Got some cute lady lined up for tomorrow night?"

Interesting timing. It was Patsy Cline's turn on the jukebox, signing about being crazy for feeling lonely. Probably should get back up on the horse and at least look at the landscape.

"Nothing too exciting," I said. "Thought I'd make a few calls to old friends, see how they're doing."

"Well, you take good care," the man said. "And stay in touch." He handed me his glossy business card that featured a caped crusader who resembled the Wizard of Oz. "Our company can use older guys like you to get our word out."

When he eased away, I stood, eyed an empty phone booth, and sat back down. "Christ," I whispered.

Doug must have overheard the "cute lady" line. "How long's it been, Ernie?" His eyebrows drew closer together. "Since Cathy passed away?" He wasn't a close friend, but he apparently felt close enough to ask. I admired him for broaching the topic.

"Too long. Just too damn long," I said, unable to maintain eye contact. "But thanks for asking."

I spanned the room, hoping to stretch the long day out of my neck and shoulders. Where was our food? I patted the pockets of my jacket, searching for car keys. I planned to wolf down my chow and hit the road.

The television on the wall scrolled college scores. I was particularly interested in the Ivy League. A smooth player from Bainbridge Island was getting some major minutes at Princeton. Just as *SportsCenter* returned to the Northeast region, Harvey Johnston blocked my view and shuffled toward our table. He looked like he'd spent thirty minutes in a sauna.

"Close quarters in that old phone booth," Harvey said. "Ever spent any time in there?"

"What are you doing here?" I said, realizing Harvey was the person Hazel mentioned. "Are you still working or coming from a game?" I introduced the detective to Doug.

"I called Greg Smithson at the newspaper looking for a phone number," Harvey said. "Said he was on deadline, but he'd be down here later. Also mentioned you'd stopped by to see him earlier. So, thought you might find your way down here."

Doug excused himself to speak with a retired referee. I stared at Harvey, palms up. "What's going on? Don't tell me you drove all this way just for a phone number."

He looked like Columbo after losing his car. He twisted in his chair, bloodshot eyes working the room. When he placed his elbows on the table, I could smell he could use a shower. "We got a call late this afternoon. The body of a Realtor was found last night in a home for sale at Lake Wilhelmina. Somebody bashed in his skull."

I felt like a fighter surprised by an explosive, left-right combo. I tried to focus on Harvey and cranked my head back, uncertain I'd heard what was just said. I could feel my eyebrows inching higher. "You gotta be kidding me. Was ..."

"We'll know more when we get the ME's report. Not a pretty scene, though. The perp took a big-league swing. Victim was from some hotshot brokerage here in Seattle. I came down from North Fork mainly to talk to his boss."

I leaned forward, my forehead not far from his. "Nothing like this has ever happened up there. It's a sleepy, little ..." I gathered myself and attempted a whisper that came out far too loud. "You're not telling me it was the Dolan place?" A guy walking by eyed me warily. Apparently, I was too close to be whispering to another man.

"Nope, five doors down," Harvey said. "The Sherrard house. Actually it's quite the fashionable retreat. Fancy-smancy."

"Talk about a retreat," I said. "Wait until the word gets out at the lake. People will be running for the hills."

"Tell me about it," Harvey murmured. "Calls are coming in like crazy. Lot of lake residents already packed up their cars and headed out. Scared to death. Some headed to Arizona for the rest of the winter; others staying with family members anywhere but the lake."

"What do you figure happened?"

"Who knows," Harvey said. "Looks like the agent—this Mark Rice—met the murderer at the house. Probably thought he was working with a potential buyer and ..."

The news hit me like an elbow to the head. For a moment, I didn't know if I could speak. "Pee Wee Rice? Oh my God, Harvey! He was just in the office the other day!" Suddenly, the heaviness returned to my feet, and my hands barely felt my forehead resting in them. "Tell me this isn't happening."

Harvey lowered his voice and moved closer. "God, I'm sorry. I had no idea he was a friend of yours."

"More of a professional acquaintance, really. Good man. Honest, reliable. Believe me, not all agents are that way. Guy had a network bigger than CBS."

He shook his head and picked at a napkin. "Could happen to anybody," he said. "Hey, think about it. Some hot prospect calls and wants to see the place right away. Agent meets him at the house. You guys do it all the time, even the old ladies."

Five doors down from Dolan's?

"The owner, guy named Emory Sherrard, came up to the lake on a lark and found the victim in an upstairs bathroom," Harvey said. "If he hadn't, the body probably would have been there for days, maybe weeks."

"Maybe Pee Wee happened on a burglary and things got out of hand," I said.

"Doesn't look like it," Harvey said. "Appears Rice was in the house when the killer arrived. But I need to do a lot more digging and legwork, talk to people. More so now, given how well you say he was connected. But as I say, this just came down."

"Did it look like there had been traffic on the lot? Maybe car tracks from agents showing the place?"

"Tough to tell it because it was getting dark, and I wasn't there that long, like the other night at Dolan's. I just stopped by there briefly to meet the yellow-tape guys on the way here. Most of them parked on the road and steered clear of the scene."

"Bet those lake folks loved that circus. Especially with what's going on with Linn."

Hazel brought our food, and I waved to Doug, who was holding court at the bar, instructing anyone who would listen on the finer points of boxing out under the bucket. I snitched a couple of Doug's potatoes. Other people's fries always seemed to taste better.

When Hazel left, Harvey sighed, stretched his arms high over his head and returned his attention to the table. "There's only a handful of homes for sale at the lake."

"Right," I said, nodding my familiarity of the inventory. "Couple of expensive mansions, two tear-down shacks, and one in-between. Been in all of them."

"I'm sure you have. My point is that there was a dead guy in one of them and another guy, one Linn Oliver, missing from another home about a nine-iron away."

I flipped my fork on the table. A different sort of emptiness had replaced hunger and fatigue. My head began to ache, and I knew I was approaching overload. "Are you telling me that you think the two situations are related?"

"No, Coach. I am just stating what we know. Sometimes it's best for me to get the obvious out on the table and do a little thinking out loud. I haven't even begun to paint. Just wondering what could go on the canvas."

I pushed my platter toward the middle of the table. "Harvey, what do you think the chances are that ..."

"Look, we have no reason to jump to any conclusions or assumptions. Tell you what. I am heading back up to the lake tomorrow afternoon to look through the house, talk to some more folks. You should join me. I could use your advice as a property professional."

Other than morning hoops, my Saturday was wide open. As usual. "Meet you there," I said. "I'll figure two p.m., unless I hear otherwise."

Harvey nodded and rose from the table in sections, unfolding his disheveled upper body until he leaned back into a truncated stretch, hands on hips. It was painful to watch.

"Tell me, have you spoken recently with Dr. Oliver? One of my detectives called down to Arizona today and just got his machine."

"Haven't connected, but he should be in North Fork by now. Got a message he was heading north today. If he's not staying with his brother, he'll probably be at the Cranberry Tree. I'll find out. Offer my spare bedroom."

"Might be better if I talk to him first. In light of what happened to ..."

I shook my head and stared across the table. "Harvey, you barely know the guy. Let me do this. He's going to be anxious and scared, and the last thing he needs is the crime chief grilling him about his kid. Let me visit with him, feel him out."

Harvey scoffed, stood, and started for the back door. "No way. Another example of you being official when you're not official." He stopped and stared at me. "I can't allow you to pose as some sort of professional investigator."

Embarrassed that two bar-sitters overheard him, Harvey sunk lower. I reached for his elbow and pulled him around. "Look. This man is different. Robert Oliver's been a lot more to me than a star player's father. I've been in life-or-death situations with him twice and a hell of a lot of stuff that's more than you'll ever want to know."

"What? Well, maybe I do want to know. After all the time we've spent together ..."

"Don't start on me. Not with this. Just trust me that I'd get more useful information from him before you can or anybody else from your office."

He shook his head and looked down at the floor.

"Harvey. Just let me do this. This one time."

He shrugged, yanked his rumpled collar higher on his neck, and took one step toward the parking lot. "I better not hear that same pitch again. Like on the next guy you want to corner and question."

"That's a deal. I pass everybody else on to you."
A moment later, the screen door slammed.

WHEN I GOT HOME, I headed straight for the sack, spewing clothes across the bedroom floor. In less than a minute, I could feel the weight of my eyelids and welcome notion that heavy slumber was just around the corner. The phone rang, jarring me upright.

"Hello," I groaned.

No reply.

"Hello. Who is this?"

I heard two heavy breaths. Then the line went dead.

TWENTY

I BLEW OFF THE EARLY MORNING HOOP game, figuring at least one of my friends would ask questions about Linn that I could not answer. The on-off feeling in my feet, heavy and listless, clicked back on. I didn't want to run the risk of stumbling while cutting into the lane or falling behind on a fast break.

My night of sleep had been sliced into random anxious sections over the idea of discussing with Robert Oliver the possible consequences of Linn mixing his drugs and then exploring the role that drugs might have played in his son's disappearance.

Cathy had made certain that the line on the off-white phone was long enough that she could pull it into the kitchen and talk with one of her girlfriends when I was studying a tape of an upcoming opponent in the den. She also constantly wiped and cleaned it, fearing the remote possibility that a visitor might speak into a dirty receiver. The phone now usually sits on the coffee table opposite the television, its uneven loops of extra line spilling out from underneath the narrow table and often catching my size thirteens. The receiver rarely is clean.

I settled the phone in my lap to make the call and flashed back to the countless times I'd seen Robert Oliver dash out of games, school plays, restaurants, weddings, and Sunday Mass, responding to the unexpected pleas from females of all ages who were experiencing the mind-boggling event that no man would ever truly understand. An obstetrician in a one-man shop, the only time Linn Oliver's father was "off call" was during his two-week family vacation at Lake Wilhelmina. Even then, he treated patients who called with emergencies.

I vividly remembered how Dr. Oliver, by way of one incident that I witnessed, chose his hectic life over the family businesses of timber harvesting and railroad shipping. In the darkest hour of my life, he told me he had fully intended to stay in the forests. He believed it to be a healthy, challenging, and rewarding place to be. His older brother William, along with William's wife Lucretia and their two sons, operated the MacTavish & Oliver Logging Company that their grandfather had started with Wallace MacTavish in 1882. Lucretia's two brothers now handled the family's Linnbert railroad business, which had been parceled out to several regional carriers.

Like his father, Robert not only married late in life but also chose a woman nearly twenty years younger. All four of their children worked for Uncle Bill in the family lumber business for extended periods during high school and college but, again like Dad, eventually pursued different careers.

During the summer of my sophomore year in high school, I escaped the Yakima heat and took a weekend shift as a brakeman on a logging train working the MacTavish & Oliver camps. The job came through my father, who contracted to move a lot of fruit on a partner line and who persuaded the powers that be that his six-foot-four son could pass as a company-required eighteen-year-old. One night while waiting for linemen to repair a rail at Camp Ten near

Lake Wilhelmina, I saw Robert Oliver perform an emergency delivery of a premature baby. The long, harrowing night changed his life—and had a lasting impact on mine.

The evening began when the woman, Ellie Phillips, collapsed while restocking the dinner chow line. Ellie was young, broke, and single. The Olivers had gone out of their way to find her a safer job on the crew when she announced she was pregnant and her choker-setting boyfriend had disappeared from the logging camp. When Ellie passed out, I helped move her into the converted freight car used as the camp's school to get her out of the heat and commotion of the cafeteria tent. Annette Zuliger, the camp nurse, soon arrived and announced that Ellie had gone into labor. The heated debate of whether or not to move her to a mulligan, hook it to the Shay engine, and power into North Fork without a log load was interrupted by my engineer, Tag Shurbart.

"We ain't going nowhere until that stick of rail west of Brookens Gorge is fixed," Shurbart said. "So everybody just keep your shirts on 'til we get word."

"She shouldn't be moved anyway," Zuliger warned. "She should stay right here and give birth to this baby. Besides, Robert probably knows more about this than that old barber we got for a doc in town. If something isn't done soon, we could lose them both."

"What?!" Robert yelled, shaken by the possibilities. He'd earned degrees in Agriculture Science and Veterinary Medicine at Washington State University and then headed back west to consider his long-term options with the family business. "Now, I've delivered some fillies and calves, but this is entirely different. This woman needs professional care and ..."

"And you are a professional, in a related field," Zuliger said. "You're the best person around to do this, so get in there and deliver Ellie's baby. Now!"

Shurbart held the most seniority within the group and made the final decision. We would ready the train and depart as soon as possible for the hospital in town with Ellie and a ragtag skeleton team of medical assistants led by Oliver and Zuliger. Shurbart told me he thought the repair would be completed by the time we got to Brookens Gorge. I helped Annette turn the school car room into a temporary infirmary, setting up a clean cot with fresh sheets and plenty of soft towels. She sterilized the camp's best kitchen knives with alcohol and gently applied compresses to Ellie's forehead. The young woman was frantic, in and out of consciousness, and unaware of her circumstances. Moments later, Shurbart quietly slipped through the door and whispered to Zuliger that the train was prepared to leave.

Shurbart bent down and spoke softly into Ellie's ear. "Ellie, we are going get you to North Fork as soon as we can. You are going to have a baby tonight, and we want you to be as safe as possible."

We lifted Ellie into the heated mulligan and fastened the bottom of the cot to the side rail of the freight car. I placed two small stools opposite the cot for Robert and Annette. Shurbart brought in a small rectangular table with a stack of white towels, a pitcher of warm water, knives, and several bandages, and returned to the engine.

The firebox of the Shay engine glowed the mesmerizing orange of a desert sunset. Primed and ready to roll, Shurbart kicked the iron lid shut, checked his pressure gauges and eased onto his stool. The three-car train determinedly chugged away from the camp in the dark, quickly gaining speed as it headed west. The mulligan click-clacked comfortably over the first rails, the lack of a heavy log load allowing the train to roll smoothly along the straight sections of track. Without a car coupled behind it to provide ballast, the rear of the mulligan twitched slightly coming out of the turns, shaking the contents on the table adjacent to Ellie's cot. The flames of the two oil lanterns danced higher, shooting brief, jagged silhouettes up the rough-sawn cedar walls to the car's ceiling.

As the train slowed approaching Brookens Gorge, I leaned out of the mulligan's sliding door to see the locomotive's spotlight pick up lanterns swung across the track by the Linnbert Railroad repair crew. When the engine hissed to a stop, I was instructed to swing down out of the car, jog quickly up the tracks, and inform the laborers of the emergency.

I stumbled twice in the dark trying to find my footing in the jagged track-side rip-rap until I entered the coverage of the train's pie-shaped beam. When I reached the five-man team, all were obviously caught off guard. A stranger walking toward them from an unscheduled train was not something they saw every day.

"We got a gal onboard, and she's about to ready to pop with a baby," I said. "Don't know how long this kid is gonna wait."

The crew chief peeled off heavy gloves stained in creosote. He pulled a floppy rag from his hip pocket and wiped a combination of dirt and sweat from his cheeks and the side of his neck. "We're in the middle of it here, son. Sure as hell didn't expect anybody at this hour."

"Things got bad in a hurry in camp," I said. "Tag didn't see another option. Wants to bust it down to headquarters."

"Hell's fire," the crew chief murmured. He surveyed the mound of ties, rail, and spikes that had been spewed beside the track.

"How's the mom doin' in there?" one of the linemen asked, resting a sledge hammer against his thigh. "She gonna make it?"

"She's one tough lady," I said. "Guess you'd have to say she's doing as well as could be expected."

The chief winced briefly into the glare, gave a half-hearted wave, and spat at his feet. "What the hell, boys. We can clear it up now and finish at daybreak. We're camping here tonight anyway. That new rail should be strong enough for the Shay."

His eyes darted to mine. I took it as a sign to return and relay the news.

"You got a doc on that train or somethin'?" the chief shouted.

"No sir," I shot back over my shoulder, heading for the smoking engine. "We're rollin' with the camp nurse and a vet. One of the Oliver boys."

I reported the results of the conversation to Shurbart, then checked in with the pensive passengers in the mulligan.

"Robert, this poor girl can't get much hotter," Zuliger snapped, one soothing hand on Ellie's forehead, the other embracing her left palm. "Believe me, I've seen this many times before. It's simply not going to come regular; you're gonna have to take it."

Oliver took a deep breath, unlatched the cot from the side railing and cautiously shimmied the portable bed to the middle of the car, allowing sufficient room on both sides of the cot. He stationed Annette on one side, instructed her to begin removing Ellie's work shirt, then dragged a stool close to his first human patient.

"Go tell Tag we're going to do this right here," he said. "We all wished we had more time but we simply don't have it. This baby needs to come out, and we're not going to wait any longer."

I bolted out the door, hopped down the three-step iron ladder welded to the car, and delivered Shurbart the message. I returned to find Oliver huddled silently over Ellie, his hands folded perfectly like a kid preparing for his First

Communion. After a moment, he turned and pivoted toward the door and motioned to me to jiggle rubbing alcohol over his calloused palms.

"Everybody's nervous, son," Oliver said. "Including me. But this woman needs us right now. Take a deep breath and do the best you can."

Oliver wrung them slowly, his fingers ultimately pointing toward the ceiling as the liquid dripped down his wrists before evaporating on his forearms. I yanked a pocketknife from my coat, poked a hole in the middle of a white towel, then ripped the white cloth down the center. I rolled it in half, wrapped it around Oliver's sweating brow, and secured the ends in the thick brown hair on the back of his head.

"Damn it, Robert!" Annette screamed. "Would ya stop getting ready? There is no more time! You're gonna need to cut her or she'll rip herself apart."

Oliver balanced a heavy silver knife in his left hand, gauging its weight and length and mulling the pressure he would need to apply. "Ernie, pin her legs to the cot and don't let go," he said.

Moving to the foot of the cot, I wrapped my fingers around her hot, slippery ankles, arched my back and pushed down, locking my wrists into a straight line with my forearms. "She's going to try to turn on her side, so be ready."

Looking down at the writhing young woman, Oliver performed each incision of the uterine layer with precision and found the uterus quickly with a minimal loss of blood. Ellie's frantic shrieks turned to mumbled moans.

"Easy, now, Robert," Annette said. "This ain't no old mare who's been down this road before."

Oliver shifted his weight and shuffled his feet, solidifying his stance.

"Annette, move the lantern to the left. No, too far. There, right there. Ernie, now ease up on your grip. Just hold her in place."

Making his final cut through the uterus, he reached through cloudy amniotic fluid into the pelvis, and lifted a wet and red baby girl from Ellie Phillips. Oliver snipped the umbilical cord and carefully laying the infant into Annette's towel-covered arms. I stood behind Oliver's right shoulder, wide-eyed and open-mouthed, tasting the tears running down my face.

"Robert, Robert, Robert," sobbed Annette, gently swaying the baby before resting her in Ellie's arms. "Those hands don't belong in the forest."

Oliver methodically collected the placenta, respectfully folding it into an extra blanket. Ellie beamed as her child wailed into the Skagit Valley night. Robert's composure remained remarkable; his steady hands truly impressive. *How could someone do that in a train car?!* Exhausted, soaked with sweat yet still on task, he smiled at Annette and nodded at me, his silent gesture of thanks. Poised and confident, he retraced his steps with sutures.

Ellie Phillips completely altered Robert Oliver's career plans. Three months later, he enrolled in two biology courses at the University of Washington and then applied for medical school the following term. After medical school, internships, and residency, he returned to the logging camps only to visit family and friends. He became quite comfortable delivering North Fork babies for the next thirty-one years.

WHEN I ACCEPTED THE coaching and teaching position at Washington High, I learned that Robert Oliver had set up shop in North Fork and become the most respected obstetrician in town. Years later, he was the easy choice when Cathy became pregnant with our first child.

Unlike Ellie Phillips, however, Cathy Creekmore never got off the table. She died of an ectopic pregnancy at the Skagit Valley Clinic after unknown hours of internal bleeding. She'd laughed at my jokes, put up with dumpy, moldy hotel rooms in tiny towns, and even scouted an upcoming opponent when I was stuck at a parent-teacher night. Her favorite line, delivered countless times to family and friends when a meaningless tournament kept me from a wedding, funeral, or reunion, carried equal parts of sarcasm and charisma. *"I'm sure Ernie loves basketball more than me, but at least there's a chance he loves me more than golf."* She was thirty-seven.

After she was gone, I still looked for her in the bleachers above our bench. She had this prolonged, sexy wink she flaunted during critical timeouts just to yank my chain when a game was on the line. I'd snort and shake my head. I could have used her magic in the state title game and her comfortable companionship for the rest of my life. Didn't happen.

Robert Oliver said that he never forgave himself for not diagnosing Cathy's condition sooner. Sympathy and grief cloaked his words and expressions every time we met. Always friendly, our past had pulled us closer, but we were never really comfortable together. His presence always brought that dreadful day to the present. For years, I thought I was making progress in moving on and meeting other women until I would bump into the good doctor after church or in a restaurant, spurring memories of my once-perfect partner. Now that he lived in Scottsdale, I felt I stood a better chance. Our next conversation, though, would hit closer to his home than mine.

I dialed the Cranberry Tree. The desk clerk confirmed Dr. Oliver had checked in just before the dinner hour. The ring up to his room brought no answer.

TWENTY-ONE

9 A.M., MONDAY, SEPTEMBER 25, 1923

ELIZABETH LINNBERT OLIVER GATHERED her eight students into the mulligan car that served as a rolling schoolhouse at the MacTavish & Oliver Logging Company's Camp Eight, a few miles southeast of North Fork near Finn Settlement and the original homestead of Anders Gustaffson and Mikko Kurri.

When a former dancehall flapper who had been hired as the primary school teacher missed the Sunday night train back to camp too many times, Elizabeth assumed the role of full-time educator. Henry approved of the move, knowing how much his wife enjoyed her portable classroom, and teased her about the low percentage of time she spent in front of the chalkboard inside the stuffy train car.

"We will finish our math lesson today. After, I will need you all to help me pack up the books and secure the desks to the walls for our move," Elizabeth said to the sons and daughters of the workers. "If all goes as planned, we will be looking down at a beautiful lake on our next class day."

After years of successful cutting, limbing, and loading at Camp Eight, chief engineer Patrick O'Leary orchestrated the circus-like move to a relatively flat, generous plateau above the west end of Lake Wilhelmina with precision. As soon as the loader pulled his tongs from the last log of a fully packed skeleton car, the camp's personnel turned from logging to folding and packing. By the time an empty train returned from the log dump near the headquarters at Conway, the bunkhouses, engineer's house, foreman's cottage, cook house, latrine canvases, mechanical sheds, and various storage shacks were folded and flanking the tracks. They were arranged to be placed in their assigned area of a specific train car. Enclosed cars resting on the camp's sidetrack that had served as dormitories, offices, and workshops were coupled into a designated place on the train. Ropes, tent spikes, canvas covers, woodstoves, schoolhouse supplies, cooking sundries, bandages, heavy pots, dried food, and personal belongings all were stowed in predetermined spots. Clothing, shoes and personal items left behind by dismissed or runaway employees were tossed into a community basket for any camp resident. Tattered, torn, or oil-stained garments were burned in the outdoor pit along with old letters, individual employment contracts, and forgotten journals and diaries.

The new setting overlooked Lake Wilhelmina and its crescent sandspit, with Bailey Mountain looming like a fallen camel to the south and Glacier Peak in willowy clouds to the southeast. Elizabeth requested that the company's brush cutters fashion a trail to the beach and the remains of the Madrona community. She led her students down the path that meandered gently from the new logging site, down a knoll covered with lofty cedars, through a sunny hollow, then alongside Minnie Creek to the mirror-like lake.

"Many of you have heard stories from your parents about the famous Indian woman, Wilhelmina," Elizabeth said to the children. "This is the remains of the Madrona Resort she built with her husband, Mikko Kurri. They both were known for their generosity and kindness."

"Did they move away after their house burned down?" a boy asked.

Elizabeth glanced around to eight curious faces. "About twenty years ago, Wilhelmina lost her life in a mysterious fire that the natives say glowed all night above these hills. Mikko had taken their son to see the big city of Vancouver. When he received the news, Mikko never returned to the lake."

Mikko Kurri was last seen by a steamboat captain who had hunted deer on vacation near Lake Wilhelmina. The captain contacted Angelica Kurri, Mikko and Wilhelmina's only daughter, and told her that her father had arrived in San Francisco and was asking about the whereabouts of a wayward drifter named Vance Tyler. Three days later, Kurri had bartered his carpentry services for passage to Helsinki.

"I did hear about the fire at the Madrona cabin on Lake Wilhelmina," the steamboat captain said. "But I didn't get word of it until after I left San Francisco. I knew Mikko was looking for Tyler, but I had no idea why."

A San Francisco hotel and saloon owner, a cousin of the captain, found Vance Tyler early one morning propped up in a booth at the rear of his honky-tonk bar. A carpenter's knife pierced his heart.

TWENTY-TWO

Noon, Saturday, February 5, 1982

When I finally reached Dr. Robert Oliver at the Cranberry Tree Inn, we agreed to meet at the Calico Cupboard for lunch. Slim but lacking the gauntness that sometimes sets in during late middle age, his silver-streaked hair floating above a flaking scalp, Dr. Oliver appeared exhausted as he drummed his fingers lightly on the table. A green turtleneck topped an olive-drab windbreaker. He looked like Alan Alda after an all-nighter in a M*A*S*H emergency tent.

"Any news?" he asked before I slid into the booth.

"Nothing this morning."

He fidgeted in his seat and removed his jacket without standing. "Can't handle the AC noise in hotel rooms, so I got up early and walked around town. Hadn't seen some of those cute new shops down by the river. Realized the guy who bought my medical building expanded the parking lot. Everything else looks about the same."

A waitress stopped by with ice water and menus, oversized plastic sheets that wobbled when she dealt them. We blew through the obligatory topics—his flight up, the Arizona weather, and the best of spring training ballparks near Scottsdale—before we got around to his fourth and youngest child. In succinct yet winded sentences, Dr. Oliver mentioned he had not heard from Linn in more than two weeks and had no idea what drugs he had been taking for knee pain "or any other pain."

"The last time you spoke, did he seem down, maybe a bit depressed?" I said.

"To the contrary. Very upbeat. Maybe a little fatigued, but he seemed positive. He's been flying pretty high ever since I saw him in Scottsdale heading home from the Mexico trip." He crossed his arms on the table and leaned in closer. "You believe depression has something to do with his disappearance?"

I shifted in the booth, grabbed the bench seat with both hands, and stared into his weary brown eyes. "It's come up, Dr. Oliver, along with the constant tiredness. Some people say he's always dragging. Not long ago, one coach got a look at Linn, then hesitated about asking him to help out at a kids' clinic."

"Please, call me Robert. Now, about the drugs. You're thinking they might have contributed in some way?"

"I'm no expert, and I don't even know what he's taking."

"Patients can respond differently to certain medications. I doubt if anything prescribed for pain could possibly affect his behavior. A new drug combined with an existing one might produce some disorientation. Add to that possible dehydration, lack of sleep."

Robert reached for the pepper shaker, unscrewed the top, and checked the contents. He quickly replaced the top, then pushed the tiny container back toward its partner. "Ernie, where in the world is he?"

I sat back and stretched my arms along the top of the backrest. "I'm guessing he probably loaned somebody his car and then got in a carpool with a bunch of guys and went off to play a tournament. If he did drive on that ferry, there's a chance he went up top and walked off."

Robert dragged a hand over his freshly shaven chin. "I don't know. The carpool idea might make sense, but walking off the boat seems like a stretch. Personally, I keep going back to him admitting to me that he was burning the candle at both ends. Linn said sometimes the knee feels great, so he plays as much basketball at night as he can. Apparently, he can perform well for several days in a row before the knee becomes bothersome." He shook his head, then continued after a silence. "You know, we preached moderation to all our children, but the message didn't stick when it came to Linn and basketball. It's as if he lost the chance of playing at an elite level, but he'll do anything he can to keep it going with what's left."

Anything?

"He did cancel on me twice this year," I said. "We'd planned to see a couple of young post players down near Monroe. But some rec team somewhere needed another player, and he just had to go."

"I know what you mean. Plus he works his tail off at the Shell station, then he bails out Kelvin anytime somebody calls in sick. I think Linn feels he owes him for letting him work there during grammar school."

The waitress took our orders. Robert chose a tuna melt, and I went with a double cheese burger. We both opted for coffee.

"And speaking of owing," he said. "The awful situation with Cathy kept me from--"

"We've been over that. I hold nothing against you. So, please, can we just focus now on Linn."

He winced and waited a moment. "Please understand that Cathy was the only patient I ever lost. For years, her death blocked me from approaching you about anything, really. Even when my youngest child became your key player. With her in the back of my mind ...”

“You don't have to--”

“Please, hear me out. I never could get around to telling you how much I appreciated everything you did for him. Lord knows, I was never around in those days. Just holding off the college recruiters was a full-time job. All the counseling, ball games, fishing. Even now—you're doing stuff with him a dad should be doing.”

“Hold on a second,” I said. “We talked about how you wanted to be around, more present.”

“But it stopped right there. With my wishful thinking and should-haves. I think I was too ashamed about what happened to your wife to properly thank you for all you have been to my son.”

I rotated my water glass, mopped its slippery wet circle with an open palm, and glanced around the restaurant, praying for our lunch to arrive.

“When Linn was in Scottsdale, I told him some things I would have done differently,” Robert said. “I began to realize how many surrogate pieces you accumulated over the years. Funny, I felt embarrassed and fortunate at the same time.”

We ate mostly in silence. Later, he asked about this year's Fighting Crabs, the current coaching staff, and how many of last year's graduates enrolled at four-year schools. Before we left, I insisted that he move into my spare bedroom when he was in town.

“Greatly appreciated,” he said. “I could use the company, and I'm sure you don't have a fan that comes on in the middle of the night. I usually stay with Bill and Lucretia but, given the circumstances, it's probably better they're gone. Some convention, plywood I think. Anyway, they'd be worried sick. I will warn you, though,” he added with a sheepish smile, "that I'll get up at least once to use the facilities."

Once we got him moved in, Robert drove his rental car to Seattle to meet with an old friend, a researcher at the University of Washington medical school. I planned some research, too—into Mark Rice's possible enemies—before meeting Harvey Johnston at the lake. It seemed we needed more data on a guy everybody seemed to like and the only one I'd ever known who was killed in a home for sale, steps from where Linn Oliver was living.

ACCORDING TO A FELLOW salesperson in his office, Pee Wee Rice, age thirty-eight, had been on floor duty the day last summer when Emory Sherrard walked into Imperial National Real Estate Services at the company's flagship office in North Seattle.

Sherrard said he was impressed with Rice's marketing ideas, which included an after-work wine tasting for potential buyers on the home's deck, followed later by a weekend open house and a Saturday swim. Kids were welcomed by a lifeguard, hot dogs, soda, chips and make-your-own sundaes under the covered porch. Rice promised to print fliers and distribute them throughout the high-tech corridor and advertise the property in the Sunday *Seattle Tribune.*

On the same day that the property went into the multiple-listing association's database, he would release the information to his confidential "pocket" prospects, a group that included high-ranking officials at Boeing and Weyerhaeuser. Knowing Rice's flair for the flashy, he probably followed through on all promises.

Sherrard was quite comfortable with an asking price of $99,950, loved the idea of luring families with the Saturday swim open house, and couldn't wait to hear the response from Rice's corporate executive clients. If nobody made an offer at the original listing price, Sherrard would simply lower it by a few thousand dollars and relist the house as a brand-new listing.

But the Sherrard house continued to sit with little, if any, winter action. Until this week.

The Rice murder slid the once-anonymous Lake Wilhelmina region under the national microscope, thanks to a front-page story in the *Trib* that was picked up by every major wire service and a nationally syndicated radio feature. The National Association of Real Estate Agents, the nation's largest trade association, wanted to know how one of its own lost his life while showing a gorgeous waterfront home to a potential buyer in the Cascade foothills. This wasn't the dirty, nasty big city. This was a tight community of retired weekenders and carefree summer vacationers on an eight-hundred-acre lake surrounded by evergreens and snowcaps, twelve miles from a small town. Everybody knew everybody—or knew somebody who did.

I knew all about the house and Sherrard, a former Californian who brought his home equity and a boorish Golden State attitude with him to a software job in the growing high-tech corridor northeast of Seattle. He bought the property on a day trip, eventually demolished the older, homey cabin, and built a spec palace that featured impressive window walls, hardwood floors, an imported gas stove fit for a gourmet, plus a three-car garage to stow summer toys.

Sherrard, looking for a quick lucrative flip, contacted our office about listing his property but Elinor Cutter refused to accept his demand for a sixty-day listing. Sherrard also required the asking price be set at twenty thousand dollars more than our agents felt the market would bear. Cookie's call proved correct—the home sat on the market for eight months with little activity. Big price. Poor design. No takers.

On my way to meet Harvey, I grabbed a jacket and a pair of rubber dairy boots that I used to walk properties. I decided to head south on I-5 toward Arlington, check a few new FOR SALE signs on Highway 530 then zigzag up the Possum Road, a six-mile unpaved switchback stretch littered with empty shotgun casings, skeletons of abandoned cars, and kitchen appliances that led to the south end of the lake.

The Possum Store proved to be a convenient target for my midday road meal of Dr Pepper and Snickers. The splintered plastic marquee that hung hard by the highway ("YOU'RE IN POSSUM, AIN'T IT AWESOME!?") had seen better days, as had the Camel-smoking grandma who teetered behind the cash register in a frayed terrycloth bathrobe and slippers. The creaky fir floors held white metal shelves with two of everything tourists needed, plus cases of animal beer stacked to the ceiling and enough cartons of cigarettes to make Philip Morris smile. The coffee smelled like burned rubber.

"You a cop?" the woman said.

"No," I said. "Did you need one?"

"Slew of Smokeys blew in here this mornin'. Frickin' Johnny Law convention. Just don't figure in February."

She counted my change, hesitated, then counted again.

At the phone booth outside, I dialed Big River Realty to check my messages. The line was busy. Busy? We've got three lines. Either we've got a lot of winter weekend lookers, or the homicide had trickled down faster than I thought, and the old biddies at the office were chatting it up. I gave up, then managed to dump part of the soda on my shirt as the truck's rear wheels shimmied out of a Possum Road hairpin. The stain, coupled with a Snickers smudge on the crotch of my jeans, had me looking my normal spiffy self as I climbed down from the truck at the Sherrard abode.

I didn't feel that bad when I saw Harvey, who hadn't changed his clothes since I saw him last night at the M&J

Tavern. His mood had headed even farther south; I could tell by the way he held his forehead as he paced across the beam-framed front porch of the Sherrard lake house.

"LAST NIGHT I dreamt I WENT TO MANDERLEY again," Harvey recited as I approached.

"Opening line in *Rebecca*," I said. "A classic. Daphne du Maurier. But aren't you a Hemingway guy?"

"Yeah, well maybe it's just being around this quiet place, the still water." He limped down the steps to greet me but put little energy into his handshake. "Thanks for coming. We just arrived. Cops, detectives, don't have squat, the CB in my car's broke, and I'm freezin' my ass off. We're really on a roll."

Maybe he felt rusty from not spending more hours in the field. Recently, it seemed that Harvey spent half his time turning down full-time positions from other jurisdictions— federal, state, county, and city—or rejecting requests to travel to bizarre out-of-state crime scenes. He became celebrated in the forensics industry for making his initial pass through a crime scene with both hands in his coat pockets, careful not to disturb any material that could eventually prove critical to an investigation. The man was known to observe, evaluate, and file an expert opinion faster than anyone. His accuracy in the business was remarkable. He linked circumstantial evidence with physical propensities; time and place to speed and distance; mental tendencies to a list of likely medications.

For the moment, though, he had zilch. I gazed up at the house and thought of the countless strangers I'd met showing homes in the middle of nowhere.

"Unbelievable," I said. "Rice was a veteran agent, for chrissake. I can't imagine how he was caught off-guard in a vacant house."

"Makes me start to think the killer was somebody he knew."

I turned to face him. "Don't most homicides involve somebody close to the victim, like a family member?"

"True. In fact, the murders in my last three cases were committed by angry exes."

I propped a boot on the bottom step and folded my arms. "Harvey, Pee Wee was never married—at least that I knew about—but he was definitely a mover and a shaker. The guy had a way with the ladies. Maybe this was a neglected lover. A torrid affair gone sideways."

Harvey didn't look up; rather, he continued to peer at the ground around and under the cedar steps. He waved to a police photographer and pointed to three areas he wanted evaluated and shot.

"Heard a lot of chatter last night from his broker and a couple of agents," he said. "Not much to go on. Evidently, a few years ago, the rumor was that he was involved with the wife of a drugstore owner down in Edmonds. We found out they did mess around some, but she eventually told him to kiss off. End of story."

"Maybe it wasn't the end of the story. Maybe the flame was rekindled; the drugstore boy finds out, follows Rice to this house and pops him."

Harvey straightened up and frowned.

"Or, the girl wants back in the romance, and Pee Wee blows her off," I said. "You know what they say about a woman scorned."

"What a theory!" Harvey shook his head dismissively. "If you ever choose to give up selling real estate for a living, you could tell more of your stories and make some bad TV movies."

We shared a grin, and I filled him in on the information I'd received from the Seattle agents. All said they were stunned, figured Rice could take care of himself—or at least talk himself out of a bad situation—and never heard a word about somebody holding a grudge.

Harvey stretched his arms above his head after I completed my report. He continued to work his right shoulder like the former minor-league pitcher he once was.

"Very thorough," Harvey said. "Looks like shaking down high-school kids all those years about after-game beer parties has improved your investigative skills."

"Hey, I had an ulterior motive. Some years, I was trying to save my job, keep players eligible by being a full-time babysitter. Anybody caught at a kegger during the season— drinkin' or not—had to sit. For a long time."

Harvey climbed the front steps and began a detailed inspection of the porch windows, his nose not quite touching the double-pane glass. He worked his way down to the entry where he closely eyed the brass knob and lock.

"Why don't you walk me through how agents would unlock this door," he said. "Is there a lockbox in that refrigerator over there they call a garage?"

Before I could answer, a distinctive voice boomed from behind me in the driveway, the same raspy growl that my students and players complained about when ticketed in town. One of my guards got nailed for "reckless driving" for hovering near forty miles an hour in a thirty-five zone. All vehicles the man deemed to be in violation contained an attractive female.

"Cold garage, but a hot lunch."

Arnold Dawson, my favorite deputy in the entire county.

"Well, look who decided to join us," Dawson smirked. "Our own private ace in the hole. Looks like we pulled out all the stops now. You just being here, Coach, makes me feel so much more confident. With your vast amount of experience, you've probably already got this case cracked. I mean, we can all probably go home right now."

"Arnold," Harvey said. "Try to behave yourself."

"Harvey asked," I said, loud enough for the group to hear. "So I came up."

Dawson shot me a nasty glare, then rotated his gaze, now nearly starry-eyed, into the cardboard box he balanced on his meat hook forearms. Odds were good he'd drool on his jacket before he could unwrap one of several foot-long sandwiches.

"Right off the grill from that new Philly cheese steak place on Main," Dawson said.

"I should have figured my loyal deputy would make a side trip at this hour," Harvey said. "But do us all a favor and hand out those things at the top of the driveway, away from any possible evidence. By the way, what was cookin' at the office?"

"Two-bit stuff," Dawson said, "and a lot of curious callers about this Rice thing."

"You ready?" He nodded toward the box.

"Yeah, but give me a handful of napkins," Harvey said. "Dorothy'll kill me if I bring this shirt home with a grease stain."

"She's not gonna care," Dawson said. "That shirt's been around the block a few times. Almost ready for the gardening drawer, or Goodwill."

Harvey pointed a warning finger at Dawson and dug into the box.

"Say, Coach," Dawson said. "What was this guy Rice like?" He crammed a healthy portion of a French roll stuffed with barbecued pork into his mouth and began munching. It didn't keep him from talking. "You must have seen him at some open houses, maybe a Realtor conference?"

Repeating information was not one of my favorite pastimes, much less to a nitwit I despised. But other officers were listening.

"As I told your boss, just a nice—and successful—guy. He worked a lot with the white-wine-and-brie crowd on Queen Anne and the Eastside. Upper-end homes like this one that most of my customers couldn't afford. Down to earth, though. Usually did what he said he'd do."

"Hey, Ernie," Harvey said. "Could you make a list of other agents, maybe home-services people, for Arnold to talk to? Owners of other agencies . . ? Let's see if Rice had a run-in with any competitor, pissed anybody off."

"Will do. I'll start with the folks in my office, find out who knows who. Probably can get you some names before the end of the day."

"I'll be poking around here with the forensics people into the night anyway," Harvey said. "One of them lifted a couple of sets of prints he's trying to trace. Some guy in L.A. who had a government job."

"Doesn't surprise me," I said. "It seems half of California has moved here the past few years."

Harvey pulled a pair of wadded black leather gloves from a side pocket, crammed in one hand, then the other, and tapped my elbow. "Let's go take a peek down the sandspit. Walk with me a minute."

We turned and marched up the driveway, through the bright yellow-black crime scene tape that Dawson had just redone. Then down Sandspit Road toward the Dolan place, leaving the investigative team to comb the murder scene at the Sherrard house. In the distance, an icy fog crept below the ridgeline on the far side of the valley and rolled halfway across the lake like a fluffy white sheet pulled to one side of a huge celestial bed. A thin line of blue separated it from the thunderheads directly above.

Harvey paced with his hands jammed in his jacket pockets. We stopped at the driveway with the sign DOLANS' DAZE OFF. He spoke, not taking his eyes off the gorgeous log structure.

"Did the Dolans and Sherrard have anything in common? Maybe with old man Dolan, or Jim Junior?"

"Zero, at least that I know about. Could not have been more different. New arrival versus old-timers. Uptight city boy against laid-back, crazy lake guys."

Harvey turned and looked straight at me. "What kind of crazy?"

We walked and talked down Sandspit Road until it intersected with North Shore Drive. I told Harvey about some of Jim Senior's booze-boosted shenanigans, including decorating his classic 1952 nineteen-foot Chris Craft runabout *On Assignment* for every lake parade and holiday occasion. He always covered his bases, especially when he was playing hooky from work. He told his kids: "If anybody from the office comes by the house looking for me, just tell them I'm out on assignment."

"Senior" was well known to the Skagit County Sheriff Department and the North Fork Police Department for many reasons. He reportedly recorded the fastest time from the lake to North Fork when he sped an unheard-of eighty miles an hour in his 1966 Mercury Cougar on the treacherous section between Big Lake and the Finn Settlement. Senior was rushing to get Martha to the Skagit Valley Community Clinic after she slipped on her full-length, slit-to-the-thigh Cher ensemble and fell on the dock during a Fourth of July costume bash, knocking her unconscious and breaking three ribs.

On another occasion, a hot day in June before Linn's senior year had come to a close, Dolan got wind that the Washington High's annual Senior Lockout Party was scheduled for the following weekend at the lake. He wasn't eager to have a bunch of beer-fueled teenagers racing their daddies' outboards on the lake, so he dressed up like a state park official, complete with *Cool Hand Luke* reflector shades and Smokey hat, and blocked the entrance to the boat launch with a series of orange road cones he swiped late one night from a county construction job on the lake road. When the kids showed up, boats packed with kegs and hot dogs, Dolan calmly informed them the launch was undergoing repair.

One of Senior's more controversial annual ventures was the self-christened Pull the Plug Party, an annual late-night caper that involved a small, quiet, secret flotilla—sans running lights—that demolished the beaver dams blocking the lake from the flow of Minnie Creek.

I explained that eliminating the dams meant a lower water level around the entire lake. And that provided wider beaches, especially for folks living on or near the sandspit. But residents with short docks, no docks, or muddy lakefront objected because lower water made launching, landing, swimming, and diving more difficult or less attractive. Depending upon where you lived and the type of property you owned, the lake levels were serious business. But Senior just enjoyed the clandestine thrill of the escapade.

At dusk on Pull the Plug Night, boats began arriving at the Dolans' beach and dock. Many of the neighbors paid no mind; a gathering at the Dolans' was no surprise at any time of day or night. Insulated plastic ice chests filled with push-button cans of Rainier Beer ("Vitamin R") and the animal-logoed Schaefer ("The one beer to have when you're having more than one") were flanked by buckets of Lay's, Fritos and French onion dip.

One night, as the procession of dinghies and kayaks slowly drifted on the black passage about halfway between the lake and the small waterfall where the outlet fell into Minnie Creek, Junior and I came upon a dam that wasn't built by beavers. Somebody had hand-driven four metal pilings and crossed them with sturdy boards and wire mesh. Whoever did it got it done with a heavy sledgehammer, and thought the Pull the Plug guys would not check as far down as the little waterfall.

By the time we twisted, wiggled, turned, and cussed all of the pipes from the suction created by the mucky bottom, loaded them into an aluminum dinghy, and freed the remaining logs, we were dripping with perspiration. Our arms were covered with mud, and we were in desperate need of cold beverages.

"Jim Senior told me that night that he'd been pulling the plug for forty years and had never seen or heard of any manmade blockade," I said. "The next morning, everybody was feeling rough around the edges."

"I can imagine there were a few bodies moving slowly that next day," Harvey said.

"Got that right. We eventually got down to the dock with our coffee and found the dinghy carrying the metal pilings nearly submerged on the shore. The five-gallon gas tank, tethered to the motor by its fuel line, bobbed near the middle of the boat. Lake water covered the floor boards, blue indoor-outdoor carpet."

"What the hell happened?" Harvey asked.

"Well, it got somebody riled up. Really hit their hot button. The outboard's drain plug rested on the driver's seat. Taped to the chipped steering wheel was a note scribbled in black crayon on yellow binder paper: *Who Pulled the Plug?*"

TWENTY-THREE

5 P.M., FRIDAY, SEPTEMBER 28, 1923

PATRICK O'LEARY, THE YOUNGEST son of a legendary boundary hunter mysteriously found murdered on the North Skagit, was well aware that the smell of fresh-cut evergreens was now the smell of money. Everyone wanted a share.

"We've got people taking our stumps, gyppos cutting into buffers near the creeks," O'Leary told his fellow members of the MacTavish & Oliver Lumber Company Board of Directors. "A lot of these guys are family men looking for roof shakes on a Sunday. They bring in a buckboard with the wife, pick through a logged section, then transport a few cedar bolts back home. Fine by me. Then we got larger gyppo outfits like Virgil Knight bringing in lots of men, using handcars on track we still have in use. They cut and run anytime they please and just don't give a damn about the land."

Henry Oliver peered down at the new timber contracts he had negotiated with the state of Washington and Skagit County and looked out the window at the huge log dump adjacent to company headquarters at Camp One on the Skagit Flats south of North Fork.

"Remember, we don't own the land, Patrick, only the trees," Oliver said. "It's going to be difficult keeping some people off the land. Not only land where we have been but also areas where we plan to go."

O'Leary unraveled a crispy, cumbersome parchment from a metal cylinder, unrolled the map onto a massive round oak table, and anchored each corner with a civil engineering manual. He surveyed the company's progress: each logging camp illustrated by a miniature tent, each stretch of track stenciled across the region like tiny black sutures on a giant's weathered face. Camp Nine was to be the final stop of the Linnbert Railroad Company's push into southeastern Skagit County; however the timber adjacent to the camp proved to be of excellent quality and so easy to log that the company decided to extend, establishing three more working camps over the next five years. O'Leary rested his left elbow on the map and pointed out to Oliver the tree symbols and stick-like structures representing the logging camps and successful harvests. O'Leary ran a stout index finger along the recently completed stretch of line to Camp Nine and noted that it had brought the total number of railed miles to more than thirty. Eight more miles—a tedious stretch toward a dragon-shaped muddy puddle known as Knight Lake—were scheduled for 1924. He stepped away from the table, rolled up the sleeves of his buckskin shirt, and placed his hands on his hips. "Now that, that piece of track is going to be interesting."

It was along this stretch that O'Leary designed and constructed a spectacular trestle, using single pilings from one-hundred-and-ten-foot-long fir trees, cross-braced by twelve-inch-diameter cedar to span one hundred and six yards across Brookens Gorge. The vibration of the huge pile-driving hammer propelled by the donkey steam engine shook the surrounding trees. The heavy iron machine sat on the tracks high above the gorge, gradually extending the railway over the abyss one piling at a time. The total weight that the span could bear was another issue.

O'Leary was adamant that no train en route to the mill should cross the trestle with a load greater than one locomotive with four loaded freight cars. He was mindful of the crews' safety and instructed all inbound passengers to walk across the new trestle until the timbers had properly settled. "Nobody rides on the train across this trestle except for the engineer," O'Leary told his crew. "One engine, one engineer until the timbers settle properly. Until then, everybody else walks across."

O'Leary watched as Virgil Knight followed his every move into the mountains and forests of Skagit County. Knight's "gyppo" or "come-behind" company waited until skid roads and railroad spurs were established, then worked behind the original logging crews once they had vacated a camp. Knight kept a watchful eye over the Oliver empire, quickly realizing that the MacTavish & Oliver roads were better graded, and its crews left more trees standing, than any other Northwest logging company. Knight made some of his money by felling immature and left-behind trees, and cutting shakes from healthy, stout stumps. He pocketed a majority of his revenue, however, by taking trees beyond the boundary of an owner's timber rights, knowing that companies like MacTavish & Oliver typically cut just short of the agreed-upon border. Knight's gang slashed and processed recklessly, laying any blame for overcutting at the feet of an "overly zealous" O'Leary crew.

Virgil and his wife, Juleen, a former secretary in the main MacTavish & Oliver office, were familiar with the company's procedures. They studied every timber contract recorded at the county courthouse and noted the exclusive rights of timber owners. They recognized that Henry Oliver had initially negotiated only the ownership of "standing timber" with the county. In Knight's view, once a tree was down or deserted, it was fair game. It made no difference to them if it happened to be in a buffer zone.

As a youth, Henry Oliver had witnessed firsthand how families had fallen apart when men were away from their homes and loved ones. As long as he had a primary say in railroad and logging matters, he would find a way to get his crews out of the forests and back to their homes on the weekends. On Friday after the shift whistle had blown, a locomotive with at least one closed-transport mulligan car, complete with sitting benches and wood-burning stove, left from camp for company headquarters near the log dump at Conway. Wives, children, and friends would meet the train, greet the loggers, and make plans for a weekend. When the MacTavish & Oliver weekend train pulled out, Knight escalated his operation.

In court, Knight contested Oliver's exclusive right to use the Linnbert-built railroad. Since Oliver and his partners did not own all of the land over which the railroad traveled, why should MacTavish & Oliver have absolute use of the track and access road? Knight asked the judge. Knight's attorney contended that any improvements to county or state land should be for the benefit of all citizens, not just for the wealthy few who could afford a railroad or a road-building venture.

"There's more behind this decision than you think," O'Leary told Oliver outside the Skagit County courthouse. "What happens when one of their handcars throws a spark into a trestle? Do you really think they are going to worry about a fire or repair any damage? What if we lose one of our trains because another company created a problem on our line but didn't tell anybody else about it?" O'Leary brushed back his silver hair and stared up at the courthouse tower. He folded his arms, leaned back as far as he could, stretching his six-foot-six frame. "Henry, my men say that the judge and

Virgil been known to take a sip together, play a few cards in a warehouse down by the river. Been doing so for years."

Tempers often flared in the woods between employees of the come-behind companies and the teams of initial contract loggers when the judge granted temporary use of the rails to the gyppo operators until he "could thoroughly research the issue."

Two incidents brought the controversy to a head, and the consequences of one of those events were not fully understood until decades later.

When O'Leary closed Camp Ten at the east end of Lake Wilhelmina in 1938, the company packed up its mobile shacks and portable rooms and swung farther east above Deer Creek and the Stillaguamish River. MacTavish & Oliver signed and honored a strict extended-buffer agreement mandated by the county above the creek. They did so in the fear that aggressive logging would jeopardize the hillside and result in a possible slide during the rainy season. Knight found the safeguarded area and logged all of its harvestable trees. Included in that region were hundreds of acres on or over the crest of the ridge above the Stillaguamish River watershed. Deer Creek, the largest tributary, wound its way through miles of the North Cascades Foothills and was home to the most prodigious steelhead-spawning region in the country. Oliver publicly chastised Knight for his unthinkable "raping of the land" above the Stilly. Knight paid a minimal fine. It was later discovered that he bribed three county commissioners for the reduced penalty.

Two years later, a fireman aboard a Linnbert locomotive was killed and three others injured when one edge of a trestle gave way over Brookens Gorge. The train slid off the track and tumbled into Minnie Creek at the bottom of the valley. The mammoth, jet-black iron engine and three cars were disassembled, transported piece by piece up the steep incline on the backs of Linnbert maintenance crews, and reassembled on a spur on which O'Leary had posted signs and verbally warned Knight's crew not to log near the trestle. But dozens of mature trees continued to disappear at both ends of the span, the huge barren semicircles growing every weekend. O'Leary comforted the fireman's widow while Knight countered Oliver's negligence and misconduct claims in the press.

"Henry Oliver simply jinxed his own track by trying to forbid others to use it," Knight was quoted in The Skagit Valley World in 1940. "Now the jinx has cost the life of a good railroad man. Trying to place the blame elsewhere is ridiculous. This is what happens when one man's greed and selfishness gets the better of him."

When Virgil Knight died at age ninety-two, his wife moved into a nursing home in Texas and his sons, Bart and Billy, sold what remained of the gyppo logging business. That same year, one million cubic yards of sediment slid into Deer Creek. Its steelhead fishery never recovered.

TWENTY-FOUR

NOON, SUNDAY, FEBRUARY 6, 1982

SOMETIMES SELLING REAL ESTATE GETS in the way of scouting basketball players and teams. Or looking for former stars. I nearly forgot about an in-home appointment with Eldon and Caroline Crane to list their old Victorian on five so-so acres of tulip fields just west of Burlington. Eldon got the property from his mother's estate but did not have the patience to deal with the annual April flowers—and the tourists that clogged his road to see them. His neighbor now farmed the land, and the Cranes got a small share of a shrinking annual profit.

I eased the bus into the dirt driveway, swept a cluster of dried orange peels from the top of my fake-leather briefcase, and looked up to find Caroline cleaning an upstairs window.

"The new trim color looks great," I said with little enthusiasm. "You guys should be pleased with all the work you've done. Some buyer is going to be lucky to get this place."

She smiled, placed a blue cloth over a plastic spray bottle and pointed toward the first floor. Eldon Crane, a former assistant principal at the junior high school, greeted me in the entry and led the way into the dining room. He'd taken an early buyout five years ago when the district announced it was consolidating two of its elementary schools, then turned a long-time summer job at the cannery into full-time employment. Teachers and administrators crammed the canneries for summer jobs when school let out in June, processing peas and lima beans to make ends meet. The school district superintendent told me he was pleasantly surprised with Eldon's decision because his physical solutions to handling discipline did not go over well with some parents. Especially after he made a student duckwalk for an hour after school for hocking a loogie that landed on a female classmate's new saddle shoe.

Eldon appeared tense and unkempt in food-stained, polyester pants. The house was colder and darker than I remembered. A near-empty square bottle of Johnnie Walker Red Label rested with one dirty glass on a drip-spotted buffet. Would the Cranes also put energy into brightening the interior before potential buyers previewed the home? As I considered where to sit, I wondered if the couple had any idea how much the housing market had declined. The past two months had been devastating to the neighborhood. Six new FOR SALE signs popped up while the Cranes mulled their decision. Four of the homes were single wage-earner households. Five of the six had kids in high school or elementary school. I knew the Cranes had to sell this house if they had any hope of buying a smaller one closer to town.

Eldon dodged any consistent eye contact and chatted awkwardly about the weather and the "wimpy" National Football League for demanding more protective helmets. I tried to avoid a noticeable assessment of Eldon's wrinkled, grubby shirt, kept my distance by choosing a spot at the far end of the table, and squared up the briefcase in front of me. The stink of his body easily made the crossing.

"All right." Eldon crossed his arms over an ample midsection. "I might as well say it now. You're going to hear it anyway. I was given notice at Twin City Foods last week. The company is eliminating three mid-level managers over in Stanwood, and I'm one of 'em. Sign of the times."

I frowned and tried to picture the faces behind the nearby FOR SALE signs. All cannery families. "I'm sorry, Eldon. I really am. It seems as though we are losing more jobs in the county every day." I interlaced my fingers on top of the briefcase like an attentive student. "Did they mention any possibility of bringing you back for the green bean season?"

Crane quickly skimmed the back of his hand under his nostrils and examined the findings. "Management said I could go into part-time sales," Crane replied, apparently more bitter at having to tell an acquaintance than at the position itself. "Can't imagine sellin' sweet peas to supermarkets a few hours a week. Can you?"

His hoarse voice made me thirsty.

"After twenty-six years with the same outfit, you'd think they could find some sort of full-time place for me. Gave those clowns some great summers."

I leaned back in the chair, felt it wobble, then quickly snapped to an upright position. Most people let go at the cannery were given no part-time option. They would have taken anything, especially if it meant keeping their kids in the same school until June. "Who knows?" I said. "A bumper crop of summer tomatoes could bring full-time jobs for a lot of people."

Crane just glared at the table until Caroline entered the room, methodically folding her beige apron. I opened the briefcase and distributed copies of the agreement; it suggested an asking price in the middle range of our office evaluations.

Eldon shifted in his chair as he read the first page, then pulled the paper clip from the top left corner of the six-page set. He took a deep breath, bent the clip into a zigzag line, and ran a palm over his balding head. I knew what was coming, but I'd underestimated the force with which it would arrive.

"There's no way in hell we are selling this place for one-forty-eight," he said, his voice rising with the numerals. "The house down the street got more than that three years ago. This is a bigger home on a better lot. 'Sides, there's the cash every year from the flowers."

He did not take his eye off the page. I waited, pulled out a pen, and pointed at the filled-out forms for emphasis. "A lot of people, in our office and elsewhere, helped me arrive at this price."

"You know, if that damned Garcia kid hadn't run out and left us high and dry, we would have been on the market before those other families," Eldon said. "Probably would have got the price we were lookin' for."

"What do you mean?" I said.

"Ronnie Garcia bid our paint job, some minor repairs. Started scraping and then never came back. Took us months to find somebody else who could do it at a decent price. Pathetic painters charge as much as doctors, and they don't take insurance."

I sat back and let his comments settle. "Ronnie played for me at the high school several years ago."

"Did he ever show up for practice? Because he sure as hell didn't show up much around here."

Caroline raised her hand, smiled politely, and focused on her husband. "Honey," that's all behind us now. We need to keep moving. We *have* to sell. We have no choice."

Eldon poked at the paper. "It's gotta be worth more than this. It just has to."

Caroline gripped the side of the table with both hands and leaned forward, her face now halfway across the waxed-maple surface. "Have you been blind to the number of homes now on the market? Good Lord, Eldon, there's a new sign three doors down!"

I dropped my forearms to the table, hoping a brief silence would heal the moment. I didn't care to witness this exchange, but it came with the job. I squirmed, waiting be called upon to justify the suggested asking price, but Caroline bailed me out.

"Eldon, you've overestimated the value of this home for years. I know it was your mother's place, but our memories don't mean squat to somebody else. You have a professional telling you what he thinks people will pay."

Eldon Crane shook his head, slumped in his chair even more, and gripped the contract with both hands. He sneered like a too-proud man assigned a menial job. His eyes darted from the paper to me, then back again. "How much real time did you put into this?" His voice lowered to a near-biting whisper. "I hear all you do is eat and sleep basketball, and look for kids who've drowned in the Sound. From what I hear, Linn Oliver is gone, and you better ..."

I was on my feet and in Crane's face in a heartbeat. It wasn't until I had two fistfuls of his smelly polyester shirt bunched under his chin that I realized he could possibly be right. Caroline broke the moment like an early morning alarm interrupting a too-real dream.

"Eldon! How dare you!"

I pushed Crane away. The motion propelled him back, whiplashing his neck above the top of his chair.

"You have no right to talk to him that way." She turned to me, chin down. "I'm sorry. And so embarrassed. Please forgive my husband."

I straightened up. Caroline Crane whipped a wood-armed chair closer to her husband. She plopped down, one knee bumping his thigh. He turned toward her like kid knowing a lecture was headed his way.

"Eldon, sign the thing," she snarled. "We need to move on with our lives. We are not in the position of hoping for more, and we might be lucky to even get an offer at this price."

ELDON CRANE SIGNED the listing at one-forty-nine-five. I drove back to the office, thinking maybe he saved a little face by not signing at one-forty-eight, despite his wife's scowl and sermon. A fifteen-hundred-dollar ego massage that Caroline would probably never forget. I thought the original price was too high, but it's human nature for sellers to think their home is always worth more. I had a feeling Eldon would end up paying for the price bump in more ways than one.

I rambled through the back door of the office. Cookie should enter my new listing into the multiple-listing computer database before the end of the day and maybe get a property sign ordered for the Crane's yard.

Edith looked up from her desk, her gray hair stacked in a mini-tower that looked like some sort of ancient gray vase. "Oh, Ernie," she muttered. "We really have to get you a new attaché piece for Father's Day. It would make you so much more impressive to our clients. And that shirt. The frayed collar will make people think you don't shave, and we all know that you do."

"Edith," I said, stopping directly in front of her. "I'm not a dad so a gift that day might be odd. I was just thinking I would junk this case for a nice brown shopping bag from the Red Apple Market. Probably easier for me to carry than this, and I wouldn't have to fool with any latches that sometimes don't like to open. And my shirt still fits, so I wear it."

"Well, I know my place." She snatched a copy of *House Beautiful* from beneath a silver letter opener and laid the magazine across her desk, chin higher than usual.

"Frankly, Edith," I said, striding toward Cookie's office. "I wish you did."

Elinor Cutter slammed the receiver to the phone as I entered. "Work my tail off to sell the guy's house, and he wants me to cut my commission because *his* price was too high?" she said, surveying the clutter on her desktop. "Already came down half a point." She looked up, knowing I was in the room but not caring in the least. "Now, what the hell do you want?"

"Got the Crane listing." I handed the documents to her.

"Geez, Coach." She slumped at the asking price on the front page. "Can we sell this sucker at that number? Half that side of town is down 'cause of the damn cannery layoffs."

"The idea was to start at a tick lower. Caroline was in our corner, but you know how it goes with Eldon. Just had to dicker; come back higher than what we suggested. Didn't surprise me at all, but it sure wasn't pretty sitting through it. Caroline got a little testy with the old boy."

"The guy's a piece of work. Doubt if he ever leaves that house anymore. I'll get this to the multiple this afternoon." Cookie flicked a curly set of bangs from her forehead with a quick neck twitch. "You got any live bodies who might be interested in this place? Speak now before other agents get a shot at it."

"Can't say as I do. My people who aren't looking for vacation property are mostly like the Cranes—trying to move out of bigger family homes into smaller ones. Thought about some of my customers' kids with families but they all seem to be set for the time being. I'll keep after it."

She glanced up, then randomly pawed about her desk. "Speaking of keepin' after it," she mumbled. "Harvey Johnston is after you. I've got the messages here someplace." She yanked a pink piece of paper that had been covered by a black three-ring binder. "Wants you to call him. ASAP.''

I took the paper, looked at the phone number, and stuffed it in my pocket. "Didn't you say 'messages?'"

"I did." Cookie continued her rummaging. "I actually spoke to another guy. He was calling from Mexico and sounded like he was talking into a tin can on the other end of a string. Absolutely lousy reception. Said he'd be here this week and was trying to get in touch with Linn. Terry somebody."

"Rausch. Terry Rausch."

"That's the name. Says he's flyin' into Sea-Tac in the next couple of days, I think. The doggone note was right here, someplace."

Her phone rang again. She dropped into her tacked burgundy leather chair, spun away so that I only viewed the top of her head, then proceeded to chew out an appraiser. It was her "humble opinion" that he was standing between one of her customers and a bank loan because his valuation of a spiffy three-bedroom rambler "was lower than the depths of hell."

TWENTY-FIVE

3 P.M., SUNDAY, FEBRUARY 6, 1982

HARVEY JOHNSTON'S HOME PHONE WAS busy on the third try so I decided to postpone the visit until the morning. Instead, I stopped by Ronnie Garcia's house to see if I could connect a few dots about basketball, Barbara, and the night Linn went missing.

I could tell by Harvey's questions yesterday at the lake that Linn's life and family were about to be put under a microscope. Harvey planned interviews with big-city doctors—including a sports-medicine expert—as well as former trainers at the UW, coaches and teachers. People worshiped former sports stars, especially hometown heroes, and I knew Harvey had to pull out all the stops. Perhaps my visit to the Garcia place would help.

Ronnie played hard for me for two years at Washington High, but only after I clearly explained the goals and roles for everyone on the team. I usually found the young man quiet, often sullen, but once a person connected with him indicated an interest, he was game for just about anything.

Ozzie and Harriet could have lived in the Garcias' brightly painted Craftsman. With a white picket fence and a clean walkway, it was clearly one of the nicer houses on a cul-de-sac just off the highway northeast of North Fork. A few bikes and trikes down the block hadn't made it out of the rain. Most driveways dead-ended into two-car garages with basketball hoops mounted on square backboards above. Always a positive sign to me.

Alberto Garcia answered the knock in clean Levi's, brown alligator cowboy boots, and a red plaid shirt. His smile came easily; his handshake was genuine. Alberto was a self-made man, revered in the community, and an innovative grower. He had built one of the first homes in the neighborhood, lived there for twenty-seven years, and raised five children.

"Good afternoon, Coach," Garcia said. "What a pleasant surprise. To what do I owe this honor?"

"Mr. Garcia," I said. "You are always much too kind--"

"Coach, please. It's Alberto." He stretched an open palm toward his den. "Please, please do come in."

I followed him in and took a seat on a comfortable brown sofa. The captivating aroma drifting from the kitchen—I guessed chili peppers and onions simmering in a pan—made my mouth water.

"I am sorry to bother you. This has been an interesting week, to say the least." There was no room for fancy intros; Alberto had always been a straight shooter, and I needed to reciprocate, especially now. "I assume you have heard about Linn Oliver's disappearance."

"Yes, I have. What an unfortunate situation. Has anything new been reported?"

"Not that I know of, but the police are talking to more people all the time. I've been circling back with a few former players, seeing if anybody may have heard from Linn. I was thinking he might have had an emergency, maybe a trip out of the area."

171 | Cold Crossover

"Perhaps Dr. Oliver has taken ill and Linn went to see him," Alberto said. "But surely somebody's contacted his father by now."

I recapped my visit with Robert Oliver.

"He's a dear man. He brought all of our children into the world. I remember how my Paola cried when she heard Dr. Oliver had retired. She said a woman's bond with her doctor is like no other. Perhaps similar to you with your players, no?"

I felt myself slouching, then jerked forward, Alberto's instincts were close, if not right on, and the realization hit close to home.

"Speaking of players," I said, "I understand Ronnie entered a team in the Montlake winter league. That's a long drive just to play hoops."

Alberto laughed softly and sat back in his chair, legs crossed. "That's exactly what I told him. But he said he had signed up to take an afternoon class at the UW, and the games were on the same days. I don't know how many games he's attended or how the team has done."

He suddenly looked down, shook his head as if he'd forgotten a major appointment, and pulled himself to his feet, the veins in his strong brown hands highlighted like dark blue rivers on a tiny map. "I am such a poor host. Can I get you something to eat or drink? Some coffee, perhaps?"

"No, thanks. I'm fine," I said. "I'll just be a moment. How did Linn look the last time you saw him? Anything different about him that you remember?"

"Well, let me see. It's been a while. I know I saw Linn in the parking lot behind the school gym during the little kids' holiday tournament. He was limping a little and didn't say much. Seemed kind of down. And I don't really remember if I've seen him since then."

"How about Ronnie? Do you know the last time he might have seen Linn?"

"I assume the boys have played basketball together several times lately." His eyes were wide, eyebrows arched. "They are, you know, on the same team."

I nodded. "I drove down to Montlake on Thursday night. Neither Ronnie nor Linn showed up for the game. Seems Ronnie didn't make it to Tuesday night's game either. That's the night Linn went missing."

"Really? I will try to locate my son and find out what he's been up to. He's working and renting a home down on the Skagit Flats with a couple of guys. I'm sure he will lead me to believe that all of his time is taken up by school or work. Tell me, did Linn play in that game Tuesday night?"

"Yes, he did, but he left early," I said. "One of the teammates said he took a few shots, saw the game was out of reach, and headed to the Bremerton ferry. That's the last anybody saw of him."

Alberto folded his arms across his chest. "Now you truly have me wondering about what Ronnie has been doing with his time."

I knew I had to get to the possible romance link, but I didn't want to sound like a cop in getting there. "Alberto, I know that Ronnie has been seeing Barbara Sylanski. Do you think there was any jealousy or anger involved with either of the young men regarding her?"

Alberto rolled a fist under his chin and stared right at me. "It's possible, but I never sensed anything negative from either one of the boys. Barbara and Linn seemed to be off and on so many times. I'm sure Ronnie would not have gotten into the middle of that if he had known Linn was still involved with her."

We sat silent for an awkward moment. Over the years, I felt Ronnie and Linn had some edgy competitive moments on the floor but nothing that was terribly concerning. There was Linn's career-altering injury in the forest, but that awful incident appeared to be behind them. After all, the two were teammates again.

"I will speak with Paola about Ronnie and Linn to see what she can remember," Alberto said. "To be honest, Barbara showed a special interest in Ronnie from time to time. Are you suggesting that some sort of resentment could be a part of all this, and that Ronnie was possibly involved?"

"I'm just wondering out loud. I've been around kids for years and know that girl-guy relationships can push different buttons in everyone. I am simply accumulating as much information as possible that might help point to Linn's whereabouts."

Alberto appeared semi-satisfied and eased forward in his chair. "We are scheduled to have dinner with Ronnie this week," Alberto said. "I don't know if he's bringing a crowd or not. I will try to have a private conversation with him about Barbara. I will also ask him when he last saw Linn and if there was anything peculiar he remembers."

"We would appreciate that, Alberto," I said. "You never know, but something that seems very insignificant could turn out to make a difference."

"With all due respect, Coach, I'm a bit confused why these questions are coming from you and not the proper authorities."

I stood opposite him, arms folded. "I thought because I had a history with some of the people involved, that I would save the detectives a few steps."

Alberto squirmed in his seat. "I don't know what Ronnie knows or where he was that night. But I'm not liking what I have heard today, and there are a couple of policemen in this town that have been known to jump the gun when darker-skinned kids are involved."

I nodded, stood, and extended my hand. He shook it firmly and looked me in the eye. "Coach, if you come back about this, make sure somebody official is with you."

As I drove home, I kept wondering why the cops had yet to question Ronnie Garcia at least once. And as I did, I realized that I was already jumping to too many conclusions about where he was the night Linn Oliver went missing.

TWENTY-SIX

5 P.M., SUNDAY, FEBRUARY 6, 1982

THE SOFTBALL DIAMOND THAT SERVED as the parking lot for the North Fork Grange Hall was crammed with minivans and pickups. Some drivers chose creative spots, unaware they'd blocked several vehicles. A young father in a Hawaiian shirt worked to corral his son and wrestle with the zipper on the youngster's jacket at the same time. His wife darted toward the entry, a glass-covered casserole dish wrapped in a yellow hand towel, while attempting to keep her ankle-length muumuu out of the mud. I turned off the VW's engine and looked down at my usual potluck contribution: store-bought oatmeal cookies from the Red Apple Market. Kids don't care when it comes to cookies.

The much-anticipated Winter Luau Cinder brought together the entire Lake Wilhelmina community and various residents of North Fork. The reason: to celebrate the biggest treasure ever found that was believed to be left behind by the early railroaders, loggers and gold-seekers who visited the region.

Last summer, while fishing for crawdads with nylon drop lines wrapped around thin alder sticks, Cindy Wagner, Poppy Kurri, and Jessica Schroers pulled in an old leather satchel first thought to be a young lady's shoulder bag. The girls dunked the bag back in the water several times to remove the muck before lifting it into their rubber raft. They rubbed away the remaining slime with their hands and discovered the name *Tyler* branded into the flap just above where it attached to the main pouch. Inside, they found several gold nuggets of various sizes. And a larger stone later determined to be a Burmese ruby.

The marshy outlet of Lake Wilhelmina and birthplace of Minnie Creek is well-known as a haven for young children in small boats. The kids use the shallow area to land their rafts, play hide-and-seek, and build forts on the bank with fallen branches and strips of cedar bark pushed like tiny log booms through the cloudy three-foot-deep water.

Even when dams reduced the stream to a mere summer trickle, parents considered it a safe zone because the outlet was away from the roaring powerboats and jet skis that often churned the middle of the lake into a chaotic chop. If the kids wore life jackets and were headed for the outlet, entire afternoons could lazily pass before they would emerge from the overgrown reeds and paddle home.

I learned these stories and more from my former players at our preseason team retreats. These private, revealing tales of adventures away from the basketball floor paid huge personal dividends worth more than my measly coaching stipend. Flashlight tag was played on slender ribbons of land that separated the narrow outlet from adjoining private property. Groups sat cross-legged, sneaked cigarettes, and shared scary stories. Boys stole kisses from giggling girls and asked them to go steady, often offering a St. Christopher medal on a silver chain as a sign of the sacred union. The summer romances that were fervently initiated while floating in rowboats often dissolved on the same stagnant water six weeks later. Once-precious trinkets were hurled back in anger or tenderly returned into sweaty palms.

I surfaced from memory lane just as Poppy Kurri, the youngest girl, pranced toward the stage. Pink ribbons gathered two shiny brown pigtails. She grinned and waved; no stage fright was in sight. She was joined by Skagit County Sheriff Griff McCreedy.

"I'm going to be brief because I know you all are ready to taste to that pig we've got roastin' out back," Sheriff Mac said. "As many of you know, our county attorneys informed me that such a treasure trove as the one these girls found belongs to the owner. Since the owner in this case presumably would be Tyler, as shown by the markings on the bag and other confidential information submitted to us, we attempted to find any and all of the possible descendants. We published a notice as required by law and conducted what we felt was a thorough and complete investigation for related persons.

"Since we did not discover any indisputable family members—and I will point out there were several attempts to prove legitimacy—the finder gets the rights to the property. Finders keepers."

The crowd mulled the statement and chatted quietly, like the scene in a courtroom following the testimony of an expert witness. The state of Washington owned the land on the south side of the outlet, while the Knight family held a sizable section that bordered the north.

Months ago, the attorney assured Bart Knight that they could make a case that the treasure was found on Knight land, and that the kids trespassed on his property to obtain it. And, since Knight was the property owner, he would have had a right to the treasure before the finder. The county, however, ruled against Knight on both counts. It maintained the treasure was actually found on state land and that the finder held priority.

"So, you get an idea of the complexity of the case," McCreedy said. "The county did not have an easy time arriving at a conclusion, which was the main reason we took months before we made any announcement. And now, let's eat!"

As the crowd turned toward the serving tables, I noticed an abrupt shoving match just inside the back door.

"The only thing complex about this case," yelled Bart Knight, strutting down the center aisle with his cantankerous attorney in tow, "is how our elected officials cheated a taxpaying citizen out of his rightful property! Those damn stones are mine, and I'm here to tell all of you people that this ain't over."

McCreedy sidestepped a young family with a crying child and met Knight in the middle of the hall. "Bart, you know the decision is final. Both you and your attorney were informed in writing and in person."

"Mr. Knight intends to seek damages from the state and personally from every person who voted on this decision," said the attorney, the only person in sight with a white button-down shirt.

"Look, Counselor, this isn't the place or the time," McCreedy said.

"I'll choose my own place and time, mister," Knight said. "Figured everybody would be here so I could put them all on notice that I'm not done. And God help anybody I find on my lake property."

The pair turned and stormed out the back door just as Stan O'Leary ducked in, his apron slathered with a rust-colored sauce. Stan collided with Knight's attorney, who elbowed him away, but not before leaving an imprint on his white shirt that resembled Whidbey Island. Stan wiped his sweaty brow on an open palm and looked around the room.

"Geez, Coach, what's wrong with those guys?" O'Leary said. "Anyway, we should have enough pork to feed 'em all, but it'll be close. Mind grabbing those metal buffet pans and takin' em to the fire pit? Wide Load will fill 'em up and get them into the kitchen."

I stacked the stainless-steel trays under my arm and headed out the door to a covered area behind the building, to where Mitch Moore had already begun carving a whole pig he'd removed from a steel spit. The smells were usually reserved for summer. From five feet away, I could feel heat from the massive grill fashioned from a fifty-gallon metal drum.

"Hey, Coach," Mitch said with a surprising amount of energy. "What's shakin?"

I took a deep breath, avoided eye contact, and swung an arm toward the heavily laden tables. "Time to feed the masses."

He turned toward the fire pit and adjusted his sweat-stained skull cap crafted from a yellow and red bandana. A ragged Washington High School sweatshirt flopped over the beltline of his baggy jeans.

"Haven't seen Cheese here," Mitch said and tipped me a curious wink. "I'm sure he's probably tied up. With work or something else."

"Yeah, I hoped he'd show," I said. "Seems like the whole lake was inside that hall, though."

He held his knife and fork down at his sides for a moment, dipped to brush the perspiration from his nose with his shoulder and stared off in the distance.

"Did you see that sorry-ass Crab team the last couple of weeks of the season? Looked like some of those boys just gave up. Mailed it in."

I placed the trays at the end of the table and began to unstack them. "No, I didn't. Heard they had a tough time putting the ball in the hole. Didn't two of the kids get hurt?"

Moore returned to his cutting chores and plopped chunks of juicy pork into the pan closest to him. "Yeah, but that's no excuse for how they finished. I think some kids were afraid to step up."

O'Leary turned the corner of the building with a bottle of Bud in each hand. "Stop talking and keep cuttin', Mitch. Kids are already getting plates, and the parents will be right behind 'em."

"Well, maybe you could get the Coach to call a timeout," Mitch said. "Lord knows he's got at least one left over from the state title game."

I shot Moore a what's-up-with-that stare and took a step toward him before O'Leary moved in between us. He faced me, his free hand on his hip.

"You know, Ernie. I was hopin' Cheese would make it to this thing, too. I was thinking about his dad just the other day. I had the post-hole digger out, punching some holes for a new split-rail fence behind our lake place near the road. Doggone if I didn't dig up a cigar box some old logger or railroad man probably had left behind. Had a silver pocket watch, rosary beads, and one of those things docs wear around their necks? You know. A stethoscope? Anywho, made me think of Dr. Oliver and the care he gave my dad and granddad."

I smiled at the mention then peered into the cooling embers of the big black drum "I heard your grandfather was one of the reasons this town succeeded. He helped a lot of folks get started." I started for the chow line inside. Three steps later, I caught myself and pivoted back toward the fire. "By the way, did either of you guys see Ronnie Garcia today?"

O'Leary placed a hand under his chin. "Don't believe I did, but I wasn't looking for him, either. Mitch?"

"Naw," Moore mumbled without looking up.

BARBARA SYLANSKI GATHERED the remaining utensils scattered on the picnic tables that stretched across the length of the Grange Hall, then began peeling the white butcher paper from each table top.

"Coach, did you see those little kids dive into those desserts?" Barbara said. "It looks as if they spilled more than they ate."

I helped her roll up the ice-cream-sopped paper. We both moved quietly past Sheriff McCreedy, who was talking to a reporter from the *Bellingham News*. After trashing the paper, I returned to the main hall with a push broom, collecting a pile of sauce-soaked napkins, plastic straws, foam cups, and garlic-bread crust.

When the man with the shiny star was finished with the reporter, he turned to find Barbara standing behind me with a dustpan, appearing more apprehensive than the setting dictated. Barbara glanced quickly around the room, looked blankly at the floor, then tried her best to maintain some semblance of eye contact with the sheriff.

"I dropped by my mom's house this morning after church," Barbara said as we both moved closer to listen. "Thought maybe I'd surprise her with some flowers and her favorite Danish. She's been a real help, especially this past week. I mean, everybody looking for Linn—and me. Well, I went out to the garage to get the pruning shears, and, it was gone. My dad's '57 Chevy. It's gone. I called the North Fork police and gave a statement."

"What? I'm so sorry," I said. "When do you think the break-in occurred?"

"It was really more like a walk-in. We always keep the side door to the garage unlocked. It's so hard to say because we never go back there. My mom parks her car under the carport in the driveway. A couple of weeks ago, she took four days to visit my aunt in Olympia but returned for the school week. I can't imagine anybody thinking they could drive that car in North Fork in broad daylight."

"Right," McCreedy said. "Quite a few local residents would know that car. Maybe it was one of those nights when your mother was gone. Is anything else missing? Cookie-jar cash? Maybe jewelry or your mom's good silverware?"

"Whoever it was didn't even go in the house. Besides, Mom's entry doors are fairly thick and the locks have deadbolts. At first, I thought only the car was missing, but when I went to the back of the garage, I noticed our little safe was wide open. All of our other papers were still there— passports, baptismal certificates, deed to the house. The only thing not there was the title to dad's car and an old diary we found several years ago."

"I'll go over to police headquarters and read the full report," the sheriff said. "I'll get Harvey to get a detective on it right away."

McCreedy pulled a notebook from the top pocket of his brown county shirt and began scribbling some notes. "You figure the car was hotwired?"

"Oh, no," Barbara said. "Dad always kept the key under the floor mat. It has been there for ages. Everybody in town knew it. We never really locked the safe, either. Just closed the metal handle."

McCreedy frowned. "OK, what else comes to mind?"

Barbara looked down, then lightly touched a finger to her lips. "It's that old diary that's puzzling. I can't think of anyone besides Linn who would even care about it."

TWENTY-SEVEN

8:30 P.M., SUNDAY, FEBRUARY 6, 1982

THE LINES AT THE GAS 'N GO'S THREE pumps were longer than usual, mainly because some of the folks driving home from the Grange event realized that the minimart now had the cheapest fuel in town, four pennies less a gallon than stations near the I-5 on-ramps. The familiar dark blue GMC Jimmy in front of me glistened in the moonlight so I leaned on the horn to see if I could get a rise out of its driver. I did. He bounced in his seat, nearly conking his floral scrub cap on the headliner.

"Why did I know it was you?" said Dr. Timoteo Mesa as he sauntered toward my bus, still in his blue hospital-issues after another weekend shift in the emergency room.

"Maybe I'm the only person in North Fork who recognizes genuine celebrities."

He laughed and eased a bare forearm on my door just below the rolled-down window. "You know, your bus's beep is pretty wimpy. Guy like you could use a more macho horn. And I like the new ding on the back panel. Really stands out."

What ding? I leapt from the bus to look. Great. Must've been the cozy Grange parking lot.

Timoteo laughed at my discovery as I surveyed the damage. He's been at my side often. The man attended more games and examined more Washington High athletes than any other physician in the county. You could fill a football stadium with just the kids that "Tim Table" had stitched and taped. I've seen him wrap a cast in the back of a school bus at two a.m., traipse to the far end of a hilly cross-county course in the snow to piggyback home a runner with a fractured ankle, and make countless ambulance rides from high school venues seem not so daunting for the fallen and frightened. He related with the kids because he'd been there, done that. His bedside—and benchside—manner put youngsters at ease.

We discussed the Grange dinner and Bart Knight's theatrics.

"I guess he felt like we had to hear again how he was cheated out of his 'due reward'," I said.

Timoteo chuckled and glanced around the lot. "Some people are not very accepting. Bart came into the ER one night, blood streaming down his neck from a gash at the back of his head. It appeared somebody had conked him with a bottle, but he told the in-take nurse it was a work accident in his shop. When I came in the room, he got up and left. He told the nurse on the way out that the clinic needed to hire doctors with lighter skin."

The car in front of Timoteo's pulled away from the pump. He flashed a wait-a-minute finger, jogged five steps to his rig and nuzzled it close to the nozzle. As I edged the bus close behind his bumper, I thought about how far he had come and how much he had given.

The son of a Mexican migrant who journeyed north to work the potato fields of Southwest Washington, Timoteo starred in soccer and track at Ridgefield High School and led the Spudders to a state soccer title before earning an academic scholarship to the University of Portland. After medical school, he filled a vacation relief position in the Skagit County Clinic's emergency room and never left.

He also filled an unofficial position as my trainer, his black bag always behind our bench jammed with Ace bandages, rubbing alcohol, tape, tetanus shots, and suture thread. Just as important, he had an uncanny way of soothing the refs during games, especially after my first technical foul. For more than fifteen years, Timoteo Mesa kept me on the floor with his diplomacy; he kept my players on the floor with his professional skills.

The heavy metal nozzle clicked and released, signaling the tank had reached its max. Timoteo squeezed in a few more ounces until it flinched again and replaced the hose on the pump. "Adios, mi amigo." He waved. "Vaya con dios."

I stuck my head and left shoulder out of the driver's window and anchored myself with one hand on the steering wheel. "Timoteo, you in a hurry?"

"No, not really, Coach. What've you got?"

I popped out of the bus. And told him about the crazy sensations in my hands and feet. "No real pain but some numbing that seems to come and go," I explained. "Maybe I'm just getting old and paying the price for years of running on bad basketball floors."

Some guys would have told me to take two aspirin and call their nurse in the morning. Not Timoteo. Which is probably why he lived in a modest brick rambler on the Skagit Flats near Conway and not in a fashionable Seattle high-rise overlooking Elliott Bay.

"How long's this been going on?"

"Hard to say for sure. Certainly felt it when I was having dinner at Tony's Place on Wednesday night."

He folded his forearms over his chest. Even when relaxed, his muscles and arteries beamed from his smooth brown skin. "Do you remember falling down playing basketball with the Saturday morning gang? I think I've missed three straight weeks, so I wouldn't know. Any acute incident that you can recall?"

"There's nothing I can really pinpoint, but ..."

Timoteo insisted I meet him behind the store after we pumped our gas. He had the rear passenger door open with a faded beach towel covering the flat back behind the second seat. He dug deep into his black bag, pulled out three silver instruments then shoved the satchel against the right wheel well.

"Take your shoes and socks off and sit down here a second," he ordered.

Timoteo tapped my knees and the crooks of my elbows with a tiny stainless-steel hammer with a head that looked like a rubber orange tomahawk. He then poked around the bottoms of my feet with a dull safety pin, gauging the degree of feeling in several different spots. I jumped at a few random jabs, barely noticed a few others. He repeated the process on the back of my hands, palms, and forearms, and did it all again with a metal pinwheel that could have passed for a miniature pizza cutter.

"Well, your reflexes are good, but you clearly have more sensation in some areas than in others." He turned his right palm toward the sky. "For example, the pinkie and ring finger on both your hands are not as responsive as the area around your thumb and index finger."

"So, do you think that's what the ladies at the office mean when they say I'm insensitive?"

He chuckled.

"So, what does all this mean?" I said. "Are we talking some sort of nerve damage?"

"Possibly, but I'm not an expert in any of this. Rather than me guessing about the prospects, go see a specialist who deals in this kind of stuff every day. Let them run a few tests. They may want to get an MRI to better understand what's going on."

"Do I need to attend to this right away?"

"I don't think you're in any immediate danger, Coach. But I've always thought it was better to find out sooner rather than later. That way, at least you'll know. Then you can choose to deal with it as you please." He thought a moment. "There's a new neurologist office in the medical square next to the Skagit Valley Clinic. Name's Crehan. Elmer Crehan. He's had a practice in Seattle for years but is working up here two days a week now. Bought a home in Warm Beach a couple of years ago. Plans on living there most of the year. Go see him; see what he says."

TWENTY-EIGHT

JESSIE MCQUADE HAD THE BUCKS TO shop until she dropped, and she always dressed to the nines, even in Harvey Johnston's dismal county office. The classy, cute strawberry blonde took her ex-husband to the cleaners when he ran off with a younger woman, and the downtown Seattle Macy's and Nordstrom loved him for doing so. With a master's degree in communications, she kept her boss on his toes.

"Ernie Creekmore! Well, just make my day!" Jessie smiled. "Have a seat, Coach. He'll be right with you."

Her spotless white blouse was conservatively buttoned; her perfect lightweight flannel pants probably came direct from Saint John Knits. Cathy had one pair. Only one, in black.

"Some guy's on the phone from Baltimore wanting Harvey to fly back there pronto to look at blood spatter and footprints. Can you imagine? Cross-country flight to look at blood and dirt?"

"What can I say?" I said. "The man's got a famous rep."

"And everybody knows that you are famous for teaching youngsters to play basketball. I know you're probably somehow still involved ..."

"Only from the stands. Don't know if I'll get back on the bench with the kids."

She smiled, sat up straight at her desk and cocked her head slightly, like an elementary school teacher posing her first question to a new class.

"Ernie, there's an interesting independent film being shown at the Lincoln Theater tonight. The director is an older French fellow that I have followed for years and truly enjoy. Would you have any interest in seeing it with me? I believe it screens at seven."

For some reason, the invitation really hit home. "Let's see. French films. Lots of colorful flowers and clueless, skinny guys wearing black?"

"Very funny, but I'm certain there's more to it than that. In fact, there's a small group staying around afterward to discuss the film with a professor from Skagit Valley College. I wouldn't ask if I didn't think you were good around people."

I shrugged and widened my stance. Maybe she just pitched the tiny confidence-builder I needed. But did I remember how to do this stuff? With single women?

"You know, Jessie, I'd like that. I'll swing by and pick you up a little after six-thirty."

She stood, grinning. "Well, that's, that's just wonderful!"

Harvey Johnston had one hand on his forehead when he opened the door to his inner sanctum. "Coach, come on in," Harvey said. "Need to bounce some more stuff off your real estate-oriented brain. Mine doesn't seem to work in that category."

"Not working? That's a first," I said. "But I have to warn you. Sometimes what I got upstairs doesn't want to work at all."

Harvey flashed Jessie, who was trying to get his attention, a what's-the-matter glance. "And?"

"I'm getting more and more inquiries from radio, TV, and newspapers wanting your time," Jessie said. "Some of those older men can be rather forward. Asking me for a date 'n stuff. How would you like me to handle them?"

"Anybody who asked you for 'n stuff should be handled like the jerk they are," Harvey roared. Once he settled down, he continued. "Now, are there any *real* reporters out there doing real research, or are there just a bunch of radio and TV guys looking for a five-second sound bite?"

"They don't seem to care just about the Rice case, sir," Jessie continued. "They all want you to go on the record and say that what happened to Linn Oliver and Mark Rice are related."

"Yeah, well, dream on, because *I* don't even know! These people sure want all homicides tied up in a neat little package. But you know what? There is no evidence to link these two situations unless one of your new media buddies knows a hell of a lot more than this office does."

Harvey walked toward the window and glanced down to the street. He interlaced his fingers behind his head, spread his feet and stretched side-to-side, pendulum-like.

"Well, Greg Smithson called earlier today," Jessie said. "He's on his way up here now from Seattle and would like a minute. I'll just tell him to ..."

Harvey turned back and managed a faint smile. "Smitty? From *The Trib*? Send him in when he gets here." He folded his arms and squinted at me. "What do you know about buying a listing?"

Squirming and stretching, I had forgotten how uncomfortable the county's visitors' chairs could be. "Means an agent priced a home higher than anybody else, hoping to impress the owner and get the listing. Some sellers are impressed by big numbers, pumps their ego. Usually bad for everybody else, though."

"How so?"

"If the asking price is too high, the home will just sit on the market. The Sherrard place is a good example. His number's in the clouds, so there's no action. Cookie had a shot at it but didn't want to bust her butt marketing a property that's unreasonably priced."

"So, Mark Rice bought the listing?"

"Maybe, but Pee Wee's not that kind of an agent. Frankly, there's a lot of other agents who would have done the same thing."

"No money changed hands?"

"No," I said. "'Buying a listing' is just an expression. Why are you so interested?"

Harvey rolled up his sleeves and leaned back in his chair. "I'm wondering if Rice turned somebody's crank in getting that listing. Maybe stepped on somebody who thought they were in line. Sizable commission's at stake, right?"

"Yeah, a nice payday. When it sells. And that can be a long, hard when. You talk to Sherrard?"

"Yeah. What a hard guy to like. Has more people screening his calls than a politician. All he did was whine about how long his house was going to be off the market because of the investigation. Said I was keeping him from earning a living. There might have even been a threat in there somewhere."

"Think he's a suspect?"

"Sure. Just about everybody is right now! Except he's higher on the list, given his jerk factor." Harvey paused. "So, you were saying if the home doesn't sell, the owner gets another agent who tries another price?"

I understood where this was going, but the gamble was just too great for the reward.

"But would you really pop somebody, Harvey, just for losing a listing? Agents lose listings all the time. What's done is done. You move on. Just like you do after losing an important game."

Harvey looked at me as if I had just landed from Mars. "All people don't work that way, pal.. Some get angry and stay angry. Many crimes don't have any logic involved whatsoever, but ..."

The intercom buzzed, jolting Harvey's focus. Simultaneously, a tiny white light above a series of rectangular phone buttons began to blink. He punched one near the middle then leaned down near the speaker. "What? And, please make it quick."

"Mr. Smithson is here to see you, sir," Jessie announced. "Would you like to have him wait until ..."

Harvey's face relaxed, as if someone had just picked up his tab for a cold beer and a French dip. "Well, please show him in, Jessie."

The sportswriter arrived in his ubiquitous blue cotton sweater and casual corduroys, a reporters' notebook stuffed into a hip pocket. Harvey greeted him politely, as did I, and waved him to a seat. Smithson flicked open the narrow spiral binder, then thumbed to an empty page and gripped the top of a black felt pen temporarily between his teeth while he scribbled a few unintelligible lines. Once he was set, he pushed his thinning hair off of his formidable forehead and sat in the chair opposite the county official. From the way he moved, his chair appeared about as cozy as mine.

"I know you've got a full plate these days," Smithson began. "I've talked with the state patrol on several occasions trying to get as much information as I can regarding Linn Oliver. He certainly was a special kid, and people sure remember his name. By the way people talk, it's as if half the state saw that title game."

Tell me about it. It was incredible how many people said they were sitting at halfcourt when the final shot went up.

Smithson continued, "I seem to have hit an impasse. Has the state patrol passed along any additional information you might be able to give me?"

Harvey slumped back in his chair. "Thank goodness the first question out of your mouth was not about connecting the two cases. You probably are aware that we are restricted from commenting on the specifics of an ongoing investigation, but WSP hasn't given us squat. Don't quote me on that. In fact, put your pen down for a moment and let's go off the record."

Smithson stopped writing, capped the pen, and placed it on Johnston's desk, indicators he'd accepted Harvey's request. I wasn't the only guy in the room who was old-school.

"Oliver's yellow station wagon was pretty much no help at all," Harvey said. "Lots of filthy socks and tees in that vehicle. A couple of pairs of sneakers, different sizes. Lots of fast-food wrappers. We had our best guys comb that vehicle from stem to stern and couldn't come up with any substantial signals that showed whoever was driving was rarin' to jump off that ferry boat. Quite frankly, it looks like somebody bought himself a Northlake Pizza and went to play some buckets."

Smithson had gleaned similar accounts from other authorities, including his contacts at the state patrol.

"So his game jersey wasn't in the car?"

"Game jersey?" I laughed. "At Silverdale Community College? Those boys have been known to go shirts and skins."

"Seriously," Harvey said. "He could have put his shoes, shorts, and maybe an extra shirt in a gym bag or backpack and got out of that car after the Bremerton ferry got under way. Then maybe he caught a ride with another player on the boat and forgot his car. Who knows? Nobody remembers seeing him in the main cabin, that's for sure."

Harvey told Smithson that cops from other counties on Puget Sound and on the nearby islands—Vashon, Whidbey, Bainbridge, Blake, Maury—had not reported any bodies or gym bags washing ashore. Not all the coastlines are accessible, however, and many property owners are seasonal occupants, leaving unchecked private beaches as possible landing points.

"Coach Creekmore and I will be talking with as many of Linn's old friends and teammates that we can find. I know Ernie had been concerned about the player's well-being, but again, please keep this stuff out of the paper."

"Will do," Smithson said. "But I've got to write something. Even the wire services are screaming for some sort of update. It's difficult to make them happy by rehashing the same old stuff. I just hope something breaks in the case soon."

"You and me both," Harvey murmured,

Smithson reached for his notebook and eyed his pen.

"Coach, I don't get your involvement in all of this. I mean, I understand the visit to my office but you're here, too? I'm wondering if my next story is about Linn's former coach becoming an official part of the investigation."

"Let's be clear on this," Harvey cut in. "Nothing Ernie is doing, has done, or will do, is official. He asked some preliminary questions because he has a long history with Linn. And, quite frankly, with you. He also knows about houses and what drives people to buy and sell them."

"Seems to me he's asked a lot of preliminary questions of some other players, too."

Harvey glared at me. "Such as?'

"Well, Robert Morrell down at the Coast Guard said Coach was 'on him' right away about why there was no helicopter to search the Sound near the ferry crossing that night. Seems Coach thought Linn had been missing long enough ..."

"Ernie!" Harvey yelled and stomped a foot to the floor. "Didn't we talk about this? What the hell did you do? Walk into the U.S. Coast Guard station and represent you were the Skagit County Crime Division?"

I pulled a closed fist to the side of my chair and took a deep breath. "I called Robert to say hello. He's a young man I truly enjoyed coaching." Harvey smirked and glared at me. "Hey, we talked about some of the old Crabs, some regional teams, that he was one of the better on-ball defenders ever to play for the school. And *then* I asked him what it takes to get a bird in the air."

Harvey shook his head and momentarily rested it on the top of his desk like a kindergartner ready to play 7-Up. He returned his back to the chair, sighed and offered a what's-next smile.

"Well, tell us, Ernie. What did Mr. Morrell have to say?"

I cleared my throat and noticed Smithson was taking notes. "Is this on the record?" I asked.

"Greg, if you would," Harvey said. "Just background for now. Lord knows how much I want to see Coach's quotes on this in the paper. He's such an expert on the subject."

Smithson nodded and put down his pen.

"Search boats went out later that night but getting a copter was a problem," I said. "Seems the one they wanted was stuck at the Naval Air Station up on Whidbey Island and it took forever to find a backup. By the time that was arranged, some kid crashed his car in Kingston and had to be airlifted to Harborview Medical Center. So, no air search took place that night, but a copter did go up Wednesday morning and afternoon. No trace of anything unusual. I know the Coast Guard boats still were active yesterday but they've begun to feel they have done all they can do. That's about what I know."

Harvey stared straight ahead, appearing confounded by the amount of information I'd obtained. He broke the gaze and squinted my way. "Yes, that is the approximate intel this office has received."

Smithson glanced down at his notebook during an awkward silence and then rose to leave. Harvey walked Smithson away from the desk and promised to stay in touch.

"Mr. Johnston, just to let you know, the paper plans a full-blown series on the case starting later this week," Smithson said. "The managing editor put me in the middle of it even though it is not technically a sports project. Actually, I'm surprised the paper waited this long because of the speculation. Interviews with the parents, siblings, former teammates, opponents plus a history of his injuries, docs, the whole nine yards. He's also not a juvenile and ..."

"I know, I know," Harvey said, steering Smithson toward the door. "I promise I'll be back to you soon."

"And, Coach Creekmore, I'd like to get some more time with you for that series," Smithson said. "Shouldn't take long. I've got that stuff from Friday night at the paper and a ton in the files."

"Sure. Give me a minute to finish up with Harvey, and I'll meet you in the hallway."

Harvey patted Smithson on the shoulder as the reporter left the office. I was curious about what Harvey didn't say, but I wasn't ready to ask. He did not mention how long he would wait before actively backing off the Linn Oliver case. And, given the circumstances surrounding the Mark Rice murder, I wondered if he already thought Linn was dead. I also wanted to know how much time Harvey had spent considering the possibility that a serial killer was at work in his county.

He also had not said a word about a bloody towel that the state patrol found in the front seat of Linn Oliver's car.

"Ernie, you know how young people operate. Probably better than anybody I know." Harvey pushed away from his desk, stuck his hands in his hip pockets, and peered out through the uneven Venetian blinds to the street below.

"If Linn Oliver ran back to Mexico—for whatever reason—would Barbara Sylanski tell us?"

"I would think so. But those two are so tight."

"Ah, yes. And I thought the lover's concerto was a thing of the past."

I looked away. "Now that I think of it, "Lover's Concerto" was a song recorded by The Toys. Pretty much one-hit wonders." Then, eyeing Harvey, I said, "I'm sorry, I didn't get the feeling that you thought you were being played here."

"Damn it, Ernie!" He turned toward me. "We gotta guy dead in a lakeside home, another missin' who lived pissin' distance away, and we don't have jack on either one! Somebody's playin' somethin' and it don't sound pretty!"

TWENTY-NINE

ANGELICA KURRI CRUNCHED HER County Squire wagon over the acres of gravel road leading to the MacTavish & Oliver Lumber Company's main headquarters just south of Conway on the Skagit Flats. The region's colorful tulips were long gone, replaced by the irrepressible aroma of garlic and onions.

"Is Charley available?" she asked one of the Oliver offspring at the desk. "I know I've asked your name a thousand times, hon, but that's what old ladies do."

"It's Jodi, ma'am. Actually Joanne Elizabeth. Got my grandmother's name there in the middle. And I know my uncle would welcome the chance to visit with you."

Charles T. Oliver, chief executive officer of the timber operation and head of acquisitions, ambled his six-foot-two frame into the reception area in a short-sleeved, button-down shirt and tan trousers.

"Lord, you're looking more like your father every day," Angelica said.

"Thank you, Mrs. Kurri," Oliver said. "If I didn't have a customer from out of town this morning, I would have snuck in here in shorts today. Supposed to be eighty-five this afternoon."

"It's Angie, Charley, and I won't take much of your time. Is there a place we can talk?"

Oliver led her to his modest second-floor office overlooking the log dump where trains both loaded and delivered massive evergreens from all over western Washington. He seated her on a small sofa opposite the mahogany table trucked down from the original headquarters on North Fork's riverfront. Oliver scooted one of the chairs from the table opposite her and sat.

"I've been thinking about this for some time, but I would like to divide my property at Lake Wilhelmina," Angelica said. "It's really the only source of retirement funds that I have. I'd also like to put something away for my daughter. You know all about short plats and such, so I want to hire you to do this for me."

Oliver raised his eyebrows and swayed in his seat. "That property is going to be extremely valuable someday. I mean, there isn't even a paved road into the lake. Once more people can get access to it, your holdings are going to be worth far more than they are today."

Angelica frowned and wrung her hands. "I had a delightful day on Sunday, riding a horse to the sandspit from the old house at Finn Settlement," she said. "When I got there, I couldn't believe my eyes. A middle-aged woman had hired a couple of men to dig for lost items, and they had left holes everywhere. Now, I've seen a couple of holes before and thought it was just campers leaving a fire pit, but this was different."

"Maybe they thought they were on state land," Charley said. "Every time a landowner up there finds a porcelain dish in their backyard, it shows up in the newspaper. People start digging all around the old railroad camps. Couple of my boys were up on the south shore for the Fourth just down the way from old Camp Eight. They didn't say anything about digging or holes."

"What young men do? Anyway, I pointed to the madrona trees and both ends of my property, showed them where I thought the state land ended and my property began. Even showed her the property stakes by the outlet where the Knight family purchased last year. Didn't make any difference. This woman, Mavis somebody, was hell-bent on digging where she darn well pleased. She was even on the beach, not fifty feet from the lake. Even had the gall to ask me what I was going to do about it."

Charley looked away as a logging truck pulled into the yard. "I'm sure once people in the area hear your land's available, you won't have any trouble selling any of it. But won't you reconsider? Part of what you have there is the largest—and nicest—waterfront parcels on the entire lake. Plus, it's so close to the Old Finn Trail."

"I'm grateful, Charley," she said. "I truly am. But I go up there so rarely, can't really watch over it and prefer to have other people enjoy it. I'll keep something, but not much."

THIRTY

THE HOUR WITH SMITHSON PASSED quickly, and I headed home. As soon as I turned the corner at First and Van Ness, I could see the black-and-white unit in my driveway. There was no sign of Robert Oliver's rental car. The proud, portly figure walking away from my front door was none other than Arnold Dawson. I could tell by the way he tried to locate and adjust his underwear. So much for my quiet lunch.

"Now, Coach, you can't ever say that I've never done anything for you," Dawson said. "You left your house unlocked. But don't worry, I checked it out. Seems fine. I needed to pee anyway."

I winced and came around the side of the bus. I slid open the cargo door and picked up listing sheets that had blown off the stack on the shotgun seat. I noticed a person sitting in the back seat of Dawson's patrol car, but the tinted glass made it difficult to see inside.

"Left it unlocked for my house guest."

He smirked. "Yeah, there's a buzz all over our building about you and Jessie McQuade. Man, what I'd give to get that woman in my boat for a Sunday spin. Betcha she could really beat up a bait box."

Shaking my head, I approached the car. "She's not the guest."

Dawson strutted closer. "Geez, not even a thank-you? It's a good thing this guy sitting in my car didn't know about your unlocked doors or he probably would have been sitting in your living room, maybe lifting a few of your valuables."

"Valuables? What valuables?" I scoffed. "High school coaches and teachers don't have valuables, Arnold. Unless you're talking about family photos and the two-dollar bill my grandmother gave me when I was five."

Curious to know the identity of my intruder, I hurriedly gathered and straightened the pile of papers, stashed them in my bag, and sauntered toward the police car. The face was familiar but the straggly red beard threw me for a moment until I could place it on a warm day several years ago at Lake Wilhelmina. Terry Rausch appeared dazed. The red blotch under his eye had the makings of a full-blown shiner.

"Jesus, Arnold, let him go," I said. "Open this door and let him out before he tells his buddies he was unlawfully detained for looking up an old friend."

Dawson shepherded Terry from the cruiser and pointed him toward the front door. "Well, I guess I'll be on my way then, Coach," he said. "Just to let you know, very little gets by me here in 'ol North Fork. Especially on this block."

"I'll be sure to remind my neighbors we're in good hands."

While Dawson dipped into his cruiser to answer a radio call, Terry explained that the shot to the face was a deliberate elbow, delivered when he first refused to sit in the patrol car.

"You know how you see officers guide a suspect's head so they don't hit the top of the car when entering the seat?" Terry said. "Well, this was just the opposite. I stood near the door, questioned why I had to sit in the car. Before I knew it, he turned and elbowed me in. It was as if the guy needed somebody to hit."

"More than anger issues," I said.

"Tell me about it. The guy also spent a helluva lot of time in your living room looking at stuff. My sense is that he did a lot more than just go to the can. If he went at all."

Dawson emerged from his vehicle, shimmied his thick black belt up higher on his soft midsection and eyed me warily. "Coach, I didn't check your garage yet. Why don't we take a minute and do that now?"

I stared at him, dumbfounded. "Check it for what? Everybody in town knows it's never locked."

Dawson strutted down the driveway. "Then come on and humor me, just for a moment." As he opened the side door to the garage, Terry and I headed that way and continued our conversation about his long journey back to North Fork. Dawson's voice rang out as we approached the entry.

"Well, looky here," Dawson said. The motor to the large automatic door began to hum, coming to a halt with the door fully extended. "Seems the 'ol Coach has been doin' a lot more up at the lake than showin' homes for sale."

I could not believe my eyes. A Yamaha motor sat on a portable carrier next to the refrigerator with several water skis, ropes, lifejackets and new gas cans strategically placed around the motor. The area looked like it had been staged by an REI professional.

"What the hell?" I murmured.

"And look at this," Dawson said, pointing to a custom-carved table I had never seen. On top of the table was a gorgeous dark walnut case. Next to the table sat a five-drawer Craftsman toolset in a black steel cabinet. Dawson swung open the clasp on the walnut case, then glared at me.

"There's an elderly couple at the lake looking for their precious silver," Dawson sneered. "Shit's even engraved. You got a lot of questions to answer. But first, I'm going to inventory all this shit then call my boss and ask him what he wants to do about it. You remember Harvey Johnston, don't ya, Coach?"

FIVE MINUTES AFTER Dawson left, Robert Oliver arrived with beer and lemonade. When he saw Terry, he prepared an ice pack to his eye. Both men recalled memorable times together and seemed to genuinely enjoy the reunion.

Terry said he had not worn long pants in three months, and his tanned legs left little doubt the claim was true. A former high school athlete from Wisconsin, Terry met Linn Oliver in a dormitory on the UW campus and the two quickly hit it off. Terry became a frequent visitor to the Oliver family home in North Fork.

"Some young men go to Paris; I went to Mexico," said Terry, lounging on the sofa in my living room. "I knew water was important to me as a kid, but I didn't really understand the *warm* part until I got to Loreto."

"Linn told me you had it figured out before most young guys," Robert said. "I'm sure there's a lot to like down here, but I don't know if I could take the heat during the summer."

"It's not just about the weather and the warm salt water," Terry replied. "In fact, I'll head back up to the lakes in Wisconsin during the summer. Mexico's about the total package, how you want to spend your days. The people are honest, hardworking, and they respect each other."

"And what about the *mañana* attitude? I don't think I could ..."

"*Mañana* does not necessarily mean 'tomorrow.' It simply means 'not today.'"

But there was a topic that couldn't wait until tomorrow, and Robert got there first. "I don't know how much ground you guys have covered," he said. "But Terry, I need to know. When's the last time you saw Linn?"

Terry rubbed his chin and glanced toward the ceiling. "Well, he only came down once and that was last year. So, it's been several months. I'm trying to think of the day he started driving back."

"But no contact in the last couple weeks?"

"Nope. I was hoping to see him on this trip and was surprised to learn you'd sold the family home. In fact, I came here from there. New owners of the house even brought me over."

Robert sighed and looked away. "They're accommodating people, aren't they?" he said. "Leaving there after all these years was a difficult decision. You know, since I retired, we just weren't using the house that much. They've done a good job with the old place. I don't believe the lawn has ever looked better." Robert checked Terry's cold compress, ambled to the kitchen, and returned with more ice.

"Ernie, there's a crack in the open window above the kitchen sink," Robert said. "Did you see it there this morning? Is there a chance the police officer ..."

"I doubt it," I said. "Young sparrows, finches bonk it all the time. They see the trees, bushes reflected in the pane, especially with the first blast of sunshine in a while. If they hit their beak just right, it cracks. It's happened before."

"Wouldn't put it past that cop," Terry said, "to try and force that window open. I was dropping my gear in your backyard when he came along. So he walked down the driveway by that window at least twice."

"Naw," I said. "Probably not." I dragged a palm across my forehead, leaned back in my chair, and returned to the earlier topic. "We listed the Oliver place in town last year and it sold faster than we thought. Linn needed a place to live, so I found a home up at the lake, owned by the Dolan family and ..."

"Any relation to the woman who died off of Loreto?" Terry asked.

"Yeah, same family. Most everybody up at the lake knew them. Their place was headquarters for a lot of late nights."

"Coach, a friend of mine chartered them the boat down there. I'm told there was more tequila involved than a Cinco de Mayo celebration. Mexican authorities had to wait for the others onboard to sober up just to interview them. I guess her husband, Mr. Dolan, was a real mess."

"That's Jim Senior. Still is, in a lot of ways," I said. "Although I heard he quit drinking."

Terry shrugged and shook his head.

I continued. "Anyway, I was wondering if Linn might have got a wild hair and jumped on a plane and headed down to see you."

Terry momentarily closed his eyes. He then pulled out of his slouch, elbows on top of his thighs, and stared out the street-side picture window. "God, I don't think so," he whispered. "But he always said he would be back. What are the chances he would come down when I was heading this way? He probably thought it was a safe bet that I would stay put in February."

"I have to admit I'm a little surprised you chose to come north at this time of the year," Robert said. "It's prime time in Arizona for us."

Terry stood up and arched his back. "My youngest sister thinks she wants to attend the UW." He shifted his weight from one leg to the other. "I encouraged her to see the area and visit the school during the dark, rainy time of year. I promised her that if she ever came out, I would meet her in Seattle. So I'm keeping my end of the deal with my little sis."

Terry declined my offer of a sandwich and a soda but reached for a bowl of mixed nuts on the coffee table. "I'll tell you what, Coach. When Linn packed up that station wagon and left Loreto, I'd never seen him quite as happy and content. He was at the top of his game, and I don't mean basketball. The guy was flyin' high, and it was great to see."

"It's surprising what a little heat and fishing on deep blue water will do for the soul," I said, searching for something to say while picturing the abandoned Subaru on the cold Bremerton ferry.

"He left Loreto and drove straight to Scottsdale?" Robert said.

"Yeah, he planned on taking the wagon on the overnight ferry from Santa Rosalia to Guaymas," Terry said. "It's pretty much a straight shot from there to the border and on into Arizona. He was fired up to see you and his mom."

He nodded toward Robert, who smiled momentarily and then leaned forward in his chair. "Terry, do you recall Linn taking any sort of medication down there? I know it's been awhile, but anything? Even over-the-counter stuff?"

Terry squirmed. "Yeah, he was on the sly with something. Seems he had one of those little brown containers in his pocket at all times. At first, I thought it was Dramamine for sea sickness, but he was taking it all the time."

Robert frowned and peered out the front window toward the street. "I spent most of the morning in Seattle talking to some old friends. Orthopedic guys who are up on the latest procedures, drugs. I'm really out of the loop on this stuff. It's just not my area. Consensus is that nobody associates typical anti-inflammatories with depression. Some of the newer, fancier non-steroids can cause depression in a tiny percentage percent of people." He took a moment and then continued. "Without getting too technical, steroids like prednisone pills or similar stuff in joint injections are used for anti-inflammatory effects and can commonly cause emotional instability including everything from mania to severe depression."

The room fell silent. Linn apparently reached the Mexican boat in time to make that crossing of the Sea of

Cortez. I kept wondering if he drove that same wagon last Tuesday night on the Bremerton ferry from Seattle. And, if he did, what he was thinking, and feeling?

THIRTY-ONE

1:45 P.M., MONDAY, FEBRUARY 7, 1982

ROBERT PLANNED TO SPEND THE afternoon at MacTavish & Oliver Logging Company headquarters, quizzing some of Linn's former co-workers who were still dialed in to all the local moving and shaking. I drove Terry to the Greyhound station in downtown North Fork. He slung an old army duffel bag over his shoulder, then scribbled a Seattle phone number where I could reach him. He grinned and cocked his left eye, like a guy betting a fifty-to-one shot on a muddy track.

"You tell Cheese I came after him and expect him to make good on that the one-on-one game he promised me. He can run, but he can't hide."

The wind chopped the Skagit River, now a dirty light tan and running a few notches below flood stage. As my tires buzzed over the heavy steel grate on the Division Street Bridge, I guessed that the local rivers would be unfishable for several weeks. Fishermen grew edgy when their favorite river ran high; fast murky water was about as bad as not having the time to fish at all. Harvey Johnston would not be pleased with the fishing outlook—and with the dwindling possibility that Linn Oliver was lounging on a Mexican beach.

I knew Johnston would hit the roof if he got the news from Arnold Dawson and not from me that Terry Rausch had been in my living room, so I decided on another quick visit.

"Well, look at this," Jessie McQuade said. She removed her black-framed reading glasses and stood behind her desk. "Talk about dying and going to heaven ... Ernie Creekmore twice in the same day."

"Didn't expect to be back, Jessie," I said. "I'm sorry to bother you but ..."

"No bother," she whispered, strolling toward the door to Harvey's office and brushing my sleeve on the way. "Really, no problem at all."

She clutched the round brass doorknob with one hand; the other rested on her right hip, highlighting candy-apple red fingernails. Gleaming black booties, shoulder-length apart, anchored a subtle stance that could have stopped a train. Her hazel eyes combed my face and blinked slower than my neighbor's cat. "The boss wants to see you." She smiled.

"Well, as much as I'd like to spend a few more moments right here, I'm sure he means sooner than later. Business before pleasure."

"Your boss, not mine. Cookie called during the noon hour looking for you."

"Really? That might even be about actual paying business. Any other secrets you might be holding from me?"

Jessie edged away from the door and narrowed the gap between us to where I could smell her post-lunch toothpaste. Arms calmly at her side, she tilted her head back and looked straight into my eyes. "Absolutely." She laughed. "Where would you like me to start?"

Intrigued and more than interested by the possibilities, I rebounded to discover Harvey Johnston's silhouette out of the corner of my eye behind the etched-glass office door. I reached out and pulled Jessie toward me so the bottom of the door wouldn't clip her heel as Harvey entered.

Harvey's head was down, nose in a yellow legal notepad, one hand on the knob.

"Jessie, try to track down the number in Olympia for the state ..." As he glanced up, he looked like the host of a neighborhood party whose guests arrived an hour too early. With questionable new partners. "Ernie, I didn't expect you back so, so soon." His gaze darted from me to Jessie, then back again. He crossed his arms, hugging the notepad to his chest.

Inside Harvey's office, I assumed my usual spot in a chair opposite his desk.

"Terry Rausch was at my house after I left here," I said. "He'd left Mexico to see his sister in Seattle. She's visiting colleges and Terry told her ..."

There was a gentle knock at the door. It swung open slightly. Jessie slipped her head in.

"What?" Harvey snarled.

"Sir, Cookie's here and says it won't take but a moment."

"Gawd, she was just on the phone!" he snapped. He took a deep breath, stood, and tucked in his shirt. "OK, please send her in, Jessie."

The diminutive dynamo bolted to the partner chair next to mine and opposite Johnston. "I need to talk to you after this, Coach," Cookie said. "So don't go away."

She told Harvey that the multiple-listing service was now requiring all sellers to complete a new residential-property-information form when a property was listed for sale. She said the intent was a move to help protect sellers and agents from lawsuits. Questions on the form are about basic sewage, heating, repairs, termites, boundaries, and neighborhood conditions.

"Cookie, I'm fairly certain you didn't come here to talk to me about termites and sewage," Harvey broke in, his right eyebrow arching.

"No, Harvey, I didn't. But this form also wants answers to questions about any known 'crimes of violence' on the property, suicide, or death from other than natural causes. Well, a crime isn't included on the form in the Sherrard listing material. Those big-city Seattle agents don't want to include anything that might be negative to their precious waterfront listing on a lake in the middle of nowhere."

"Wait a minute," Johnston said. "The Sherrard place is still a crime scene. There's still blood on the floor. How can they be concerned about what's in a real-estate listing when it's in no condition to sell?"

"The Sherrard listing expired last weekend. As soon as your guys are out of there, the owner wants it spiffed up and back on the market. At the price he's asking, he's feeling that a buyer will likely be from out of the area. Some big-bucks hotshot from California probably doesn't care about the history because they're star-struck over that gorgeous waterfront. Besides, somebody's going to buy that place, eventually."

"So, what they don't know won't hurt 'em?" Harvey said. "Just keep it out of the listing."

"Exactly," Cookie said. "The crime would certainly mean more to some people than to others. Locals would care more than out-of-staters. But the state now requires the disclosure of a felony to everybody."

"We can get the real-estate office to comply with the new regs," Harvey responded. "I'll get the licensing guys in Olympia to give the broker a call."

"Good," she said. "The Seattle brokerage should disclose a murder happened to have occurred in the Sherrard house and get on with it. The house is still going to sell. Period."

"So, let me get this straight," Harvey said. "You don't think the murder will bring the value down, or slow interest in the home?"

Cookie removed her rimless glasses and glared at the lead investigator. "Well, that's really why I'm here, Harvey. I'm no criminal expert, but they say some killers have been known to return to the scene of the crime. Do you want to know when anybody in my office tours the place from now on? I've shown that home more than anybody else, and I'm sure I'll be showing it again soon. If not before, certainly during spring break. Lake homes get a ton of activity then from families who want to be owners by summer."

"Sure. Good suggestion. Anybody interesting on the line?"

"No, not really. First, it depends how long the cops have it yellow-taped. I've got some customers coming from California in ten days who want to see any affordable waterfront on a lake they can water-ski on. I've got a hermit-looking guy who says he wants to hole up and write the Great American Novel, and one of the local construction guys had somebody else asking."

"OK," Harvey said. "I'll see if my people can wrap it up by the end of the week. But be careful up there and not just in this home. Take somebody with you. And let me know your take on hermit-type characters."

THIRTY-TWO

COOKIE NEARLY TACKLED ME COMING out of Harvey's office. We huddled in the corridor near the first-floor water fountain as several sad-faced county employees skirted past us.

"An offer came in on the Dolan cabin. Hand-delivered by an agent from a small office in Fairhaven. I didn't look at it closely, but it's from that Bellingham family that has been sniffing around up there for months. Both husband and wife have signed. I didn't know if you wanted me to call Jim Junior or if you wanted to handle it. The deal is in a manila folder in your inbox at the office."

I wasn't stunned, just pleasantly surprised. "Yeah, gotta be the same people," I said. "I'm glad they finally did something. They've been hanging around so long just kicking tires that the Dolans had begun to think they were flakes."

"Have other agents shown the place recently?" Cookie said. "I haven't heard any other rumblings in our office."

"Not that I know of," I said. "These people are really the only ones out there. Problem is, they probably know it and might turn the screws pretty tight on the price."

The buyers had done their homework, having inspected every waterfront property on the lake at least once since Labor Day, and settled on the Dolan place after carefully checking the amount of sun on the lot during different months.

The buyers examined the Dolan place so frequently that the locals took for granted that a deal had already been done. Linn Oliver no longer was surprised when they showed up at his door more than once a weekend. Since none of the Dolan clan had been there for months, many residents assumed Linn was now renting from "those nice people from Bellingham who bought the Dolan place."

"Do you know what Linn's agreement was with Dolan?" Cookie said. "If this sale closes, the new people may no longer want to rent it to him. From what I've heard, they are going to want to start making their own changes right away."

"Nothing written," I said. "Month-to-month on a handshake. Certainly no long-term lease the buyers would have to worry about."

Cookie glanced down and slowly dragged the toe of her tiny white sneaker in a semicircle over the vinyl floor squares. She lifted her head and stared over my shoulder. "We're going to have to get his stuff out of there," she said. "That is, if we can't find him. We'll give it a few more days, but if this deal gets signed all around, we might want to look at the calendar and pick a day to go up there and pack it up."

I turned away and tried to stretch, but the tightness in both legs would not subside. I pictured Linn's room at the lake, the contents of the closet, the stale smell of his sweat clothes strewn on the carpet.

"Let's not worry about it now," Cookie said. "I'm late for an appointment in Marysville. You take care," she said, hustling down the hall. "And get that Dolan deal signed."

In the office, I looked over the offer. It wasn't full price, but it was in the ballpark. It had a lot going for it, including the fact it had come from a local buyer. Nothing upset a lake resident more than a lowball offer from an out-of-state speculator. Especially one from California who could care less about the people and history of the region. I had not been involved before with the buyers' Fairhaven agent but had heard some positive comments about the office. The deal was fairly clean with no off-the-wall stipulations. And it was the only one I had received in writing.

The offer was contingent upon a structural inspection. It required the Dolans to physically locate the property corners and provide seller financing for three years. The last condition drew some consternation from the Dolans because the family—especially the women—preferred to be cashed out. The buyers were willing to make a thirty percent down payment but preferred to wait until they became equity partners in a hardware business before applying for another bank loan. The request was logical; they feared rejection by a conventional lender and did an admirable job of explaining the situation in a cover letter to the Dolans. Frankly, I knew the Dolans would be relieved to finally get the offer on paper.

I rinsed the dried grounds from the bottom of my Washington High coffee mug, filled it halfway with hot office fuel, and closed the door to the meeting room behind me. After I read through the meat of the offer, I knew I'd encourage Jim Junior to take the deal on behalf of the family. While I anticipated more activity from potential buyers during the summer months, the possibility of a fatter price seemed like a long way down the road, especially given the strange and tragic events of winter. I also wondered if the buyers realized that the young man living in the lakefront cabin they wanted to buy was the former high school basketball star that was now missing.

I left Jim Dolan Jr., a phone message. The purchase-and-sale agreement requested the sellers to respond within three business days and I suggested that the family consider the deal soon so that the siblings could accept, counter, or reject in a timely fashion.

"Even if you don't want this deal at all," I said. "I always like to give the other party the courtesy of knowing what you decide."

Junior called back thirty minutes later, saying that he had polled his siblings and that the consensus was to take the deal as proposed.

"Kelsey whined a little bit about carrying the paper," Junior said. "She was looking forward to her full share. Said she wants it for the down payment on her new home. She eventually consented but wants us to hold fast to the three-year cash-out. No extensions."

"Got that," I said. "I'll make sure to hammer that home with their agent. It's a big deal to ask any seller to carry the financing for any time period."

"Timing is a big part of this, Ernie," Junior said. "Had things been different, we may have countered to full price, but this year's county tax statement just arrived, and nobody wants to write the check. I know a brother and a sister that don't even have enough money to write their share of it. The tax has become a drain, along with the insurance. And now this murder down the way? Could keep values down for a long time. I don't want our place being clouded by a neighborhood killing. I'm looking at this offer as a bird in the hand."

We agreed to meet at Weller's Restaurant off Interstate 5 just west of Arlington at 6:30 a.m. The early get-together would allow Junior to scoot up I-405 and miss the Boeing traffic heading for the Mukilteo plant. The place would also allow me to sample at least one of Mrs. Weller's early morning pastries.

"I'll be in the office until at least seven tonight, and then I'll be heading home," Junior said. "So let me know if there's anything else you need before tomorrow."

218 | Tom Kelly

"It would be helpful if you could bring the power of attorney that gives you authority to sign for the family," I said. "If I think of anything else, I'll let you know. And bring your dad. Tell him I'm going to introduce him to a hot cinnamon roll he won't believe."

"Will do," Junior said. "If I can get him to answer his phone. He really needs to get out. Sits in that dark basement and watches game shows and ESPN. Say, what have you heard from Cheese Oliver? Have you told him that he might have to move?"

I lifted a hand behind my head and massaged the back of my neck. "We still haven't found him, Jim. I don't know where he is."

"Jesus, Ernie. What do the cops say? Do you think there's any hope that ..."

"I don't know. They've had APBs out the past few days all along the Pacific Coast and in Arizona and Nevada. Not a word. The chief investigator hasn't said anything, but I get the feeling he's starting to lean toward suicide."

THIRTY-THREE

6 P.M., MONDAY, FEBRUARY 7, 1982

THE PHONE CALL CAME AT THE DINNER hour, prime time for telemarketers or family and friends who haven't checked in for months. Pick it up and hear a pitch for the lowest mortgage rate in the free world, or pass and hear later from a former player about how he'd been trying to reach me for weeks but can't ever seem to catch me at home?

"Ernie?"

"Yes, speaking."

"This is Jessie. I am so sorry, but ..."

The rustling in the background sounded like the Seahawks' stadium on a football Sunday. "Hi. Just getting ready to come get you for the movie. But I can barely hear you. Can you speak up a bit?"

"Sorry, there's quite an early-dinner crowd here tonight. I'm at the Big Lake Bar and Grill."

"OK, but I thought ..."

"It's not by design. Believe me. I've had a little accident."

"Are you all right?"

"Yes, yes. I'm fine. A little embarrassed, but fine. My car's in the culvert near the restaurant and I was wondering if you had time to tow me out."

"Sure, sure. I can be there in fifteen minutes. Are you able to drive the car?"

"I think so. The back rear panel is dented, but everything looks in pretty good shape. I hit the brakes too late and slid on in."

"Did some guy blind you with his brights turning into the parking lot? I know that stretch is pretty nasty, especially when it's raining."

"No, it was all my fault. I was on my way home and turned to see ... Ernie, I'm fairly certain I saw Ross Sylanski's '57 Chevy cruise past me. I couldn't see who was driving, but I loved that car for so long. Those chrome wheels. I just remember so vividly how that car looked on the road."

"Stay where you are. I'm on my way."

THE RESCUE TURNED into a meal, and I found myself gazing at Jessie McQuade over a light dinner at the Big Lake. I'd discovered that one of her compelling qualities was the ability to focus on her conversational partner, despite possible chaos or boredom. Harvey could be having a heart attack three steps from her desk, but her eyes rarely left the speaker in front of her. When they did, it was to provide the needed interlude that separated interested eye contact from mindless staring. More importantly, she never peeked over your shoulder to see if a better option had just entered the room.

As the flame of red-glass candle on our corner table danced a thin shadow across her face to the wall, the size and energy of her eyes captivated me. Even after she settled down from retelling the harrowing car sighting and subsequent plunge into the roadside culvert.

"So, you're probably thinking this stupid accident at least got you out of seeing a film with a bunch of stuffy intellectuals." She smiled.

"No, no. I'm a movie guy. It's just that I haven't gotten out much lately."

She set her elbows on the table, made a triangle with her arms, and rested her chin in her folded fingers. "What's your master plan, Ernie Creekmore? Where are you going from here?"

I shifted my weight in the uncomfortable captain's chair and glanced around the Big Lake's dining room. The pieces to my big puzzle still seemed scattered and distant. Oddly, I felt no qualms about discussing them with the person opposite me, even though I knew little about her.

"Good question," I replied. "It's probably time to put more effort into figuring things out. I enjoy the liveliness of young people yet I'm not terribly eager to get back into the classroom. But coaching... Well, I'd say a re-entry is likely and probably not far down the road."

Her eyes glowed brighter. She reached across the table and briefly touched my hand. "Coach Creekmore back on the court. How exciting! Wait until I tell ..."

"Now hold your horses, lady. I'm not quite ready to see it in the paper this weekend."

"Well, I know, but it will be big news around here. Have you informed the high school that you want to come back?

"It's not that easy. And I wouldn't want to disrupt what Coach Morais is doing with the Crabs. He lost a ton of seniors, and he's in a new league. Despite what some boosters say, he's got a lot out of those kids."

She sipped her chardonnay and dabbed a red napkin to her lips. "Speaking of kids," she said in a near-whisper, "what's your honest take on Linn Oliver?"

Honest take? Did others harbor the notion that I've been fooling myself? I wrapped both hands around my Rainier bottle and leaned in closer. "His competitive passion is my main concern. The young man lives for playing at an elite level. How far would he go once he gets a taste of what could still be possible? And, would those measures—whatever they might be—make him crazy?"

She nodded slowly and then said nothing for several minutes. I felt comfortable in her silence; she apparently had the gift of quiet. But when she decided to break the silence, she shattered it. Big-time.

"You mentioned re-entry into coaching. What about re-entry into a relationship?"

I could feel my eyebrows move higher on my forehead. "Truthfully, I haven't taken the time to even consider what might fit. Cathy and I were really partners, and so many couples I see today are not. I guess I've been using that as an excuse not to try."

She smiled and touched my hand again, this time for a moment longer. "Well, this is the third time I've spoken to you in the same day. I was hoping there just might be some merit to what they say about the third time being the charm."

THIRTY-FOUR

6:40 A.M., TUESDAY, FEBRUARY 8, 1982

BY THE TIME JIM DOLAN, JR., FOUND me in a booth against the back wall of Weller's Restaurant, I'd scribbled my to-do list for the day, including giving Harvey a rundown on what Jessie had said about Ross's Chevy. I'd also inhaled a cherry strudel square about the size of Seattle. My fork rested on a dessert plate sprinkled with sugar flakes and a trail of gooey pink jam.

"Just couldn't wait, eh?" Dolan said.

"No discipline when it comes to baked goods," I said. "So, couldn't convince the old man to join us?"

"You know, I went over there, and the old Pontiac was gone. My guess is that he's made a road trip to visit one of the sibs. Anyway, at least he wasn't catatonic on the couch, glued to those damn early-morning reruns of *Bonanza*."

I showed him the purchase-and-sale agreement and pointed to the critical lines.

"Look, Ernie, I'm not going to counter this thing," Junior said. "Maybe these people"—he fingered the first paragraph—"would go for a higher price, but a few more thousand dollars would not be worth another property-tax payment or the anxiety of gambling until after Memorial Day for a potential stream of new lookers."

Junior pulled a pen from his shirt pocket and began initialing and signing at every yellow-highlighted place. "Take this to the other agent and see if you guys can get the final signatures. Should be easy because I don't think we have changed a thing. I know I am going to miss this place in August, but it doesn't even enter my mind on a stormy night in February."

He sat up and pulled his feet closer to the chair. "Tell me something. I understand these people know what they are doing and really want to be at the lake. But if they sign, can they walk away from the deal simply because they get cold feet about Linn being missing? Or, can they nitpick the structural inspection to disguise their concern and get out of buying the place?"

My buyers did not walk away from deals. I knew most of them, coached and taught with many of them, and guided them through escrow. These buyers were not my customers, but I saw nothing bogus about them.

"If a buyer really wants to get out of a deal, he is going to find a way to do it," I said. "Just like anything else. If a burglar wants to break into your home bad enough, they are going to find a way to get in. Given all the publicity in Linn's case, you would think the buyers are already aware that he is missing."

I didn't know if I wanted to believe what I just said.

"Is there any information I need to update or clarify since I signed the listing back in September?" Dolan said.

"Nothing comes to mind, but I'll be sure to corner Cookie today, get her take on it, and go through the file. You are certainly not selling *because* Linn went missing. The house has been on the market nearly six months, and he was living there most of that time."

THIRTY-FIVE

7:45 A.M., TUESDAY, FEBRUARY 8, 1982

I HEADED STRAIGHT TO THE OFFICE and arrived much earlier than usual. An old flycaster friend of my dad's had left a message on the answering machine about listing a cabin I had never seen, off the Jim Creek Road near Trafton. Not only did I have to get up to speed on the place, I also needed to make an appointment with Dr. Crehan about the on-and-off sensation in my fingers, follow up with the buyers' agent regarding the Dolan deal, and get on Harvey's schedule about Ross Sylanski's Chevy.

I dialed my dad in Yakima, hoping to catch him before his morning tour of the orchards and quiz him about a property owned by one of his longtime fishing buddies on the west side of the Cascade Mountains. When he answered, I forgot how much I loved hearing his early-morning snarl. "Are you going to have some decent Tiltons this year, or am I going to have to go elsewhere for good apricots?"

"They'd be better if you came over here and picked 'em this summer. Son, it's good to hear your voice."

"Same here, Dad. Say, I'm heading up to see the McCord place off the Jim Creek Road. Have you ever been in it?"

"Yeah, tight as hell, and Bob keeps all his stuff in tip-top shape. If he's sellin', somebody's going to get a great getaway. You might put some of your A-list guys on notice because there are fishermen who would snap that place up."

"Great. That's what I needed to know. Any dates this weekend?"

"Nope. Still can't find anybody to match your late mother. Sorry, son, but I don't want you be as lazy in that regard as me."

"Right, right. Got that. Now, switching gears ..."

"OK, shoot."

"Did I ever run off and play hoop without telling you or Mom?"

"Well, you did all the time. But do you mean, overnight or something?"

"Yeah. When I didn't check in."

"Twice. No, wait, once. Your mother forgot that one time when her memory was starting to fade. But you went to Bellevue at the last minute with some AAU team, and we didn't know until the next day or so. I'm glad you reminded me 'cause I'm still pissed."

I laughed. "Can't believe I didn't call and at least leave a message."

"Yeah, it wasn't like you, but I remember you got caught up in some last-minute shuffle. Your mother and I thought you were at the Yakima Y all night. Say, I got the truck runnin' outside. Call again, soon, OK?"

"Right, Dad. Thanks."

I put the phone down and picked up the newspaper. As soon as I reached the local roundup, my heart sunk and I laid the paper out on the table in front of me.

Search for Skagit County Man Called Off

The U.S. Coast Guard and Kitsap County Sheriff's Office have called off the search for a Skagit County man who has been missing since his abandoned car was found last week on a Washington State ferry.

"There was no reasonable expectation that he was going to be found alive, unfortunately," said Judith Slattery, Coast Guard spokesperson. "As you can understand, the Puget Sound—we all know what it's like—can be quite cold and unforgiving especially this time of year."

Slattery said a ground search will scour the shorelines in the next few days in the hopes of recovering the body of Linnbert (Cheese) Oliver, 23, who was last seen participating in a recreational-league basketball game near the University of Washington campus.

Oliver, a highly touted high school athlete from North Fork, accepted a scholarship to Washington after a vigorous national recruiting competition.

Slattery said that while the incident is still under investigation, the case is now being treated as a suicide.

The paper slid from my hands and floated to the floor. My arms flopped to my sides. I coasted backward on the chair's tiny wheels and stared at the ceiling. This was it? The first step to closure for the best kid I'd ever been around? I was now two-for-two because I had not gotten over the loss of the best woman I'd ever known.

The office phone buzzed. I rarely answered the office lines, but I picked it up immediately, hoping the caller would address an entirely different topic. No such luck. Austin Ragsdale was on the line.

"Say, I saw couple of the players from our rec league at the Husky game Sunday afternoon at Hec Ed," Austin said. "Anyway, I got to talking with these guys at halftime, and it turns out an old buddy of mine moved to the West Sound a little over a year ago. Took a job at the Puget Sound Naval Shipyard. Interesting guy. Had gone all over the world just fixing props. You know those big cruise ships that run aground on a reef in the middle of some exotic island, well, Bobby ..."

"Sounds like quite the life, Rags, but I--"

"Well, it turns out that I introduced Bobby to Linn at a three-on-three tournament in Spokane three or four years ago. He ended up playing for us on the last day when our third guy got hurt. Bobby and Linn stayed in touch and Linn even invited him up to the lake last fall when Bobby was heading to Vancouver--"

"All good, Rags, but tell me how--"

"So, once Bobby gets squared away on the new job, he recruits some players at the shipyard to play buckets one night a week at Bremerton High. They decide to enter a team in the Silverdale Community College winter league, but they always need players. Some of their guys are in sales and have to travel out of town for work."

"So you think Linn was headed over there to play for them last Tuesday night?"

"From what I heard at the UW game, they were counting on Cheese, but he never showed. Had to start the game with only four guys. Funny thing, they actually ended up doing OK. Ran this four-man box defense until a fifth player floated in the door midway through the second quarter. I guess Holly was more concerned than pissed about Cheese and the lack of bodies for the game but ..."

"Austin, slow down," I said. "You lost me at Holly."

"Bobby Hollingsworth," he said. "Holly's my buddy who moved over there and organized the team. I should have thought of that the other night when you asked me, but you were asking me about a girl."

THIRTY-SIX

10 A.M., TUESDAY, FEBRUARY 8, 1982

THE TITLE COMPANY INFORMED ME that a preliminary report on the Dolan property was already in the works, thanks to an earlier request from the buyer's agent. I reluctantly dialed Mitch Moore to get on his schedule to pump the septic, per county requirement when a home is sold, but his message machine was full. There were better servicers but Mitch recently had paid Cookie a pretty penny for the "first right to pump" on all of our deals east of I-5. By making the call, I had done my duty.

I debated when to drive over and track down Mitch and couple that trip with a visit to Harvey Johnston about the call from Austin Ragsdale. Peggy Metzger tapped me on the shoulder as I hunkered down in my cluttered cubicle. "There's someone holding for you on line three."

I shrugged and punched the line.

"Yes, Mr. Creekmore, I am the agent representing the buyers in the Dolan transaction." She sounded like an efficient executive who made lists and then checked off the completed items with a sharp pencil. She got to business. First, we agreed on a title company.

"Now," she continued, "according to the contract, the sellers are to physically show where the property lines are located to my buyers. I know they have found two of the corners—there are steel stakes in the ground where the lawn meets the beach—but he has yet to locate them on the road side of the property. When would Mr. Dolan be available to accommodate us, or might you prefer to handle this task in his stead?"

I remember finding all the corner stakes last year when I listed the property but feared the county might have covered the roadside markers when it repaved the lake road in October. Besides, if a guy as thorough as Schwager, a fastidious accountant, couldn't find them, they probably weren't there.

"Tell you what," I said. "Let me know when you want to meet up there. I've seen them and know where they should be, but I don't know if we can easily find them. If we can't, the width of property is also marked by the power poles at the road. I'll also fax you the most recent survey for your files. Shows the poles, too."

The agent spoke as if she approved of my plan and promised to call me back with a time her buyers could meet us at the lake. We covered other business, which was routine until we hit upon Mitch Moore's unavailability for the septic pumping. She wanted to move the deal along and suggested another septic person who often worked with her office. I couldn't really say no.

"Thank you, Ernie, for helping me expedite this process. I can tell it's going to be smooth sailing working with you. If we can pull all of this together by the end of the week, I don't see any reason why we couldn't push the closing date ahead. My people would really like to gain access by spring break so that they can begin adding their personal touches. They're very creative people."

Creative people. Creative financing. Pushy agent?

THIRTY-SEVEN

NOON, TUESDAY, FEBRUARY 8, 1982

HARVEY TOLD ME TO MEET HIM FOR lunch at the Streamliner Diner, a popular lunch-only joint a block from the courthouse. As I yanked open the side door to look for him, I nearly pulled Jesse McQuade to the ground as she left the restaurant. I lunged and caught her before she lost her balance, gently steadying her from behind. Her leather jacket felt soft and cozy.

"Whew, that was close," Jessie said, removing a shoe and checking its heel. Her cheeks grew rosy as she rolled her head to the side, straightening her hair.

"I am so sorry, Jessie," I said. "I was in such a hurry to catch Harvey."

"Oh, no worries, whatsoever. A coach such as yourself might say that was a nice save, or something along those lines. And again, thanks for the save last night."

She hand-brushed, then inspected her pleated pants and smiled the way a woman does when she's not concerned about using the correct athletic phrase. She looked over the shoulder to see Harvey hobbling down the sidewalk toward us and leaned closer, pulling my arm to her side.

"You know, I did enjoy being with you last night, and I appreciated you following me home. I also need to find a way to make up for that missed film. Perhaps we can catch another movie, maybe dinner, in the next few weeks?" She released my arm and swayed away, swiping quickly at her bottom for unseen dust. She was not the type of woman who would look back to measure the effect.

"What was that all that about?" Harvey said, sliding an arm into his brown topcoat. "And don't tell me she was asking you who would win the Pac-10 title."

"Probably those kitty-cats from Arizona," I replied. "But, no, it was more about last night. She mentioned you had an especially fat wallet today and would be more than happy to buy me lunch."

Harvey fastened the belt of his coat and turned up the collar. "Wrong on both counts, but let's grab a bite anyway."

We sat at a window booth, and I started to review the previous evening with Jessie and what led to my towing her out of a ditch. He cocked a questioning eyebrow. "What kind of odds you giving it was Ross's?"

"It's hard to say. But I don't see Jessie as somebody with a flighty imagination." We ordered our food. After the waitress left, Harvey went back to his window stare.

"I'll talk to the sheriff," Harvey said, "but it's just another stolen car at an extremely busy time. Besides, it was dark. Navy blue could have easily been seen as black. Look, I know everybody loves that family and all, but I've got a couple of other rather pressing issues. The heat is coming down every which way for me to make some major progress, at least somewhere. We sure as hell aren't getting inundated with useful material, especially in the Rice homicide."

I pushed back in the booth and rested my head against the wall. "I'm surprised you didn't mention Linn's situation in that mix."

Harvey leaned in over the table, reducing the distance between our faces. A shower of rain crashed against the window, but he ignored it.

"The Kitsap County Sheriff's Office called last night about eleven p.m.," he said. "Some waterfront owner near Fort Ward State Park on Bainbridge Island was clearing driftwood after dinner. Afraid the stuff was going to get into his boathouse. He's tossing limbs and kelp, comes across a vinyl bag with one handle. Zips it open and finds a leather basketball. The guy yanks the ball out and finds some loose change, a set of keys, and a wallet belonging to one Linnbert Oliver. Driver's license, coupla credit cards, few bills. I sent one of our guys down to pick it up. He should be back by now."

My shoulders tensed. "No body?" I said, bracing myself for the worst.

"No body."

THIRTY-EIGHT

1:30 P.M., TUESDAY, FEBRUARY 8, 1982

I WAS IN NO MOOD TO PREVIEW PROPERTY, but I'd known the potential buyer most of my life. Plus, I could use the drive to clear my head. The address was on a road that angled away from Highway 530, but I didn't know how much of it was paved. Given the amount of water on the city's streets, I figured it best to drive the old Travelall. As I reached the top of a grade overlooking the I-5 bridge, I could see an ominous storm front moving in from Puget Sound. Great call on the truck.

I headed east on I-530, past the three-mile stretch of dairy farms and corn mazes into downtown Arlington, then turned left at the Fountain Drive-In and followed the highway sign toward Trafton, Possum, and Darrington. The rain slowed momentarily, giving the sun a chance. The two combined to offer a brilliant arching rainbow whose pot of gold appeared to be securely planted on Mount Pilchuck's northern shoulder.

Trafton, Washington, is a wide spot on I-530, just this side of a highway sign that reads RESUME SPEED. The burg is composed of two longtime establishments: Olson's Saw

Shop—not a bad place in Snohomish County to buy a seasoned cord of wood any time of the year—and the Trafton General Store. Just off the highway on the Jim Creek Road sits tiny Trafton Elementary and its century-old schoolhouse.

I passed aging double-wides, tight little Craftsmen houses, and a tiny brick Tudor on ten acres with a hand-painted FILL DIRT WANTED sign. Nails had rusted through the plywood, leaving brown streaks in the white paint as if dumped soil had creeped up the sign. Most structures were in better condition than I expected and a good distance from the noise of the highway and far enough out of the flood plain that the nearby Stilly rarely soaked their front yards.

The property for sale was a vacant, cute Lincoln-log structure on a couple of well-kept acres with raised flowers and more than a dozen mature alder and maple trees. The well-landscaped driveway zigzagged to a two-car garage, partially hiding the main entry from the road. A newer composition roof with two skylights topped the house. The heavily lacquered wooden door with two etched glass panes beamed as if framed by lights. I parked on a concrete slab adjacent to the garage that cried out for a basketball hoop and followed a stone-lined bark trail. It wound through a low, compact meadow until it ended near an old green bench littered with maple leaves overlooking a swirling creek. I imagined an older man teaching his son or grandson to cast from the bank below the bench in late autumn, a warm afternoon sun breaking through the yellow-turning alders. It certainly would be a setting my potential customer would enjoy seeing. It was the sort of spot I would've loved to have shared with Linn Oliver.

I found no key, but a walk around the house told me all I needed to know. It was beautiful and in move-in condition. All this place needed was groceries. I jumped back into the truck, eager to show the property to my dad's friend, especially before other local agents found out about it. I

236 | Tom Kelly

rambled up to the payphone outside the Trafton General Store and called the office for the numbers of other possible prospective buyers.

"Say, have you spoken with Cookie?" Peggy said. "She was looking for you a little bit ago."

"I'll get back to her soon, but I need your help right now. Can you go over to my desk and grab the Sauk file and the Trafton file?"

She put me on hold and, when the music cut off, I was surprised to hear Cookie's voice.

"Coach! Thank god you called. You've got to get up to Lake Wilhelmina right away."

"Might have to wait. I've got somebody who'll be really interested in this new Trafton listing. It's a cute--..."

"Forget the frickin' Trafton listing! The septic guy called from the Mountain Market. He was able to start the Dolan job today."

"That's great. I was hoping he could get up there today or tomorrow. Maybe we can get the deal to close early."

"You might ... Coach ..."

"I might what? What's the matter?"

"Might prepare yourself." She snuffed and wept, struggling to gain enough breath to speak. The phone receiver seemed to be muffled by her hand, or periodically held to her chest. "I'm so ...''

"What?" I yelled, wondering how much I was missing in the clamor of the passing logging trucks. The dirty spray from their trailer tires nearly hit the sides of the red Plexiglas booth. "Tell me what the hell's going on!"

There was a moment when neither of us spoke.

"It's Linn, Ernie," Cookie whimpered. She took a short, staccato breath. "His clothes clogged the little pump truck's line. The driver's gotta go back, couldn't finish the job because his tank was full from another stop. But ..."

"No way. How does he know it was Linn's stuff? Could be anybody's clothes."

Cookie sniffled and continued in a barely audible whimper. "It's his gas-station shirt. The one with *Linn* stitched on the lapel? Black work shoe, too. Harvey and the sheriff are headed up. But there's ..."

"He's been working at that Shell station for years," I said, grasping for some level of calm and logic. "Those things could have been sitting in there for ages. Dumped in there a long time ago."

There was another pause, this one long enough that I thought the call was lost. "Hey! I screamed. "Cookie, are you still there . . ?"

"There's more, Coach," she said. "They found ..."

"Speak up! I can hardly hear you. It's loud, raining, and I'm on the side of the freaking road."

"A FOOT ... Coach, they fished a man's foot out of the septic tank. Apparently it's been severed just above the ankle. It's hard to tell."

"What? Was there any more that would show ..."

"The pump trucker thought he had vacuumed up another shoe. He told me more than he was supposed to, but cops are going to somehow sift through his load up at the Whatcom County plant and go back tomorrow. Oh, Ernie, I am so sorry."

I didn't remember dropping the receiver, but the next thing I knew, it swung slowly beneath the Yellow Pages on its silver coiled line. I felt hauled from a warm and treasured place, disconnected from anything safe and tangible. There was no strength in my knees and thighs. I propped the top of my head and hands on the wall above the phone to stay upright.

IN THE TRUCK, I yanked an old white towel from behind the seat and wiped the tears from my face and the rain from my hair. I sat silently behind the wheel, feeling the cloth's cool softness on my cheeks and mouth while weighing the rugged possibilities of the late afternoon.

Moments later, I pulled out onto Highway 530 and headed farther east into the Stillaguamish Valley toward Darrington, taking solace in the snow along the ridgelines of the Cascade Foothills. I remembered as a boy riding in my father's woody station wagon, my wonderment of what could be found just beyond those ridges, the mirror-lakes, golden meadows and fort-like beaver dams on trickling creeks. Now, the naive awe had turned to a stark, unconscionable reality so foreign to any and every experience that I'd associated with the region. When I reached the Possum Road cutoff, that reality suddenly was just over the hill.

The going was brutal through the switchbacked roads, requiring all my attention. But as the truck rumbled up abend, I again lost my hold on the present. My cherished times with Linn—fishing the Stilly, critiquing opponents, downing pizza at Tony's—surfaced like a string of consecutive baskets in a fourth-quarter comeback. I recalled the number of times Linn Oliver had come out of nowhere to bail our team out of nearly impossible situations. I yearned for just one more reprieve, but my gut filled with the familiar emptiness of loss.

Soon after, the lake was on my left, calm and deep blue. Covered boats sat on rusted trailers in driveways. Through the evergreens, I spied a lonely fisherman, hunched in green rain gear, one arm poking out under his hooded slicker. The sight made me shiver, despite the warm air blowing from the truck's dashboard heater. As I approached the corner of the sandspit and the stretch of land where the community of Madrona once prospered, I was startled by the number of police and emergency vehicles, flashing lights, and the volume of yellow crime-scene tape stretched across the road.

Harvey Johnston huddled with two other detectives in the middle of the road, curiously out of place in trench coats and ties. The sun was long gone and the trio tried to warm themselves by wringing their hands and rubbing their sleeves. Harvey saw me approaching the barricade and motioned to the officer on duty to allow me to pass. As I walked closer, I overheard a cop speaking into a portable receiver.

"Yes, there was a crowbar in there, too. Yeah, what we saw was well-preserved because it had sunk to the bottom of the tank."

Harvey looked into my eyes for a moment, then turned his face toward the ground, hands stuffed deep into the pockets of his charcoal overcoat.

"Just tell me what happened, Harvey. From the start of the afternoon."

He sighed and glanced toward the lake. "The pumper came up here with a pretty heavy load from another stop. Thought this was a small job. He couldn't take all that's here and he's gotta come back and pump late tonight." He turned and faced me. "He did suck up a bunch of clothes that apparently belong to Linn. We'll know a lot more tomorrow, but there's little doubt that they're his. I can't tell you how ..."

"What else, Harvey? Don't string me along here. What else did they find?"

He leaned back on his heels and folded his arms. "Couple of body parts. They took a foot and what looked like a ring finger to the lab. White-coat boys just took them to town. I wished like hell the damn driver would have had the sense to call us first instead of Cookie. Said he felt obligated to contact both real estate brokers because they hired him.."

I could barely breathe and felt slightly dizzy. I finally managed to exhale. "You're that certain it's Linn?"

"Seems clear," Harvey said, staring off over my shoulder. "But like I say, we'll know more after the tech guys go through tests. Got his Shell Oil shirt.. Also a hoop jersey, some old black sweat pants. Stuff was pretty nasty comin' out of there."

"What tests will they do tonight, just to be sure?"

"Depends what time they can get back to the lab and get started. Once they filter through the material, we'll see what we have and go from there. We'll eventually get started on the radiographs and bring in the dentist–the forensic odontologist. Processing any teeth we get first can speed up the paperwork. Most of that stuff's SOP."

I shuffled my feet, the soft mud sucking at my boots. "Then what?"

"Our guys will also have to sort through the stuff he collects late tonight. It's going to be a long evening for a lot of people."

Arnold Dawson sloshed over to me and pulled the lid of his Smokey hat down closer to his nose. "Looks like we won't be needing your investigative skills any longer, Coach," he murmured. "As valuable as they were. Now, if you wouldn't mind moving out of the way, this is an official crime scene. Tell you the truth, I never considered you even close to being official anyway."

While I felt like breaking his nose, there was no reason to waste time and energy on the likes of Dawson. I turned and stepped toward a stand of evergreens on the other side of the road. I could feel the closeness of my old grief, like a massive swamp lingering just beyond the trees. Then I caught myself and turned and faced the growing turmoil of vehicles and officials. "Is there anything that I can do for you, Harvey?"

"Absolutely. You can get me a few minutes with Ronnie Garcia and Bart Knight. Nobody has seen either one of them for a few days. Drove down Knight's lake driveway earlier, and a Doberman nearly jumped the fence and took my face off. Gate was padlocked. That family has so much property around here he could be anywhere." He straightened up, narrowed his eyes. "And, that reminds me. Alberto Garcia said you were over there earlier this week asking questions about Ronnie?"

"He's a former player. Thought I'd see how he was doing."

"And when you found out he wasn't there, you continued to interrogate his father?"

"It was a casual visit. We talked about my helping out."

"You grilled his dad! In his own house! Not exactly on the casual scale." He shrugged and lowered his voice. "Look, if you want to help, find Bart Knight and Ronnie Garcia and call me immediately. Other than that, I'll see you in the morning." He waved a police cruiser down the road and then continued. "I'd like to bring you back up here tomorrow but first I told Sheriff McCreedy we'd start with coffee in town at nine a.m. sharp. I'll save the specifics for later."

"Robert Oliver is going to want to come with us. He's been chomping at the bit to become more involved.

Harvey was silent for a moment and looked around the crime scene. "I did speak with him after our lunch, before I came up here. All of this has really begun to get to him, to all of us." He kicked at the mud and then stared at me. "I'm going to let him ride with us up here, but I'm not going to tell him what we found today until our guys break down that truck's entire load. You got that, Ernie? I'm not going to ask a father to ID anything about a son until we know what else was in that tank."

THIRTY-NINE

8 A.M., WEDNESDAY, FEBRUARY 9, 1982

ANXIOUS, RESTLESS, AND NOT KNOWING how long we would be out with Harvey, I drove to the Red Apple Market for donuts and fruit. The banner headline of *The Seattle Tribune* in the box outside stopped me in my tracks.

Cheese Oliver: The Early Days

I crammed a quarter in the machine, yanked out the top copy, and sat on a pallet of charcoal briquette bags just outside the sliding glass doors. The two-page feature at the back of the sports section was the first of a three-part series on a "Northwest prep basketball legend" by Greg Smithson and contained old photographs of Linn when he was barely bigger than a basketball under the family's driveway hoop. It also had interviews with elementary school classmates, coaches, and teachers, and it speculated about a secret bout with depression. I wondered when the material I gave him would surface and what he would choose to use. I would soon find out.

The one-paragraph introduction, set in large type, explained how Linnbert "Cheese" Oliver had been the most talked-about high school basketball player in Washington state history and now was missing for a week after his abandoned automobile was found on the Seattle-Bremerton ferry: *The state patrol was expected to announce in the next 48 hours that the incident was officially a suicide.*

I leaned against the market wall and read on.

By the time he was ten, Linnbert Oliver dribbled balls everywhere he went on the sidewalks of North Fork. He pestered his way into pickup games with boys twice his age at Hillcrest Park. On nights after the high school gym was swept and dark, he went home and fired Nerf balls at tiny hoops around the house till way past his bedtime.

As he grew older and stronger, he crafted imaginary championship games in the driveway. According to his siblings, Linn used the garage door as his give-and-go partner, flinging his ball against the wooden wall. Retrieving the ricochet, he would leap and snap off one of the dozens of jump shots he attempted every day. He mentally timed this sequence, first with bounce passes that hit the pavement before each attempt, then with rapid-fire chest passes that gave him little time to catch and shoot. He strove to better his time on every execution. When out of earshot of his siblings, he imitated the voice of veteran Seattle SuperSonics' announcer Bob Blackburn to describe his exploits before a roaring capacity crowd at the Washington State High School championship game.

"This building has never seen a game like it folks, and the young kid from George Washington is puttin' on a show! Oliver, on the dribble-drive, cuts off a blockbuster screen and takes the ball ALL THE WAY TO THE HOOP. . ! Just listen to that crowd! Oliver has brought the Fighting Crabs back from twenty-two points down to just three and has all of these people on their feet ...

"Oliver stops, elevates and lets fly with a twenty-four footer, that rattles home at the buzzer! Oh, Lordy! The crowd is going wild. They are mobbing the kid in the middle of the floor. I don't think I have ever seen a comeback like this one.

Whoa, Nellie! What a game folks, for the Washington State championship ... !

A four-column picture anchored the page. It showed Linn and his St. Brendan School teammates, beaming ear to ear, kneeling behind a Catholic Youth Organization championship trophy that was bigger than a few of the kids. Sister Mary St. Germaine, the St. Brendan principal, stood beside her triumphant team.

St. Brendan looked dazzling that day in their controversial new uniforms that included full-length satin warmups that boasted *Gaels* in sweeping white cursive on the back of their snap-on button jackets. Unis are a big deal to kids, even bigger for the nuns.

Smithson wrapped up the section with a provocative piece on Linn's early recruitment. It detailed how longtime Husky assistant Keith Kirkwood first observed Oliver's skills as a sixth-grader.

I stopped by a parochial tourney on Thanksgiving weekend to support one of my nephews playing for a Snohomish team," Kirkwood said. "This one kid had parents buzzing when he converted his first four shots, all from long range. I couldn't believe what I was seeing. I stayed for the second game, and then a third. The hair on my forearms began to tingle. Was I, a college assistant coach, seriously scouting a twelve-year-old? While I had the perfect cover—my nephew—I remember ducking behind a set of bleachers, looking for other coaches. Secretly, I hoped I was the only talent evaluator in the building

A bold-face line at the end of the section told readers the second installment of the series—"The High School Years"—would appear tomorrow and include several of Linnbert "Cheese" Oliver's memorable games, including the 1977 state championship loss to Flintridge.

I folded the newspaper, strolled to the VW bus and stuffed it under the front seat. Robert Oliver didn't need to see it before breakfast.

FORTY

AFTER PANCAKES AND SAUSAGES AT the Calico Cupboard, Harvey said he'd like to see the stretch of road where Jessie found herself in the ditch en route to revisiting the area around the Dolan cabin.

"It's on the way so I thought we would cover as many bases as we could in one trip," Harvey said. "From there, two, maybe three waterfront sites. I really don't know what I'm looking for, but Ernie's Realtor key code might come in handy in getting us into some homes."

The sheriff glanced around the restaurant and then down at his watch. "I should be clear to go with you, at least for the next several hours," the sheriff said. "Any noise from the medical examiner and septic plant should come through loud and clear on your CB. I can keep you all informed of any findings."

Harvey nodded. "Let's take two cars in case I need to hang around or head off in another direction." He turned to me. "Ernie, why don't you and Dr. Oliver jump in your bus and lead us to the spot where Jessie's car went off the road. After I check it out, we'll swing back to Dolan's place. Again, you guys just might have to bear with me because I

247 | Cold Crossover

might spend a lot of time at the house where Rice was found and also back at the Dolan place. If you choose to follow me, stay outside the yellow tape."

As we pulled away, the dark, dank morning felt more like early evening. Robert appeared pensive and mostly stared out the window at the green hills. I could only imagine how many times Robert had been on these roads, at all hours of the day and night making emergency calls.. He had never, though, searched for a missing son. When he spoke, it was a sort of nervous chitchat, comparing Arizona and Washington landscapes; its purpose only to break lengthy stretches of silence.

When I approached the Big Lake Bar and Grill on Highway 9, I slowed and downshifted, then pulled over directly across the road from the spot I hooked up Jessie's Lexus. Harvey guided his county-issued Oldsmobile to a stop just behind my bumper. Rising from behind the wheel, he pointed out the first set of skid marks to Sheriff McCreedy and reached for his jacket in the back seat.

"It's a good thing she didn't have too far to walk to the bar," Harvey said.

While he limped head down around the scene in the rain, the sheriff slid into Harvey's shotgun seat and pulled the CB receiver to his lips.

I looked at Robert and pointed to the bus. "Sit tight while I go in and use the restroom." A few minutes later, I darted from the bar. My breathing quickened as I approached Harvey's car window. He cranked it down.

"Change of plans," I shouted. "We're going to a different part of the lake. Follow close because the access is hard to see."

Before Harvey could respond, I was halfway to the bus. I turned the key and quickly ground through the gears as we sped toward the Lake Wilhelmina cutoff. I nearly put the bus in the ditch by trying to take the turn too fast.

"Goodness," Robert Oliver said. "Something obviously changed back there. Why the speed ride?"

"It's complicated," I said. "I'll explain when I can, but right now I need to keep this bus on the road. As you just saw, she's not known for great cornering."

We barely slowed through the fire station speed zone at Finn Settlement and continued the pace down along the lake's North Shore Drive. I angled off the pavement on to a fire trail road adjacent to the beaver ponds at the east end of the lake, the road twisting for more than three miles up and away from the old MacTavish & Oliver Logging Company's Camp Ten. A few deserted trailer homes sat behind broken-down fences on rough outcroppings and rocky plateaus sprinkled with a few spruce or cedar.

I reduced speed and lost Harvey for a moment, the bus scooting around a blind hairpin turn. We veered right, the road now flat and parallel to Deer Creek. As we drew near a wide spot in the road, a trio of alders marked the opening of an overgrown lane angling toward the creek. I steered the VW into the high grass behind the alders and turned off the motor. Just ahead, I could make out the outlines of several cabins plus assorted sheds, barns, and outbuildings. Unlike the access to the Knight compound from the south, the road had no locked gate ahead. I eased open the door to a chilly graveyard smell. Harvey glided his car to a wide spot a few feet away.

Sheriff McCreedy held an index finger to his lips. Other than the howl of periodic gusts up the creek valley, it was as quiet as a school library at spring break.

"I'll walk on down and poke around," McCreedy said. "Harvey, stay several yards behind until I know what's what. Don't want to spook anybody. You guys"—he pointed to Dr. Oliver and me—"stay put."

Slightly crouched, McCreedy stepped quickly down the side of the arching driveway that served more than one creekfront cabin, his dark boots and flat-brimmed Stetson making him seem even taller as he darted away. Harvey turned up his collar and hitched his trousers, ready to follow. I huddled beside the bus while Dr. Oliver remained in the passenger seat with the door open, one leg dangling outside, constantly checking his watch like a coach at a track meet.

As the sheriff disappeared around the curve, Harvey said, "Just sit tight."

A lone blue jay swooped down in front of the bus and drilled on a dried pine cone. I grabbed the VW's roof ledge with both hands to stretch the tense drive from my legs like a long-distance runner, slowly alternating each heel to the ground. Dr. Oliver pulled a pair of black ski gloves from the pocket of his knee-length down coat. A moment later, I arched my back, face to the sky, and extended my arms behind, trying to shake the tightness from my shoulders and the numbness from my hands.

"Another minute, and I'm waitin' in the car with you," I said. "It seems the temperature's dropped."

"We got a runner!"

It was the sheriff's voice and a good distance away. Harvey hobbled toward the corner of a rundown pole barn and quickly out of sight. I bolted from the side of the car, arms and legs churning down the driveway toward Harvey. I covered the gap between us quickly and caught up to him on his left side, my gut in my throat.

Harvey slowed and turned.

"Ernie, you and Dr. Oliver stay with the cars! Here, take my key. And, don't move until you hear from me."

Retreating to the bus, I tossed the keys on the floor near the accelerator. As I closed the door, I could hear Harvey yell "Stop!" in the lower creek bed.

I shot Dr. Oliver a glance, then jogged back toward the cluster of buildings.

"Ernie! Get back here!" the doctor howled.

Silently moving around pine and maple, I approached a tiny lane of shacks anchored in the middle by a huge metal building about the size of a high school gym. A well-worn dirt road led to the chain-locked double doors. Peeking through the gap created by the slack in the chain, I could see shelves stacked to the ceiling with auto parts; heavy engine blocks and pistons on the floor, fenders, chrome bumpers, and door panels at eye level, radiators, generators, and stereos up high.

As I wiggled the chain to increase the crack between the two doors, a black Doberman slammed into the doors, showing his snarling teeth through the tiny space. The surprise blow sent me reeling onto my back in the wet pine needles, the dog desperately pawing the doors to break free. Scrambling to my feet, I hugged the side of the building and jogged toward the last structure of the group, a plywood-sided cabin with peeling turquoise paint. Smoke billowed from a black stovepipe in the middle of the roof. A single light glowed in what appeared to be a rear bedroom.

I moved as quietly as I could toward the house. Faded beer cans and chewing tobacco lids were strewn near the foundation wall, along with kindling, a splitting maul, and uprooted shrubs as dry as sagebrush. A stained sheet served as window covering for the only room that faced the lane. I inched along one side of the house to find dusty, thin blinds blocking any chance of looking inside through an aluminum-framed window twice the size of the window on the lane. I ducked lower and tiptoed as best I could toward the deck that ran the length of the front of the house, its three entry steps caked in slippery green mold.

On hands and knees, I peeked around the front corner and found a camping chair turned to face the creek below. The door leading to the house was open and swayed intermittently in the wind. I bobbed up quickly once to glance into the deckside window. The living room and kitchen areas appeared to be deserted. I heard Harvey shouting down in the creek-bed but an enormous madrona blocked my view.

I rose to my feet and slid through the back door when the wind again pushed it wide. Brown linoleum bubbled near the deck door and again a few feet from the potbelly stove in the corner. Given the condition of the floors, there was no stopping the creaks beneath my steps.

An old Hotpoint refrigerator purred in the kitchen; greasy, mustard-stained plates littered the sink. The remaining space on the main floor appeared to be two small bedrooms and a bath. The stairs to the dormer appeared to have been carved out of the bedroom closest to the driveway. The bathroom door was ajar, and I tapped it farther open but chose not to enter. I could see splotches of black mold crawling up wallboard on the side of the shower and two tattered throw rugs bunched up below the toilet.

Across the hall, I knocked twice on the first bedroom door, waited, and knocked again before yanking it open and leaping away. Hearing and seeing nothing, I flicked on the light. I could smell the musty sleeping bags and canvas camping gear from the hall. Steelhead poles leaned against the far corner, flanked by a stack of tackle boxes of different colors and sizes. Two metal cots topped with bare foam cushions were pushed against other walls.

The other bedroom had no door, only a multicolored, beaded curtain of strung glass pieces straight out of the sixties. The room could barely accommodate the unmade queen-size bed, a side table and the switchback stairs to the dormer. The stairs to the dormer led to a closed door. I reached for the metal knob and heard a curious buzz coming from the room, the sort of sound a radio makes when it's between stations.

I flung open the door. A horrible stench sent my shoulders forward, palms to my thighs, as I braced to control a deep gag. Cupping a hand over my mouth, I pivoted through the entry and discovered the back of a man clothed only in a t-shirt and underwear. He was bound to an oak dining chair, his wrists secured to its splats and rear legs with weighted nylon crab line. His neck and shoulders remained still, and I doubted if he was breathing.

His skin, the eerie gray of dried grade-school paste, turned pink where it met the rope. A dark pool of urine and liquid excrement filled the seat and surrounded the chair, trickling off in two tiny trails on the uneven plywood floor toward the near wall. Under the chair lay a coiled noose fashioned from a heavy hemp marine line.

The man's head was tilted forward. The tails of a blue paisley handkerchief knotted the back of his thick oily hair. The chair faced a mammoth black Sharp television topped with a video recorder. The screen's snow static produced the indistinct droning sound I heard from the landing. I cautiously began to loop around him, noticing that the blue rag had been inserted into a now-gaping mouth that faced the floor.

A curious scar, the size, color, and consistency of an earthworm, arched around his right kneecap. I dipped down and peered closer at the scar and then slowly moved my gaze up his torso, straining to see any facial features through his cascading hair. The chin, his mouth, his cheekbones ...

No. How could it be?

My hands shook with fear and confusion. And desperate possibility. I steadied my right by reaching and placing two fingers against his forehead, gently nudging his head back until it rotated, bobbed, and stopped at an angle above his right shoulder.

Linn Oliver's puffy, battered eyes looked like they'd gone ten rounds with Sonny Liston. His bulging, crooked nose was so swollen that it appeared boiled and stuck back on his face; his split, chapped lips looked ready to snap away from the rest of his purple mouth. I leaped closer and applied the same two fingers to the side of his neck between the windpipe and largest discernible muscle, praying for a pulse.

It was faint, but it was there! Barely.

I darted to the riverside window, yanked up the shade, and spied Harvey and McCreedy about one hundred yards down the way, escorting a hooded, handcuffed person up the bank. I pushed open the aluminum frame.

"Harvey! Get in here! He's still alive!"

As I turned to face Linn, Robert Oliver bolted through the door and stopped dead in the muck, wide-eyed and stunned. He fumbled through a series of pockets before locating a Swiss army knife in his down vest and cut the salt-dried line from Linn's lifeless arms. His efficient movements and amazing calm reminded me of the scene inside the train car years ago. I flew down the stairs, ripped the sheet from the rear window and grabbed one of the sleeping bags from the musty bedroom. Without a word, we carefully lifted Linn from the chair and laid him on a clear area of the floor. Robert began CPR while I cleaned Linn up as best I could with the sheet.

"Let's go! Now!" Robert rose from his knees. "Who knows if we'd ever get any help out here. They've got equipment at the clinic in town. We can get to them faster than they could get to us."

We unzipped a mummy bag, eased it around Linn, flipped him over my shoulder, and started down the stairs toward to the bus. Robert sprinted ahead as I lumbered behind with Linn in my arms, his head bouncing like a bobblehead doll above my quick, uneven steps. We gently slanted him onto the back bench, his feet resting in the open area adjacent to the second seat. Robert climbed in, one arm around Linn's shoulder while his left hand searched for a pulse.

254 | Tom Kelly

As I slid the side door closed and skirted around to the driver's side, Harvey arrived, followed by the sheriff escorting their head-down suspect.

"Is it really Linn?" Harvey said.

I nodded on the run and climbed in.

"Then go! I'll find you in town."

I crunched the bus into reverse, and we maneuvered back to the dirt road. Reaching over my shoulder for the seatbelt, I caught them removing the suspect's hood.

"Mitch Fricking Moore?" I mumbled. "You sonofabitch!"

A STOCKY NURSE at the clinic said she'd seen plenty of retirees with coronaries, hikers with broken bones, and fishermen hooked in just about every imaginable part of the body. But she had never witnessed anyone in Linn Oliver's condition.

"Even had a guy stuck in the snow for three nights on a ridge in the north Cascades," she said. "Looked like a ghost when they got him in here. But I ain't never seen anybody who looked like your friend. Alive, anyway."

Harvey arrived. "How's he doin?"

"The nurse said the doctor should be out in a few minutes to give us an update," I said.

"How about Doctor Oliver?"

"He's on the phone. Calling his wife."

"Speaking of updates," Harvey said, folding his arms, "one of my detectives met with the medical examiner's assistant late this morning."

I drew closer so the nurse could not hear.

"That foot in the septic tank?" Harvey said. "Turns out it belonged to Jim Dolan, Senior. Cut off just above the ankle with a big-time blade. The medical examiner says it was probably a circular or table saw. I expect we'll find the rest of him, or more of him, when the pump truck finishes its work up at the lake."

I staggered over to the sofa, plopped down, and wrapped my palms around my face. No wonder Junior couldn't locate Senior.

"The sheriff's already begun questioning Mitch Moore over at headquarters," Harvey said. "I better be getting back over there myself because we're probably going to be there awhile." A moment later, he turned toward me. "Tell me something. How did you know to deadhead it to Knight's property this morning in the first place?"

I eased back into the couch and sighed. "I got lucky. Ellie Phillips was in the Big Lake finishing breakfast with her granddaughter. When I asked about Jim Senior, she said she had seen his red Pontiac Firebird on the lake road a couple of days ago. With Ross's Chevy missing, I got to thinking that might be too much of a car coincidence. I found both cars were under a couple of blue tarps in that pole barn at Knight's compound."

"Did you get to meet Mr. Doberman?"

"Yep. The building he's protecting looks like a Carquest warehouse."

A lanky giant covered head to toe in light green hospital scrubs pushed through a set of windowed doubled doors. He had a full head of light brown hair and looked like a super-sized Dr. Kildare. He looked uncertain if he should address Harvey or me.

"I'm Dr. Holland and I will be heading up his—is it Linnbert?—his care."

"Yes, that's right," I said. "We call him Linn."

"And some people call him . . ?"

"Cheese. Cheese Oliver."

"Right, well he's a long way from being out of the woods. He's incredibly dehydrated, and I won't know the extent of his facial fractures for some time. Once we get him stabilized and ascertain his condition, we may have to transport him down to Harborview in Seattle."

I shuffled my feet and looked away. I was still attempting to come to grips with the events of the past twenty-four hours and needed the back of my sleeve to blot my eyes.

"Doctor, thank you," Harvey said. "Can you tell us what is your biggest concern at the moment?"

Dr. Holland tipped his head down and briefly rubbed the back of his neck.

"Not only has he had very little to drink, but I'm afraid he's got some sort of kidney damage. It looks like he might have taken a serious blow to his side and one to his head. Quite frankly, he looks like he might have been beaten with a two-by-four, or a baseball bat. He needs to be examined by a top-notch nephrologist, and there's just not one available up here."

I got my act together and re-entered the discussion. "So he's going to make ... I mean ... be around for a while?" I said, not as recovered as I'd thought. Just as I got the words out, Dr. Oliver shuffled toward us.

"As I mentioned, it's tough to say," Dr. Holland said. "We were able to get the IVs started immediately, and he's responding well."

"Oh, thank God," Dr. Oliver mumbled. He rested his head in his hands and slumped into a chair.

"We're running a lot of tests right now and should have a more complete report in a couple of hours," Dr. Holland said. "I would suggest maybe you get a bite to eat— our cafeteria's off the parking lot—and check back later. I will be here until midnight."

"Thanks, Doctor," I said. "I really appreciate your help."

He nodded and pivoted toward the double doors. Harvey began his exit in the other direction.

I waited then said, "Excuse me, Doctor. But, how did you know?"

He turned and faced me, seemingly puzzled. "How did I know what? Oh, about Cheese?"

"Right. Seems you knew something right away."

"One summer when I was in med school, several of us reffed a tournament at Western Washington up in Bellingham," the doctor said. "Linn must have been about a junior in high school. He came up with a select team from Seattle's eastside, maybe Bellevue or Issaquah. I believe you were an assistant? Anyway, I don't think he missed a shot in the second half, all of 'em from a long way out."

"Good memory."

"It is difficult to forget something like that. I mean, it was an amazing performance. Each shot with perfect form, regardless of distance. I found myself watching instead of reffing. It was hard to keep the whistle in my mouth."

FORTY-ONE

THE PUMPKIN-GARLIC SOUP PROMOTED on the cafeteria chalkboard smelled like a winner, but I couldn't move myself to order a thing. Harvey appeared preoccupied with returning to the office and wanted me to accompany him. I was reluctant to leave the clinic.

"You guys go ahead and go," Robert said. "I'm not going anywhere and will be around when he wakes up. Here or anywhere else, for that matter."

At the cop shop, Harvey had his game face on and quickly marched into the interview room where Sheriff McCreedy signaled to us he was taking a break, a portable tape recorder blinking on pause on a table in front of him. Mitch Moore, still handcuffed, unfolded his bulky body on a bench against the far wall.

"They've already read him his rights," McCreedy said to Harvey. "And he's declined two offers to have a lawyer. He really hasn't said much of anything in quite some time."

Mitch remained fully reclined, like a first-class passenger on a cross-country flight. His eyes were closed and his round head rested against the wall. Several whiskered chins hung above his chest; his smile held more than a hint of smugness. While crossing in front of the desk en route to a folding chair on the far side of the room, I deliberately kicked the bottom of one of Mitch's black Durango boots.

"I can tell you what," I said, doubting that my mellow voice concealed its tightness. "I felt there was something strange going last week at Tony's when you offered to pay my way to spring training during state tournament time. No booster tries to influence a coach *after* he retires." I stepped closer. "What did you do to Linn? You stinking pile of ..."

McCreedy yanked me away. I straightened up, dragged my palms through my hair, and grudgingly returned to my chair. Mitch hadn't budged and continued as if he were waiting for a bus downtown.

"I only wanted to pick your brain about Lake Wilhelmina and property lines," he said. "What stuff your lake customers had found in their yards. I heard rumors for years that the Tyler treasure was near the outlet creek. That's why I sunk those steel poles in the creek and wrapped 'em with mesh. I knew the current would eventually bring any loose stuff my way. Dolan's crew yanked them out when they unplugged the beaver dams. Pissed me off. I sunk Stan Bottom's boat to pay 'em all back."

"So when Poppy Kurri and her girlfriends pulled in that satchel of precious stones," Harvey said, "they probably ..."

"Probably?" Mitch roared. "They fished that bag out right where I placed my screen. I'd been raking that area section by section for months since it thawed last spring. Even jumped in and poked around in that cold muck with my hands and feet. Doggone water's so black; can't see a thing."

"So when the sheriff awarded the girls what they found, both you and Bart Knight felt cheated," I said.

"Boy, you sure got it going today, Coach," Mitch growled. "Wish you had been this smart when the state title was in your hands. But yeah, Knight thought if he'd sniffed around long enough it would pay off bigtime."

I stood, seething. A deputy I didn't recognize at the door took a step toward me and shook his head, a casual warning for me to stay put.

"And don't think I didn't leave love notes for you all these years," Mitch said. "Those late-night phone calls? Crushed crab shells on your anniversary? Cracks in your kitchen window? How about that fender-bender at the Grange? Just doing my part for you screwin' up at state." He looked around, making eye contact with everybody in the room. "And I should probably thank you, Coach, for almost helping me get out of debt."

"What the hell are you talking about?"

"I stole so much stuff at the lake over the years, it damned near paid for money I lost in the title game. When I dumped all that gear in your garage—that damn motor and tool set were heavy by the way—it took the heat off of me and had the cops lookin at you. Ha! And the boats? Think there were four in four years—nice trailers, too—damn near paid the back taxes on my property. But, hey, what's a guy to do? Frickin' people from out of state pushing my property values. And you brought 'em here, Mr. Real Estate Agent!"

I leaped at Mitch. Before I could reach him, the same cop wrapped both his arms around my waist and swung me away while I flailed away.

Mitch laughed and interlaced his fingers in his lap.

"Yeah, you're pretty dumb, Coach, but you don't even hold a candle to Knight. Gotta be the dumbest hayseed you'll ever find. He had no idea I'd been diggin' on his land for that loot. Hell, I even trespassed over his place to set those poles and mesh. Knight thought the girls just lucked on to that ruby. But I had a darn good idea where to look for it."

Mitch wiggled his wide load, eased his head back on to the wall and again closed his eyes. Harvey pulled out his notebook.

"And, tell me, Mitch," Harvey said. "Just how did you decide where to set your man-made beaver dam in order to trap this treasure?"

Mitch took a deep breath, his cuffed hands rising on his belly above his blue work shirt. He spoke without stirring or opening his eyes, like a sunbather unwilling to give up the brightest ray on a hot August afternoon.

"Heard Cheese talkin' one night at Tony's Place about a year ago," Mitch said. "He'd found this journal, this diary, under the trestle at Brookens Gorge. Said he and Barbara had kept it. When Doc Oliver put up his home for sale, I broke in. Picked the place apart. House and garage. Figured if it wasn't there, it had to be at Barbara's."

My gut was turning with bigger questions. About murder and kidnapping. I bit my tongue and allowed Harvey to continue, knowing he was the expert with the effective routine and legendary method.

"So, you stole the journal when you stole the '57 Chevy," Harvey said.

Mitch shook his head slightly, leaned forward, and stared at the polished concrete floor. "Yes, and no. The first time I broke in to the Sylanskis' garage, I was drunker than a skunk. Too drunk to drive the car. Didn't want to hit something, dent that beautiful baby. I found the journal, ripped out some pages, and put it back. Next morning, I read all about some lady havin' a baby on a train, the Tyler gold we'd been hearing about for years, and how one of the Tylers told an old clinic nurse he'd burned down the old Madrona Resort."

"Then you went back for the car and the rest of the journal," Harvey said.

"Yeah, last week. Darn near a year later. Still don't know how you found out about the '57 Bel Air."

"Word tends to get around when someone drives one of the most popular cars in a small town," I said. "People tend to notice."

There was a knock on the door. Sheriff McCreedy turned off the tape recorder and motioned to the uniformed officer to answer it. He spoke briefly to another cop in the hallway and then returned.

"Mr. Creekmore, there's a call for you at the switchboard," the cop said. "Would you care to take it now? Or, would you like us to ..."

"No, no, I'll take it, thanks," I said. "I'll be right back."

"And Sheriff McCreedy?" the cop said. "Apparently the medical examiner would like to speak to you or Mr. Johnston."

"I'll take it, Sheriff," Harvey said. "I'll be back in a moment. Meet you back here, Ernie."

Robert Oliver sounded thirty years younger. No shortness of breath; no indication of fatigue.

"Ernie, Doctor Holland says Linn is doing really well. Well enough, in fact, to move him down to Harborview in Seattle to see experts in critical care. He mentioned a weaker man would've had little chance of making it. I can't help but attribute at least a bit of that toughness to you."

I experienced a lightness in my chest, a sensation of temporary detachment from the phone, the police station, and everyone in it. I felt free, nimble with a bring-it-on vigilance for anything down the road. Including the numbness in my hands.

"Ernie! You there? Did you hear anything what I said?"

"Yeah, Robert. I'm sorry. Lost it there for a second."

"There's a kidney specialist on call down there and I know of him only by reputation. However, Doctor Holland knows him well and has worked with him in the past. We're told he'll see Linn whenever we get there."

"I just can't believe how great this is," I mumbled.

"Right. How's it coming over there?"

"Mr. Moore is just starting to talk. Sounds like we are going to be here a while."

Robert was silent for a moment. Had the roles been reversed, I'd be screaming to know what the hell Mitch did to my kid.

"There's so much I want to know, Ernie," he said. "But I'm still too angry to ask. I'm also extremely grateful, and I need to sit with that right now."

"Understand. Try calling Harvey's car CB when you have an update for us."

When I got back into the interview room, Harvey was leaning over the desk, whispering quietly with Sheriff McCreedy. As I entered, the cop closed the door behind me, and Harvey rose to face Mitch Moore.

"Now Mitch," Harvey said. "Why don't you explain to us"—he moved to within inches of Mitch's nose—"JUST HOW MISTER DOLAN ENDED UP IN HIS OWN SEPTIC TANK?"

"That was all an accident!" Mitch cried. "None of it was meant to happen. I mean, I loved the guy."

Sheriff McCreedy pushed his chair away from the table and paced in front of me. "Sounds like you really loved the guy. Great way to show it. By cutting him up and sticking him in his backyard sewer!"

"None of *what* was meant to happen?" Harvey said.

Mitch sighed and shook his head. "Hell, after the little girls found the ruby and I got my hands on the notebook, I was certain the Tyler gold was on the Dolan property. I'd checked the legal descriptions over the years; knew the property lines darn near by heart. Dolan had hired me to extend the drain field and do other work, so most people were not suspicious that I was always digging on his land.

"But one day the old man surprises me out of the blue. Comes up to check the house, see if the FOR SALE signs were still up. Wants to know why I'm working in his yard. Sees me take a little gunny sack out of the ground and flop it on the back of my loader. Well, I won't let him open it, and he pushes me away, sayin' what's on his land is his. Next thing I know, I crank him with a shovel. And he didn't get up."

Harvey appeared equally flabbergasted and angry. He stood and flapped his notebook on an open palm in Mitch's face. "Why didn't you radio in, or use the phone at the Mountain Market. Tell 911 there'd been an accident?"

"Man, I was scared! I didn't know what to do."

"What you are is a greedy, miserable miser, Mitch! You saw the Tyler gold as a chance to hang up the hammer, maybe sell off your heavy equipment. So greedy in fact, that you cut up Jim Dolan and put him in a stinking sewer!"

"Yeah! And you would have never found him if..."

"If the deal to sell the house hadn't come together so fast," I said.

Mitch again reclined on the bench, eyes rolling toward the ceiling. "I didn't know there was a solid deal on the house and that it was heading to escrow," Mitch said. "This time of year, I guessed it would take much longer to get an acceptable offer. I figured the body would decompose by the time the system needed to be pumped, or I would find a way to handle it. I pump just about every septic system at that lake."

"I don't understand," the sheriff said. "Why weren't you there to pump the Dolan's place?'

Mitch exhaled and sneered. "Damn message machine was full, I guess," he said. "I was off trying to ditch a car. Because Coach was in such a doggone hurry to get the thing done, I guess the job went to some competitor before I even knew it. New law, making us pump before all homes are sold, has brought out a bunch of rookies looking for a fast buck."

"Sounds to me like you were just lazy and sloppy," I said. "Again."

"Screw you, Coach."

"He's got a point, Mitch," the sheriff said. "You just confessed to a murder, and we barely had to ask."

Mitch tried to stand, but the door cop hustled over and shoved him back down.

"All that gold and that ruby are rightfully mine!" he screamed. "My family put it there, and it should all have been given to me! Me!"

"Now what on earth do you mean by that?" the sheriff said.

"My granddaddy was Vance Tyler. All he left his illegitimate daughter was a sketchy, faded map of the sandspit where he thought his brother buried their loot from the North Skagit. Mother's name was Mavis. Looked for years but didn't find a thing. Said the guy she had me with stole the map before I was born."

"What became of your father?" McCreedy said.

"Never met the asshole. Mavis waited 'til I could drive, then ran off with some lonesome picker. Left me with a beat-up Chevy Nova and made me promise to look for gold at Lake Wilhelmina."

Harvey shook his head and paced across the room.

"Hey, other people were findin' stuff," Mitch said. "Then I got my hands on that diary. Couldn't stop looking."

Sheriff McCreedy circled behind the seated policeman, leaned against the wall, and folded his arms.

"Say you are a Tyler, like you claim. Why didn't you come forward and claim the satchel and the gold nuggets? If you could prove it, you would have been the next of kin."

"Yeah, right," Mitch scoffed. "Mother gone and me a bastard kid? Saw a birth certificate once, but that was years ago. Anyway, I found my gold on Dolan's property, until the basketball player got in the way. But what were the chances you would have taken all those valuable stones from that little girl and handed them to the bastard grandkid of the man who burned down her great-grandmother's cabin? With the woman in it? I wouldn't have stood a chance. Still, my family buried the gold, and it belongs to me."

The door cop stared at Harvey, incredulous.

"You might have got away with it," McCreedy said. "If you kept your mouth shut. You're certain about all this?"

Moore scoffed. "Problem was the kids. They found out when they dug up that diary. One of the reasons I ripped those pages out. They're back at the cabin in a canvas sack with some gold. Seems 'ol Vance didn't like Indians at all, liked to brag to Mavis about it. Mavis said she heard it from more of the women he slept with. I guess he was quite the servicer."

Harvey's anger jumped into overdrive. "So you popped the Realtor, too, when he found you with the gold?"

"Forget you, man!" Moore yelled. "I was up at Knight's dealing with Cheese when that guy got whacked. No way you're putting that on me!"

Harvey exhaled noticeably. He approached Mitch, bent over in front of him, and glared into his eyes. "So, you want us to believe you had nothing to do with the death of a man a few feet from where you killed another one out of sheer greed?"

Moore snickered, his top lip raised. "Think about it, mister investigator. Why on earth would I off a guy and leave him bleeding on a floor? I'm sorry, Harvey, but if I'd killed that squirrely wimp, Rice, I would have slam-dunked him and his tassel shoes in the septic with Old Man Dolan." Mitch laughed. "They could have festered together –"

"Together with Bart Knight? Bart Knight, too, Mitch? You know that call I just got? Well, the ME says there was more than Jim Dolan in there, Mitch. They found other body parts in that tank, Mitch. And they happen to belong to Bart Knight!"

Harvey clenched his fists and started at Mitch, then hesitated as the cop by the door closed in.

"Do you want to take a break, Harvey?" the cop said.

"No," Harvey said. "Let's keep this moving."

Moore continued, without any prodding, as if he didn't want to omit even the slightest detail.

"Can you imagine?" Moore said. "That stupid moonshiner wanted to part-out a '57 Chevy. Part it out! Thing is a classic and would bring beaucoup bucks, man. Now, I might understand chopping the Pontiac, but the Chev? Gimme a break. When he popped the hood to begin yanking the engine, I guess I hit him too hard with a crowbar. Cut him up in a hurry with the shop tools. Bagged him. That dog seemed to like the blood, though. Not much to mop."

Sheriff McCreedy slumped back down in a chair. back down. Harvey collapsed into a folding chair near the door and settled his arms across his middle.

"And Linn?" I started softly. Then, feeling my anger, "Just how hard did you hit him?"

"That frickin' Cheese. Been useless ever since he cost us the state title."

I jumped to my feet.

"Easy, Ernie," McCreedy said.

"Yeah, easy, big fella," Moore said. "Not cool to swing on a guy with cuffs."

I dropped my fists to my sides and groaned loud enough to draw stares. But I sat back down.

"So, he's renting there for months and questions every move I make," Moore said. "He stayed a lot in North Fork and Seattle, so I did most of my digging when he wasn't around. Last week, he comes out heading for a game in town and he sees me lifting something heavy out of the bucket of my backhoe near that big madrona tree. You know him. Always the damn helper. As if I needed help or something. Anyway, turns out it wasn't a rock I dug up, but one of the saddlebags. It rips open, and out comes this gold. His eyes about came out of his head!"

Mitch went on to explain that he tried to convince Linn to keep the discovery quiet, lest the sandspit turn into another Sutter's Mill.

"Gaawwd, I argued with that kid for more than an hour," Moore said. "Said I'd pay him a lot of money to keep his mouth shut. He just couldn't see my way of doin' things. He was adamant about telling Barbara about the gold. Said he told his stupid girlfriend about everything and this was no different. I couldn't afford to have word get out about this."

I could feel the heat in my face. I flexed my hands. "Then why not just kill him at Dolan's place?" I said. "Why go to the trouble of staging a suicide if the goal was to protect your pot of gold?"

Moore leered my way and raised his lip. "I needed to see him suffer. Yank the life out of him. Like he did to me and my money."

Before I could take a step, Harvey slammed a forearm into my chest. He turned to Moore. "So then what? You followed him to Seattle?"

"Yeah, I followed him. Told me he had a game at Montlake. I was afraid he would spill the beans, and I'd be ripped off again—the little girls had my ruby, and I had squat for all my work. I really didn't want to share my find with that loser kid. I just stewed sitting there in a dark corner of the parking lot, waiting for him to come out.

"When he finally showed, I blasted him over the head, wrestled him into the trunk of my rental car, and then drove his Subaru wagon on to the Bremerton ferry. I was lucky Barbara didn't see me because I saw her turning into the Montlake gym parking lot as I was leaving. I'm sure he couldn't wait to tell her about my gold –"

"Hold it right there," I said. "How did you know Linn would leave the gym and go to Bremerton that night?"

"I got my sources, asshole. You ain't the only one with a network, ya know."

"Difference is my sources are legal."

Moore scoffed and swayed in his seat, taxing his chair. "Since you just gotta know, I stopped for petrol early that morning at the Shell station. Kelvin told me Cheese had a doubleheader. Montlake then Bremerton. Said he was worried about the kid, workin' and playin' too hard. I told Kelvin he should be worried about him, if you get my drift."

The room was silent. All eyes were on Moore.

Harvey broke the quiet. "So, you drove the car onto the boat. What did you do next?"

"'Bout halfway over, I jammed his basketball and jersey into his gym bag and tossed it over the rail," Moore said. "It was so cold and blowy that nobody was on the car deck to see me. Then I locked the station wagon up, walked off the boat in Bremerton, and waited in the ferry terminal for the tow truck to haul away the station wagon. When the boat was cleared for the return trip, I lined up with the other walk-on passengers for the return sailing.

"When I got back to the Seattle side, I took a cab to the Montlake Gym, picked up the rental car, and drove it back up to the lake. I drove down Dolan's driveway, backed the car as close as I could to the septic tank, took off all his clothes and shoved them in."

"Was your plan to dispose of Linn the same way you got rid of Jim Dolan's body?"

Mitch sneered. "Was to begin with," he said. "Given what happened, I probably should have followed through."

"So, what changed your mind?" Harvey said.

"You know, all I could think about when I saw him coming out of the Montlake gym that night was how he lost my state title. Not the gold, that game! It was right there for him to win, and he couldn't do it. I mean, this was state, and

I bet just about every dime I had on the Crabs to win. I needed to have him *see* what he'd done. See and remember."

"So, that was what the television was for in the cabin," Sheriff McCreedy said. "And the tape machine?"

"Bingo, big guy," Mitch hollered. "Copied the last five minutes of that game dozens of times on to a five-hour VHS. Took him to the shack and set him up with his own tape session. Told him to break down his stinkin' performance in front of the biggest crowd our school's ever had. Came back every few days to check on him."

My mouth was open, but nothing came out. No one said a word.

"And the noose?" Harvey said. "Was the plan to use that rope in that room?"

"Thought he might like to go out knowing the state championship game was the last thing he ever saw," Mitch said. "Too bad you guys got there first. He was probably just a few hours away from swinging above his last shot. Then, into a sleeping bag he'd go with some cement shoes, and into a deep spot in the river."

I leapt with such speed and purpose than none of the men in the room could stop me before I landed a right-left combination to Mitch Moore's face. I felt his cheekbones shift under both punches before two huge uniform arms were wrapped around my middle, lifting my feet off the ground.

"You still don't get it, Coach!" Mitch wailed. "He had an open shot—*his shot*—and he couldn't make it? C'mon! It was state, man. *state!*"

FORTY-TWO

DR. ELMER CREHAN'S NEW ENGLAND accent and ubiquitous bowtie clashed comfortably with the flannel shirts and casual conversation of downtown North Fork.

While waiting for the MRI results, he ran me through the same tests in his exam room that Dr. Timoteo Mesa performed in the parking lot of the Gas 'N Go—rubber hammer for reflexes, pizza wheel, and safety pin for sensation. I was grateful to have completed my trip inside the claustrophobic MRI scanner, a huge donut with a tube-like coffin on one side that allows only inches of clearance and no body movement while being bombarded by magnetic vibrations that sound like the unhappy union of a jackhammer and ancient popcorn popper.

A young radiologist knocked and looped through the room without waiting for a greeting, an oversized manila folder under one arm of his creased white lab coat. The flat package was split open at the top, exposing huge sheets of black film.

"The written report's inside."

"Thanks, Sam," Dr. Crehan said, yanking the first image from the folder with one hand and jamming it into the clips of a wall-mounted X-ray viewer. He drew closer to the slide, then jerked it down and instantly replaced it with another. "That first one didn't show us much of anything, but this one does. See the difference in this area here?" He pointed to my upper neck.

The two slides looked exactly the same to me. It wasn't until he pointed to a few tiny bubble-like areas in my spinal cord that I could see any perceivable difference. Once I looked away and then returned my gaze to the area, I had a difficult time finding the bubbles again. "Well, I think so. How can you see this stuff so quickly?"

"Takes a while," Dr. Crehan said, flipping the frames into the light and then onto the countertop below faster than a Las Vegas dealer. "Here's a better one, a view looking down. From the top of your head."

I felt strangely clueless, needing an expert to explain pictures of my own body.

"You've got a few lesions in that cervical area; a couple more down a bit lower in the thoracic," he said. "My guess is that these are having a lot to with the numbness in your extremities."

"Lesions?" I dropped back lower on the table. Sounded like nasty critters that needed to be cut out immediately. "What do you mean, lesions?"

"Tiny areas where the stuff insulating your nerves is breaking down. It's a fatty cover called myelin. Think of it as the black and white stuff that covers the wires in a wall outlet."

He continued to swiftly shuffle the slides, this time checking out various images and angles of my brain. Given some of the lighter dots, there appeared to be more negatives ahead.

"Now, these don't bother me," Dr. Crehan said. "No vision problems, right? Other symptoms?"

"That's correct," I said. "Only strange stuff has been in my hands and feet."

"A lot of people, especially men, have these spots in their head and they never bother them at all. MEs cut 'em open after they're dead, see the lesions all the time."

At that moment, I didn't care about dead people and surprising factoids discovered in autopsies. "So, what does all this mean and what do we do about it?" I said.

"Means I'm fairly certain you've got multiple sclerosis," he said. "Those periodic symptoms in your hands and feet? Known as relapsing remitting, they come and go. I'm betting they're caused by those lesions in your spinal cord."

It wasn't cancer, but I knew it wasn't good. Stunned, I laid back on the table, hands covering my eyes, harboring images of wheelchairs and walkers. Being carried into Washington High's Crab Pot and secured to a seat behind the scorer's table with the aid of a guardian. Or wheeled to a remote corner of the floor with a blanket on my lap, hiding a catheter and urine bag. Besides, I'd always been an ornery and nasty patient, upset that others had to care for me.

"How long will I be able to scout kids, fish?" I said. "I was even thinking about getting back into coaching."

"Can't say for sure, but how's the rest of your life sound?" Dr. Crehan said. "Wouldn't plan on major changes; probably won't stop you from doing a thing. You might have to adjust an activity down the road. But, like I say, we just don't know how this is going to go."

The relatively upbeat prognosis startled me nearly as much as black cloud that immediately arrived above the diagnosis. "I thought MS ..."

" ... hit young women in their twenties and thirties?" Dr. Crehan said. "Yeah, it does, a lot of the time. But it looks like you got it, so let's deal with it. Suggest starting you on one of the new drugs soon. Getting some pretty good results, not

274 | Tom Kelly

like the old days. Back then, all we could do was plan a healthy diet."

While I couldn't be certain, the first known onset of any lack of feeling occurred at Tony's just hours before I learned of Linn's disappearance. At the time, I chalked it up to the stress and anxiety. "Seems the initial numbness took place around the time I got some surprising news. Could that have started all this?"

He placed my chart on the table next to me and conducted a cursory eye test, asking me to follow his ballpoint pen as he moved to different areas in front of my face. "Usually it's not started by one acute incident, but we really don't know." He slid the pen back into his chest pocket. "I'd like to do another test. Get a spinal tap, check the clarity of your fluid. It might be some help, tell us more."

"I'd be up for anything that could help tell us what I'm dealing with."

"The MRI is the main indicator. Guys over fifty usually don't get MS. You're what? Fifty-one? Puts you at the bottom of the bell curve. Your symptoms, the period between incidents, could also be very different."

I gripped both sides of the exam table and stared into his eyes, amazed at the thickness of his frames and lenses. "Can I still play hoop on Saturday mornings?"

"Play hoop whenever you want! Symptoms tend to exacerbate as body temperature rises. Be aware of your feet, hands. Don't want you tripping or dropping passes."

"Most of those guys say I can't catch anyway. So, what's next with this?"

"Let me ask my nurse when we can do this spinal tap. Maybe later today, if you're available. Uncomfortable, but fairly quick."

"OK, I can be around. Then what?"

"Then I was thinking about calling that guy at the *Seattle Tribune*. Smithson, is it? Tell him I heard on the street that Ernie Creekmore's getting back into coaching."

I snorted, unexpectedly flattered and surprised. "Why don't you hold off on that announcement for a while," I said. "Especially after this."

"This," Dr. Crehan said, "should not make a difference."

"Do you think some school or club is going to hire a coach with MS?"

"Why not? If they know, they shouldn't really care. Especially if they can get someone like you."

"Ignorance may not be bliss," I said.

"Thomas Gray," Dr. Crehan said. "English poet. And he didn't exactly put it that way."

I HEADED BACK downtown toward the office. The session with Dr. Crehan produced a measure of clarity and understanding while also igniting a definite fear of the unknown. My way of handling similar feelings in the past was to start with a healthy dose of sugar, so I cruised the Calico Cupboard just off First Street. I could smell the fresh cinnamon rolls from the sidewalk and smiled at the cute baker as she inserted a new rack in the window display case. As I stood at the rear of the four-person counter line, I spotted Ronnie Garcia drinking coffee and buried in a newspaper at a table in the middle of the café. I ordered a cinnamon roll and coffee.

"Breaking down those NBA box scores?" I said, approaching his chair from behind. His long black hair curled just above his shoulders. A long-sleeved linen shirt was rolled to his elbows.

Startled, he had the look of someone trying to identify a face from a different place and time. He rose to shake hands.

"Coach Creekmore! Man, it's good to see you. How ya doin' these days?"

I smiled, struck by mounting number of possible responses to that question. "Good, good. Thanks. Actually had been looking for you earlier this week."

"Sit, sit. Please." He removed his rain slicker from the seat of the facing chair and draped it over the back of his. "I guess you weren't the only one. My dad mentioned that to me last night when I got back to town and stopped by his place. Said it had something to do with Linn?"

"Yes, well, I was surprised that you guys ended up on the same Montlake team in Seattle," I said. "Actually headed down there one night to see you. Kind of an interesting coincidence after all these years."

He took a sip of coffee and leaned back in his chair. "Actually, it was more on purpose. Coach, the whole deal with Linn and me, there's a lot to it," Ronnie said. "We weren't best buds, didn't hang out with the same crowd, but we still talked, remained friendly. Until, well, until that day on the mountain when he got hurt."

"Remember it well," I said. "Hotter 'n hell. Best week of the summer, and he ends up in the hospital."

"Yeah, well, he never said anything, but that was because of me. That knee injury could have been avoided had I just done my job."

"What are you talking about? You can't put what happened on yourself."

"Yeah, I can. And I'll never forgive myself." He took another sip of coffee and crossed his forearms on the table. "That day, we were paired as choker partners. Crew started early, and we were all pretty well fried by mid-morning. The sun was a demon; we went through most of our water by ten a.m. When the whistle blew for lunch, we scrambled to any shade we could find. When I found a spot between two downed trees, I was so gassed I didn't even eat. Closed my eyes and didn't wake up—until I heard Linn screaming. He'd set a choker around a log, but I wasn't there to relay the mainline pull. When the cable moved, the log rotated and caught his knee."

"I knew you were partners in the woods that summer, but I didn't know about ..."

"Nobody knew. Still don't. I mean, I ruined the guy's career because I was asleep! Could never look him in the eye after that. I remember when he woke up in the hospital, leg high in this huge suspended sling. I couldn't even talk, I just sat there. So what does he do? Says 'Don't worry about it, Ronnie. Those cables can be unpredictable.' After what I did? Are you kiddin' me?"

Our waitress darted around the counter and slid a plate in front of me followed by a mug of steaming coffee. The pastry was big enough to feed a starting five.

"Well, that's a big one," I smiled, looking at the huge, sugar-coated coils in front of me. Locating a knife to help my fork, I sliced the first section of the roll. "I spoke with Barbara about you and ..."

"I wasn't trying to move in on Linn," Ronnie said. "Yeah, sure, I tried when I thought they were on the outs way back when, but she set me straight in a hurry. Which was another reason I asked him to play on the Montlake team. Wanted to make sure things were cool between us, maybe get a chance to finally talk through a lot of the BS. Much of it is me, I still feel guilty he's not playing for big-time money. We all know he was definitely good enough."

I nodded slowly, pondering the possibilities.

"Lately, Barbara and her mother were helping me get more Hispanic kids involved in community programs," Ronnie said. "Mrs. Sylanski is the best teacher I ever had, and kids listen to her. She's got a lot of connections at the schools. In fact, she was critical in getting me accepted into the Hispanic Affairs workshop last week down in Portland. Even got some grad school credits from Oregon State."

"So, you've been down there the past several days. Why you didn't play in those Montlake games?"

"That's right. I wasn't accepted into the workshop until the last minute and was actually gone eight days. I drove straight down I-5 late last Tuesday afternoon. It turned out the school did not inform Mrs. Sylanski of my acceptance. I thought she would have known, so Barbara would have known."

"Help me understand something. Why did you leave the Crane house before finishing the job?"

"Mr. Crane flat-out lied to me," Ronnie said. "I bid the repairs separate from the paint job and told him I needed two separate payments. He agreed. I bought and replaced a lot of deck boards, some stringers, then downspouts and gutters. He told me three times he would pay me before I started painting. Well, I begin scraping, and he comes out falling-down drunk saying he won't pay until the house is completely finished. That wasn't the deal, so I split. Sent him a bill for what I'm owed. Say, you're making quite a dent in that thing." He pointed to the cinnamon roll.

"Actually, I have an extensive background on most items produced in a bakery," I said. "And, big does not necessarily taste better. This was impressive, however. Not too soft with just enough raisins."

"Sounds like you know your stuff."

"Unfortunately, in here, I do."

"You know, I was thinking," Ronnie said. "Both Linn and me missed three straight games and the rest of the Fool's Gold guys really stepped up. One night they played with four players and won the game! Played a box defense, rebounded like crazy and walked the ball up the floor. Heard all about it, plenty of grief, after last night's game. We played well and beat one of the better teams in the league. All of the guys were asking about Linn. I just told them he was probably tied up."

The image of Linn bound to a chair in a rancid room returned. I pushed the plate forward. More than half of the sweet roll remained.

"Well, I know he was tied up for at least one game," I said. "Probably all three. Suffice it to say, he's just had a lot going on in his life."

FORTY-THREE

BY THE TIME I LEFT RONNIE GARCIA and rolled into the office to review the latest listings, the work morning was completely shot. When I saw Harvey Johnston's county car in our tiny lot behind the agency, I could tell that more of my workday would be put on hold. Through the window blinds, I saw him speaking with Cookie in her office. The door was closed.

Peggy Metzger dropped by my cubicle and handed me several telephone messages. "Harvey's been in there quite a while," Peggy said. "And he's not happy."

"Probably thought I was supposed to buy him lunch." I said. "Maybe he's just taking it out on Cookie."

"Not sure what it is. He did mention that Linn is doing a lot better down at Harborview Medical Center, so that can't be what's dragged him down."

"I've known the guy a long time," I said. "Sometimes he can get a little sideways just from missing his morning coffee."

Peggy laughed and headed back to her post in the reception area. The new listing sheets included a couple of surprises, most notably a three-bedroom lake-view home a stone's throw from the Big Lake Bar & Grill. The property notes stated that the house was rebuilt on the original Montborne Train Station, a primary stop on the first Seattle-Vancouver railroad.

"Another piece of history," I mumbled aloud. "Probably sell to some out-of-stater buyer who could care less. Only after that view of the lake."

"Not a good sign, talking to yourself," Cookie said from behind me. "Makes me wonder about some of the hires I've made around here."

I shrugged and offered a what-can-I say gesture.

"Harvey wants to see you for a few minutes," she said. "You guys can use the conference room." She looked as if she had a lot more to say but simply turned and marched away.

Harvey was on the phone, and I sat and waited.

"What time was the flight?" he said into the receiver. "And the return? OK, well, that's an indicator. I should be back in the office in about an hour. No, I'm not stopping at the Philly cheesesteak place! Right. Talk to you later." Harvey hung up the phone and stared down at the table.

"No longer in the delivery service business?" I said, tossing my tablet on the table. I pulled out a chair and took a seat.

Harvey shook his head. "Some of my guys think there's a potential for food anytime anybody's away from the office. But talking about a delivery service, we should be expecting a call from Linn Oliver's physician. Apparently, they are going to release him in the next couple of days and wanted to know if we might be available to help bring him home."

"Certainly," I said. "I'll make the time. Just plan on it."

"That's what I thought. I was hoping maybe we could go together, so I could talk with him on the way home. The sheriff did question him for few minutes in the hospital. As you can imagine, he said he was in tough shape for a couple of days there. Glad we got there when we did."

"What's the latest on Mitch Moore?"

"Proper paperwork's been filed," Harvey said. "The prosecuting attorney is reviewing the tapes for the second time. We should know more by noon tomorrow."

Harvey eased into the chair at the head of the table, leaned back, and slowly wrung his hands. "You know, the people in my department are pretty tight," Harvey said. "They all back each other to the hilt, and you can't say that about every cop shop. Their kids play together; wives cook together. Guys in the squad even play hoop together. It's as if they're all one family."

"Granted," I said. "But where're you goin' with this?"

"Well, sometimes you forget that other people know that, too," he said.

"How so?" I said.

"I got an anonymous call from a woman early today. Said she needed to report a crime but couldn't call the police switchboard because people would know immediately who she was."

"Why is that a bad thing? Because she's real embarrassed, maybe scared?"

"Scared, big-time," Harvey said. "So scared that she disguised her voice on the phone by speaking through some sort of cover, maybe a handkerchief. Giving me her name was out of the question. She told me to go to Scott's Bookstore for instructions on where to meet her. I went, sat down, and a salesman announced over the PA that there was a call for Harvey Johnston. I answered and was told to be at the Cranberry Tree Restaurant in fifteen minutes."

"Were you concerned this was a hoax?" I said. "Somebody playing a game?"

"No. It was her tone. Always started deep, then after a couple of words, escalated to a place between screaming and crying. Absolute desperation."

"Well, did she show up at the restaurant?"

Harvey tipped up his chin. "Get this. I took a seat by the window, near the front door. The breakfast crowd was still there; lots of Canadian freeway fliers heading to Seattle and Portland. A shiny black Lexus pulls up in the parking spot in front of the window and nobody gets out. I wait a minute, peer into the windshield, and see a person trying to get my attention from inside the car. I look around, go out, and she opens the door."

"Was she injured?" I said. "Being hounded by some jerk?"

"Bit of both," Harvey said. "She had a puffy eye. And remember the client that Mark Rice had, that wanted to see Lake Wilhelmina properties? The one he was going to refer to you, but she insisted on Mark showing her the homes?"

"Yeah, he mentioned her the last time in was in this office. What's she got to do with your department?"

"It turns out she was falling head over heels for Rice, but a guy she had dated didn't like that at all. Sometime last week, he'd had about a bottle of wine and was putting the moves on her in a bar. Anyway, he starts talking like a big shot and says he is certain that Mark Rice wouldn't be bothering her anymore."

"Did she know Pee Wee was dead?" I said.

"I doubt it. She tried to leave, but he followed her into the parking lot. When she said he couldn't come over to her place, he backhanded her in the face. One of the barmaids came out to get something from her car and saw the guy trying to stuff the woman into his trunk. Apparently, the guy realized he was made and took off."

"So why didn't the barmaid call the cops?"

"She did. The call was patched through to the deputy on duty."

I shook my head, confused. "Connect the dots for me. Is this the wife of somebody in your office, out playing the field when they should be at home with her hubby?"

"Not at all," Harvey said. "The woman was single and says the guy who smacked her was Arnold Dawson, your favorite law enforcement officer who was allegedly on duty that day."

I pushed back from the table. "I hope she's pressing charges."

"Hasn't yet. But, she believes he's got something to do with Mark Rice coming up dead in that Sherrard house at Lake Wilhelmina—a home she'd just toured with him the day he died. She said Sherrard had promised Rice a big bonus if Rice could sell it in the final days before Sherrard relisted. So, Sherrard held firm on the price."

"I never thought Pee Wee bought that listing," I said. "Knowing him, he would have given the bonus back to the woman after the sale. Still, it isn't going to be easy to prove that Dawson was involved."

Harvey leaned forward and rested his arms on the table. "It's getting easier. He was definitely patrolling the lake the day Rice was killed. When we couldn't find him this morning, I asked my friends at the Port and Customs to check airports and the borders. Turns out he boarded a flight for Houston, connecting to Roatan, Honduras. I'm guessing he waited until now to run for it because he got his latest paycheck and had the max amount of cash—ten grand—with him. Just found out now he had no return trip scheduled, plus he hadn't put in for vacation time. Doesn't look good for 'ol Arnold."

EPILOGUE

ANOTHER BACK-TO-SCHOOL DAY and a clean slate for kids. But I still felt ambivalent about not being at Washington High on the day after Labor Day. Former coaches and teachers stay hardwired to the academic year despite their change in occupation, interest, or time away from school. By the time anxious kids and doting parents gathered at the bus stop down the street, I'd pondered my possible routine— what my class load might be, the number of students in each section, whether any last-minute transfers had arrived from out of state. Hopefully, one turned up tall and extremely skilled.

As I gazed out the front window at some of the parents retreating to their homes, one such extremely skilled individual strutted up the walkway. My truck was parked at the curb behind him. Linn Oliver stopped to pick up my newspaper, then smiled and waved it at me as he headed toward the door. His shoulders appeared broader than I remembered; his forearms tan and muscular.

"Now don't think this is going to be a daily delivery service." He laughed. "At least for the paper."

"The truck run OK?"

"Yeah, thanks. That baby pulls Uncle Bill's boat like a dream. And it's the perfect answer to that public launch at Wilhelmina. So torn up, all that loose gravel. You should have seen some of those people with front-wheel minivans trying to get their boats out. Had to help one lady who could not back in her trailer. The husband was just screaming at her from the boat."

"Labor Day zoo."

"Got that right. Well, thanks again for the truck. Maybe Crab football Friday night? First home game."

"Maybe," I said. "If it's warm. No longer do football in the rain."

"OK. I guess I better head up Highway 530. I'm supposed to look at a new section of trees before eleven. What do you have going?"

I looked at the front cover of the paper, flipped it on the coffee table, and slid into the sofa. "My Tuesdays always start with a weekly injection. I get that out of the way and then look at my day. I guess first up would be that letter over there. County officials have asked me to coach a select team in the spring. They want an answer by Friday."

"Coach, that's great! Are you going to take it?" He took a seat in the leather chair opposite me and flopped a huge boot over his knee.

"Thinking positively about it. I'd like to get back in it, and this might be the perfect way. Probably would have to start scoutin' in about a month. "

"Really? You seem so certain now."

"Frankly, Linn, the MS diagnosis kind of kicked me in the ass. That and some other things this year really got me thinking differently about a lot of stuff. In many ways, it's made my life better."

As I searched for a way of telling him that the disease, coupled with witnessing his second chance in an upstairs room of a remote fishing cabin, had made my daily experiences precious and more fulfilling, he jumped in.

"Do they hurt?" he asked.

"Do what hurt?"

"The injections? I don't think I could handle those needles."

"They're not so bad, if can you find a stout muscle."

"I've had tetanus shots, various vaccines. But the needles aren't as big. Couldn't even look at steroids.''

I slid my back into the couch and sat up. "What *did* you take for the knee?"

"After leaving the UW, I tried a number of prescription anti-inflammatories. Felt like a high school sophomore again, for about three weeks. Played every night, sometimes two games, and worked ten-hour shifts during the day. Then it began to hurt more, and I eventually broke down. Wanted that sophomore feeling, bad. Got my hands on some prednisone, took some pills once. Felt and looked like a zombie and never wanted to take them again. Now, I play less, take a slug of Advil when I do and a little Glucosamine. Every now and then it seems to work, and I can really go."

"Well, I'll tell you what. You tell me anytime you're even thinking about taking a new drug, and I'll hand you a rundown of all the kids I'm scouting for the select team. In fact, I'll need your help."

"That's a deal," Linn said, rising to his feet. "I'll also keep an eye out for potential prospects when my Washington High freshman team plays this year, and there's bound to be some surprise talent at the camps I'm working for Doug Willis. But right now, I've got to get on down the road. If I miss the cruiser up on that hill, I'm toast."

"Right. Get out of here. Call me and remind me about Friday."

He grinned and bolted out the door. As he jogged effortlessly to his Datsun sedan parked two doors down for the long weekend while he borrowed the truck, I felt how lucky the school and community were to have him back and involved.

By the time I nursed my second cup of coffee, I'd cleaned out most of the closets and the bathroom. The blue recycle bin was brimming with old sports magazines, newspaper clippings, and programs.

A trash bin got all of Cathy's perfumes, bath oils, soaps, and skin creams. I stuffed her two remaining raincoats from the hall closet into a big bag for St. Vinny's and followed them in with several frayed shirts and threadbare trousers from my bedroom armoire, allowing room for the rack of plastic-covered garments I picked up from Modern Cleaners on Division Street. Before driving downtown, I erased Cathy's message from the telephone answering machine, and centered a framed picture of us taken at sunset on Warm Beach above my desk in the extra bedroom.

I parked the bus on First Street and peeked into the window of Books, Bagels & Beans while waiting for Harvey to arrive. Barbara Sylanski made a fresh pot of coffee and sorted through a box of used titles marked ST. BRENDAN SCHOOL.

Her new store recently opened its doors in a storefront owned by the Berrettonis two blocks down the street from Tony's. George charged her little monthly rent and persuaded his longtime baker to cut her the best deal possible on fresh bagels and scones. Her mother was eager to help on weekends and after school; her sister had already dropped in to help out. Dr. and Mrs. Oliver contributed two boxes of excellent quality hardbacks, plus nearly every paperback that John Grisham and Robert Parker had in print.

After just two weeks, Barbara said she was surprised by the number of professional people who scouted for specific authors and genres. Professors and students from the community college, accountants, and physicians took their time roaming the aisles in the pursuit of a special gift or a coveted addition to a collection.

The seed money to purchase much of her initial inventory and refurbish the first-floor space came from a portion of the Tyler gold that Wide Load Moore had dug up on the Dolan property. Jim Dolan, Jr., believed that Linnbert Oliver also was entitled to a portion of the money.

While Mitch testified in court that he found the bags of gold on his own before Linn appeared on the scene, Dolan said Linn was entitled to at least a share. Dolan told the court that if Linn had kept quiet, Mitch would have "given him something for keeping the secret." That "something" was a significant sum the Dolan family decided to give to Linn who, in turn, staked Barbara.

Dolan was quoted in the *Skagit Valley World* at his father's memorial that if Linn's great-grandfather hadn't established the mercantile store in North Fork and paid the original Finns to blaze a trail to Lake Wilhelmina, "there probably would not have been any treasure buried on our lot." It was an amazingly generous gesture that brought a standing ovation from the huge memorial crowd at the Lake Wilhelmina Fire Hall. A handful of the attendees donned I PULLED THE PLUG t-shirts for the day while a woman showed up as a Cher lookalike, a tribute to Martha's favorite star.

As Harvey and I entered the store, Barbara was busy at the coffee bar.

"You know, I'm a Melville guy and could use a really clean copy of *Billy Budd,*" I said, as we took seats in the café section. "Actually, Zane Grey fished these rivers, so anything you got by him I'd be interested in, too."

"Oh, Coach," Barbara sighed. "You are so thoughtful to stop by. I have been thinking about you. And, Mr. Johnston, how are you?"

"We both seem to be getting older faster than you," Harvey replied. "It sure looks like you enjoy what you are doing."

Barbara flashed a flattered grin, then served us each a hot apricot scone, their golden tops sprinkled with tiny squares of rock sugar. She then pulled up a chair next to us. "Those are Yakima apricots," she announced proudly. "Straight from the Creekmore orchard."

"Wait until my dad hears about that," I said. "He just might begin making more deliveries west of the mountains."

Barbara crossed her arms on the blue-checkered tablecloth. "Everyone's been so generous, especially the Dolan family. I have been writing thank-you notes to everyone. It's amazing the number of people who were so kind and interested."

Harvey lauded the fresh paint and trim, and the newly finished floors. "I hope you got some help with this from that basketball player." He pointed to the walls and floor.

"Actually, my biggest helper has been Ellie Phillips," Barbara said. "The little touches she's added have been amazing. She's getting along in years now and only wants to work two days a week. Plus, she can bake. Wow, can she bake." Barbara slid back in her chair and pointed to the glossy floor. "Linn spent the whole weekend on the finish coat. He said he wanted to make this as nice as the floor in the Crab Pot on the first day of practice. You did hear he's going to help with the freshman team this year?"

"A great addition," I said. "He'll be a terrific coach."

"He couldn't be happier. Back in the woods, back in basketball. Even though he's been getting home long after dark. I also heard you'd been seen after dark—in a sport coat and slacks?"

I laughed and could feel the heat coming to my face. "Had a few dinners with Jessie McQuade," I said. "Thought I'd take her down to see the Mariners on Thursday."

Harvey cringed and spread his arms out on the table. "We're going to have to talk about this," he said. "You're all she talks about in the office, and she's getting very little work done." He looked at Barbara. "Jessie, my now-distracted assistant, said you had called the office with some questions. Is there something in particular that I can answer for you?"

Barbara walked to the side of the room and opened a drawer of a large oak bureau. When she returned, she held two folded pieces of worn, faded paper in her hand. The edges were jagged and a light brown. "I got these back from Sheriff McCreedy. I copied them and showed them to Dr. Oliver."

She unfolded the pages before me on the table. I stared down, mesmerized by the first entry:

Ellie Phillips

North Fork, Washington

July 28, Skagit Valley Clinic – My beautiful little girl, Amy, arrived two nights ago. She just wouldn't wait! She was born on a train before I could get here. She's so tiny. The nurses have been taking good care of both of us. Mr. Oliver stopped by today, said I could return with Amy to the camp when I felt up to it. I need the money. I could also use the help of the other women there.

One of the retired nurses was in the building for a birthday party. Says she knew all about Lake Wilhelmina and the old resort. Said she sewed up an old drunk named Tyler one night after a bar fight. Tyler bragged his daddy, guy named Vance, burned the resort down because the woman running the place refused to return his uncle's gear. Called her a squaw. Tyler told the nurse that his uncle buried bags of Skagit gold and a leather satchel of stones near the resort and outlet crick. The man said they looked for the loot for entire years, then figured the Indian plain lied to him. This Vance Tyler fella had a daughter who snooped around

292 | Tom Kelly

for the gold some years later. She went by Mavis. Mavis Moore.

I looked up and cleared my eyes with my fingertips.

"Coach, you were there!" Barbara gasped. "On that train. I'd heard Dr. Oliver once delivered a woman in a train car, so I showed him. He said you ..."

Harvey leaned back in his chair, his mouth slightly open.

"A lifetime ago," I whispered, barely getting the words out. "And a night I will never forget. Second toughest woman I ever met."

Barbara and Harvey glanced away, allowing me a chance to pull myself together.

After a brief silence, she rolled a paper napkin in front of her and held it tightly with both fists. "Mr. Johnston, I understand Mitch Moore wanted that gold more than anything, but why didn't he ..."

Harvey finished the question. "Just keep living like he had been? Hard to say what he was thinking. Taking your dad's Chevy, constantly digging for treasure, not monitoring the Dolan house sale. It's almost as if he wanted to get caught. Turns out Arnold Dawson was much the same. At some level, he probably knew he could not continue down the same road much longer. I'm glad the authorities nabbed him at the Houston airport and we were able to bring him back here. Now, they're both behind bars. Wide Load was in a stingy, desperate panic that night in the Montlake Gym parking lot. And, in the end, he was an over-the-top basketball fan. My guess is that the combination was too much for him. In the anger and fear of the moment, he overreacted and took it out on the best player ever to come our way."

ACKNOWLEDGMENTS

THIS BOOK COULD not have been possible without the following individuals who provided creative insights and useful information for this effort. I called upon them often and their patience, interest and kindness have been extraordinary: Jim Thomsen, Danny O'Neil, George and Jean Johnston, Leigh Robinson, Dr, Michael R. Kelly, Kelyse Nelson, Dr. Meghan Sheridan, Dennis Dahlin, Alicia Dean, Craig Smith, Linda Owens, Bruce Brown, Kevin Hawkins, Paul Bossenmaier, Sara Sykora, Victoria Cooper, Adam Fuller, Amelia Ramsey, Bob McCord. James Walker Ragsdale, Dr. Robert X Morrell, Joanne Elizabeth Kelly and Dorothy Von Der Ahe Olsen. Special thanks to the Skagit County Historical Museum to the overworked, underpaid high school coaches everywhere who have their hearts in the right place.

ABOUT THE AUTHOR

Cold Crossover is the first book in T.R Kelly's Ernie Creekmore series featuring the adventures of legendary high school basketball coach turned real estate agent and amateur sleuth. It is followed by *Cold Broker* and *Cold Wonderland*.

Before launching into fiction, Tom served *The Seattle Times* readers for 20 years, first as a sportswriter and later as real estate reporter, columnist and editor. His groundbreaking book How a *Second Home Can Be Your Best Investment* (McGraw-Hill, written with economist John Tuccillo) showed consumers and professionals how one additional piece of real estate could serve as an investment, recreation and retirement property over time. His other books include *Real Estate Boomers and Beyond: Exploring the Costs, Choices and Changes of Your Next Move* (Dearborn-Kaplan); *The New Reverse Mortgage Formula* (John Wiley & Sons); *Cashing In on a Second Home in Mexico* (Crabman Publishing, with Mitch Creekmore); *Cashing In on a Second Home in Central America* (Crabman Publishing, with Mitch Creekmore and Jeff Hornberger), and *Bargains Beyond the Border* (Crabman Publishing).

Tom's award-winning radio show *Real Estate Today* aired for 25 years on KIRO, the CBS affiliate in Seattle. The program also has been syndicated in 40 domestic markets and to 450 stations in 160 foreign countries via Armed Forces Radio. Tom and his wife have four children and live on Bainbridge Island, WA, where they back the runnin', gunnin' Bainbridge High Spartans when not wrestling with three of their five grandchildren.

Made in the USA
Middletown, DE
14 April 2023